beaming
sonny home

A NOVEL

cathie
pelletier

sourcebooks
landmark

Published by Sourcebooks Landmark, an imprint of Sourcebooks, Inc.
P.O. Box 4410, Naperville, Illinois 60567-4410
(630) 961-3900
Fax: (630) 961-2168
www.sourcebooks.com

Originally published in 1996 in the United States by Crown Publishers, Inc., an imprint of Random House, Inc. This edition issued based on the hardcover edition published in 1996 by Crown Publishers, Inc., an imprint of Random House, Inc.

Library of Congress Cataloging-in-Publication data is on file with the publisher.

Printed and bound in the United States of America.
VP 10 9 8 7 6 5 4 3 2 1

I

It was the piece of picture puzzle needed to finish off the left eyeball that Mattie had been hunting for all morning. As it was, Jesus was staring up at her with a blue right eye and a brown hole for the left one. It gave her the willies seeing the poor boy like that, the way she felt when Irwin Fennelson turned up at school functions with that sewn-up hole where his left eye should be, the real one somewhere in the rice paddies of Vietnam. Aside from Irwin, Mattie could only recall one other single-eyed person, an old man, his name now lost in the annals of Mattagash's past, who had sacrificed a baby blue to working in the woods. That old man, Irwin Fennelson, and now, Jesus.

"Don't you go straining out of that good right eye now, honey," Mattie told Jesus. "I'm gonna fix you up just as soon as I find that blasted piece." She peered down through the tiny half moons of her reading glasses as she pushed a bluish chunk of puzzle into the hole before her. But no amount of prying, or rearranging the little round knobs, could make the piece fit. Mattie laid it in the pile of bluish pieces that she predicted would make up the mass of flowers bordering the painting, flowers that grew over there in the Holy Land, big blue flowers you'd only see in a florist shop in Watertown, Maine. They were prettier than the blue flags that grew in the back swamp, although those blue flags, those irises, could top any flower you put them against. They were that pretty. Their major setback was that they smelled like an open sewer. Mattie smiled, remembering how Sonny, her only boy, had been forever picking bouquets of them as a child. How many times had she looked out the kitchen window, where she'd been washing dishes, and spotted Sonny coming through the field, his blondish head barely scaling the tops of the hay, his hands full of blue flags, the cuffs of his pants wet with swamp water.

She had already found the two blue eyes of the lamb, the *real* lamb, that is, the woolly one Jesus carried in his arms. Now the only pieces left scattered on the table seemed to be the reddish-brown of the blessed earth upon which Jesus trod, his sandals a snowy white. In reality, Mattie knew, Jesus would have his godly share of dirt stuck to those shoes. Real life had its quota of dog doo, into which everyone, even the son of God, had to step sooner or later. And Mattie doubted that biblical sandals were ever *white*, considering all the blood that must have flowed thanks to that "eye for an eye" stuff. She glanced around the table at the separate piles of puzzle: the mostly ivory pieces of the robe, scattered with the scarlet reds of that scarf-like thing Jesus was wearing over his right shoulder; the yellowish-brown pieces that would go into his hair; the cloudy white pieces, with little whorls, that were sure to be the wool of the lamb; the skin tones of his face, some touched with beard hairs; and the pinkish parts that would make up the holiness of the sky on Easter morning. *Easter Rising*, the picture was called. Mattie had been given it for her birthday by Rita's children, those loud, rude grandchildren, but most likely Rita picked it out. Mattie had dropped more hints than Jesus had beard hairs that she was pretty much fed up with religious picture puzzles, ever since her whole family had gotten into such a fight while putting together *The Last Supper*, which had been twenty-five hundred pieces of pure hell. A ruckus such as you've never seen or heard before, beginning with when they couldn't find the brown piece that would become Judas's money bag, and ending with Mattie's two oldest daughters engaged in a hair-pulling fistfight over whether Judas was a Catholic or a Protestant. Marlene seemed to think that Judas had come from some branch of the Protestant tree, while Rita kept insisting he was of the Catholic persuasion, the original Antichrist, a forerunner to the *true* Antichrist, that being the pope. "I don't give a damn if he was a Moonie!" Mattie finally shouted, and she lifted the lid to her little woodstove, took the dustpan, and shoveled the whole damn puzzle into the roaring flames, just as King Nebuchadnezzar had thrown those three Jews into the fiery furnace. In it all went: earthen pottery, a table as long as a pulp truck, plates of food, chairs, silver goblets, bread rolls, Jesus, the twelve disciples, you name it. "I think something akin to sacrilege has just taken place in this house," Rita said. Rita was the oldest of Mattie's daughters. "You want to hear about sacrilege?" Gracie, the youngest daughter, asked. "Leonardo da Vinci, who painted that famous picture, was an atheist, and a queer to boot. So help me, I learned that in my Rethinking Major Art Trends class." That's when Mattie cleared the temple, you might say, by putting the correct pocketbook in each daughter's arms and then pointing all three of them to the door. Ever since Rita had become a born-again Christian, she was blaming the Catholics for everything. And so Mattie had put her foot down about picture puzzles of a religious nature. Give her the head of a good old cocker spaniel, or the sad face of a clown—she called them "breakfast puzzles" because she could always finish them before lunchtime—but don't ever give her Mary Magdalene having stones cast at her by the multitude. All she needed was for those awful daughters to start throwing rocks. It was bad enough that Marlene and Rita were fighting over religion, but then Gracie, that youngest daughter, had started taking some kind of women's studies classes at the little college in Watertown, and now she didn't like to hear about anything, not even a fairy tale, if women got the short end of the stick. Gracie needed a tall, cold glass of reality, if you asked Mattie. But then Marlene's kids, those little heathens, had given Mattie that picture of Jesus, with Easter morning all around him, and big-faced flowers the size of saucer cups, and suffering from "picture puzzle addiction"—at least that's what Marlene had once whispered to Rita—Mattie found herself putting it together in private. She kept it on a big sheet of brown cardboard, ready to shuffle it under the sofa the minute one or all of her girls drove into the yard.

"Cripes," said Mattie, fingering through the blues of the flowers, the most likely place for the eyeball to be hiding out. "I can't leave the son of God looking like one of them sailors on *Treasure Island*." And speaking of *one eye*, that's what she'd been keeping on the driveway, since she never knew when those daughters, who seemed to have nothing better to do, would turn up. Mattie was also keeping a watch on the sky over the back mountain. The driving rain that those weathermen down in Bangor had predicted for midafternoon was still to arrive. She had already been out to her little clothesline to bring in the sheets and pillow-cases that had been flapping out there since the day before. All the signs said precipitation, what with those dark clouds strung out over the mountain, the kind that even *look* wet to the eye, true rain clouds that send down streaks of rain all the way to the ground. But so far not even a light sprinkle had fallen, much less a downpour.

Mattie saw Pauline Plunkett's car turn into the driveway and pull up close to the front steps. Pauline got out with a bag in her arms, and Mattie knew that her Avon order had arrived. She could have waited on the bottle of perfume. She had ordered it only to help Pauline out in hard times.

But she needed that big jar of Skin So Soft to get her through mosquito season. She put her reading glasses back in their case and went to open the front door. Pauline looked more tired than usual.

"Here you go," said Pauline. "Here's your order, all except for the Skin So Soft. Them big bottles are back-ordered, but I expect we'll get it to you before the mosquitoes carry you off." Pauline had taken on the Avon job as soon as news went around Mattagash that several mill workers from each of the surrounding towns would be laid off, no discrimination, from the paper mill in St. Leonard. Frank Plunkett, her husband, had been one of them, along with Rita's husband, Henry. But then bad news got worse for Pauline when Frank came down with some form of cancer and could no longer work anywhere, even if he *did* have a job.

"You ought to work harder," said Mattie, looking closely at the dark rings under Pauline's eyes. "There still seems to be a little life left in you." Pauline looked older than Mattie's own daughters, even though she was a year younger than Gracie.

"That's what Frank keeps telling me," Pauline said. "But you know yourself how things are around here. They'll probably close the school down since there's only a couple dozen kids left, and then I won't have my cafeteria job. I better hope the mosquitoes don't leave town. If it weren't for Skin So Soft, I'd be in big trouble." Mattie reached out and pushed a few strands of hair back from Pauline's face.

"You lean against some gray paint or something?" Mattie

asked. "How else would all that gray be in the front of your hair?"

Pauline smiled. "You don't quit, you know that?" she said. "Now, I better run. I got more orders to drop off. By the way, if your girls keep on ordering makeup and nail polish, I guarantee you I won't starve."

Mattie nodded with dissatisfaction. "Could I talk you into putting some superglue in their tubes of lipstick?" she asked, and this time Pauline laughed a big laugh, like the big woman she was, the kind of woman who used to be referred to as "pioneer stock." Not a feather in the wind, like Gracie and Marlene, women who would blow away in a strong gale.

Mattie followed Pauline out to her car, then stood and watched it disappear around the turn. She knew that it would pull into the next driveway, at Lola Craft Monihan's house. She had seen a bag on the front seat with *Lola* written on it with a black Magic Marker. A flock of grackles, which had flown up into the trees when Pauline started her car, had resettled beneath the clothesline, their black wings shimmering blue, their straight beaks poking at the grass. If Mattie had planted a garden, she wouldn't be so quick to let those grackles be. But for the first time since she'd married Lester Gifford, back in 1945, when she'd been only seventeen and too brain-dead to know any better, she hadn't had the energy to tear open a single package of cucumber seeds. She had sat upon her front porch instead, all that sweet, beautiful spring, and listened to her neighbors up and down the twisting Mattagash road as they harrowed and hoed and planted and scarecrowed. Now Mattie could almost hear those gardens growing, could feel tendrils drilling up out of the earth, string beans and tasty leaf lettuce and pale orange carrots and tomatoes, enough to fill a million shopping bags. Later, folks would bring Mattie what they couldn't use. She would be witness to a glut of fresh garden vegetables, more than she had ever grown in her own garden. She was certain of it. And she would suffer gladly this future surplus from her neighbors. She had seen it happen a thousand times with gardenless folks from Mattagash. She herself had hoisted a million unwanted tomatoes upon her neighbors, had bid farewell to bushels of pickle-sized cucumbers. "Still," Rita had said when Mattie mentioned this larder which lay just weeks away, "it don't give you the same satisfaction as when you've done your own planting and weeding." Mattie had thought about this, all the while Rita was sitting next to her on the front porch, creaking away in her own rocking chair. But she said nothing. It was only as Rita's taillights were disappearing from the driveway that Mattie, still waving good-bye in the dusk of evening, muttered, "Cow shit." It would have done no good to try and explain to her oldest, most headstrong daughter that the best response Mattie could think of, the *only* response, had been those simple words, *cow shit*. And the last thing she needed was to let born-again Rita rant on and on with one of her now-famous "God Don't Like It When We Swear" lectures. Mattie thought again about the garden, or lack of one, rather. Soon, she would be given enough cucumbers to make mustard pickles. She would can lots of tomatoes, just from the sacks her sister Elsa would give her. She would put up a couple dozen jars of string beans, thanks to Elmer Fennelson, who never ate a string bean in his life. "I just like the yellow of them," Elmer was fond of saying. Mattie thought of all those backbreaking years of hoeing, of fighting potato bugs and aphids, of the tons of sweat she had given up to weeding.

"Cow shit," Mattie said again. She was just about to resettle herself above *Easter Rising* when she heard a car horn blasting, followed by tires mowing through the crushed rock she had bought that summer for the driveway, crushed rock that Marlene's little heathens had taken to throwing over the hill by the handfuls when no one was looking. Through the living room window, Mattie saw Rita's big black Buick, Rita just getting out, leaving the car's door wide open behind her, her head covered with tiny silver curlers. It happened so fast that Mattie barely had time to scoot Jesus and his lambkin under the sofa. But Rita was too keyed up to notice the content of picture puzzles. She burst through Mattie's front door, leaving *it* wide open, too, for whenever the rainstorm did arrive.

"Good heavens, child," Mattie said. "Calm yourself. You'll have a heart attack years before your time."

"Oh God!" Rita cried. "It's the worst you can imagine, Mama! Turn on the TV, quick!" Mattie felt her heart lurch.

They had shot the president, surely. Wouldn't that be the worst thing you could see on TV, if you lived all the way up north in Mattagash, Maine? Some cruel, crazy person had shot Bill Clinton, the best thing to happen to America since Jimmy Carter had chosen to stop planting peanuts, just as Mattie had chosen not to plant her own garden. Or was it an earthquake? An earthquake down in Connecticut, maybe, where all Mattagashers had so many relatives living. No, it couldn't be. Earthquakes were bad enough when they happened in Russia and killed Communists, back when Russia still had Communists. But they weren't bad enough to send Rita hurtling out of the beauty salon where she was having her hair permed. And Mattie could tell by looking at the funny little gizmos on her daughter's head that Myrtle Craft had been three-fourths done in giving Rita her regular perm.

"Child," Mattie said. "What kind of trouble is it?" Her mind had now come back to President Clinton, his soft voice, his deep concern for the country. Why were people so crazy these days? Drugs, that was why. And too many guns. She tried to picture Hillary, being brave for Chelsea, just as Jackie had been brave for Caroline and John-John. The world was an awful place, too awful to live in, if people could kill a president so easily. Mattie watched as Rita flung herself upon the television button, not bothering to search for the remote control, knowing that at Mattie's, the grandchildren were forever hiding it. Josh, who was Rita's younger and more heathenish child, had thrown it up onto the roof just the Sunday before. They found it only because Steven, who was *Marlene's* younger and more heathenish child, had tattled. Elmer Fennelson had been kind enough to come with his rickety ladder and retrieve the remote, along with an assortment of odds and ends that Mattie had been missing over the past year, including one blue, fluffy slipper.

"Is it the president?" Mattie heard herself ask. "Is it poor President Clinton?" He was such a nice, polite boy, one who had made his mother proud. Rita shook her head, and the loose hair still waiting to be permed bounced dramatically. Mattie was reminded of Gracie's childhood doll that Sonny had given a haircut, only to be interrupted before he finished the job.

"You're not going to believe what he's done now," Rita said as she frantically punched at the channel numbers. This took Mattie by surprise. She didn't have to ask who *he* was. She knew. She knew by the tone of Rita's voice, by that same old jealous anger mixed with excitement, that Sonny was in the middle of some kind of limelight. Mattie had heard that tone many times, all through those blasted school-age years, when Sonny was interacting far too much with the teachers, the principal, the superintendent. Mattie had come to know a parcel of people very well through Sonny's misadventures. Now she wished she *had* planted a garden. It would offer her something to do. A little weeding could be good for the soul. Dear Lord, but what could the boy have done to get himself on TV?

"Sit down," Rita was now saying, "because what Sonny done this time takes the cake." Mattie found herself dropping down onto the sofa, her hand clasping her throat, as it always did in times of heavy stress. Over the years, Sonny Gifford had caused a great deal of that throat-clasping, Mattie hated to admit.

Rita was now on the phone.

"Gracie? Get over to Mama's place, and I mean *pronto*. You ain't gonna believe what your brother's done this time. *This time*, he's outdone himself. Don't ask. Just pick up Marlene and get to hell over here." Mattie tried to focus on the television screen before her. She hadn't heard Rita swear since she'd found Jesus at the Pentecostal church a few months earlier. All Rita had planned to do was drop by quickly and pick up a sweater she was borrowing from her friend Rachel Ann, a long-suffering Holy Roller, and before Rita left she'd been saved. She didn't need Rachel Ann's sweater after all. She had found the warmth of Jesus Christ, or so she told everyone who did and didn't care. She was wrapped up snug in the wool of the Lamb. But now here she was, swearing again. Mattie tried to listen to what the newsman on Channel 4 in Bangor was saying. The scene flicked to a trailer park as the camera focused on a single trailer, a white one with a nice red stripe running down its middle. Rita flung down the phone and then cranked up the volume on the television set.

"Sonny Gifford, of 15 Trenton Street, Bangor," the voice was announcing. "Mr. Gifford is a white male, estimated to be in his midthirties." Mattie looked up at Rita for an explanation.

"Has Sonny shot the president?" Mattie asked, her heart drumming fiercely. "Has Sonny shot that nice Mr. Clinton?" This would be one little fracas she wouldn't be able to get him out of, she knew that for certain. Not when Channel 4 had their nose in it.

"Sonny ain't smart enough to shoot a president," Rita said. She dug into her enormous purse for a cigarette, which she lit in a hurry. Mattie had been under the impression that Jesus had told Rita to quit smoking, but then Jesus hadn't known about all of Rita's bad habits when he saved her. If he had, he might have let her go downstream instead.

"According to witnesses at the bank, Gifford led the two women to a waiting 1985 blue Ford pickup truck and then sped away to this trailer, at Marigold Drive Trailer Park. Neighbors have told police that the trailer belongs to Sheila Bumphrey Gifford, Sonny Gifford's estranged wife." The picture was still on the house trailer. Mattie noticed a green-and-white lawn chair leaning against the small porch railing. A child's sand pail, the toy shovel peeking above the rim, was tilting out of a tiny pile of brownish dirt in the front yard. Then the picture flicked back to the newscaster's face, which was lined with professional concern.

"Sonny's robbed a bank!" Mattie cried, but Rita waved her cigarette.

"Sonny's too lazy to rob a bank," said Rita. "That involves weeks of planning. I'm telling you, this stunt takes the cake." The screen now showed a man and woman standing in front of a gray-colored bank, their hands waving, their fingers pointing frantically. Mattie could see the words *Bangor Savings and Loan* just above their heads.

"He just sort of appeared out of nowhere," the woman was saying. "He said he had a gun and, well, I didn't look. I just covered my eyes."

"Gun?" asked Mattie. What was Sonny doing sporting a gun? Sonny hated guns, had never even fired BBs as a boy.

"He told us he had no intention of hurting anyone," the man said. He had a big round nose, bigger even than Elmer Fennelson's. "He picked two young women out of the line and they had no choice but to go with him." Well, it would be like Sonny to choose women. He had always been a ladies' man.

"Have you ever?" asked Rita. "Is this not the worst yet?" Mattie strained forward in her chair. She still couldn't understand what was happening. Sonny hadn't shot anyone. Sonny hadn't robbed a bank. So what was he doing in a bank claiming he had a gun?

"Tell me what he's done," Mattie warned her daughter, "before I slap you."

"Listen," Rita cautioned. She cranked the volume button higher.

"The suspect has given no statement as to why he took the two female hostages or what his plans are now that he's

barricaded himself inside his estranged wife's trailer, Police Chief Patrick Melon has told reporters. Bangor police are in the process of setting up telephone communication with Mr. Gifford at this time."

"My God," said Mattie. "Hostages?"

"Didn't I tell you it would take the cake?" Rita wanted to know. "This is a lot worse than when he set fire to the American Legion Hall." Did Rita have to remember *everything?* Couldn't she focus once in a while on something *good* Sonny had done? Hadn't he gone back himself, the very next day, and helped rake up all the rubble left behind after the Legion Hall burned down? And besides, everyone in town was glad it had burned. It had been an eyesore for a good many years and someone's kid was bound, sooner or later, to fall through the rickety floor.

"Hostages," Mattie said again, and her mind played with the word. Hostages were usually nabbed in strange parts of the world, by terrorists and governments run by folks in the Middle East who wore dish towels on their heads. But *hostages* in Bangor, Maine? Taken by her only male child, Sonny Gifford? Mattie's heart fluttered again, in that way Sonny Gifford could make it flutter.

Marlene and Gracie roared into the driveway. Mattie hoped they hadn't mown down the cement birdbath she had set out on the lawn just that morning, in the middle of her pansy bed. It was a little statue of St. Francis, holding a bowl in his hands which Mattie had filled with water for the birds. Marlene was first into the house, Gracie on her heels. They both flung their purses upon the sofa.

"I had no more than hung up the phone from talking to you," Gracie said excitedly, "when Denise Craft come banging on my door with the news." Rita offered her a cigarette. Marlene helped herself to one, too. They lit up. Smoke rose into the air. It looked to Mattie like some church ritual, with incense and all, a ceremony of sorts. And in a way, it was. Her daughters had always been at their best when Sonny was at his worst. No wedding, no funeral, no high school graduation had ever given them pleasure such as they got from their brother's wrongdoings.

"It ain't done me a bit of good to have quit smoking five years ago," Mattie said, "with the three of you puffing away like chimneys here in my house. That's what they call secondhand smoke." Marlene had turned her empty Coke can into an ashtray and now all three daughters were batting their cigarettes against the small opening. And it hadn't helped to hide all her ashtrays either. She was forever emptying soggy cigarette butts out of pop cans, thanks to one or all of her daughters. But the girls were too excited to care about secondhand smoke, not when there was firsthand smoke on the television screen. Mattie tried to think of Sonny. Who could she call this time? Even if her husband, Lester, was still alive, which he wasn't, thank God, he had never seen anything worth helping out in Sonny. Not like Mattie did. When Lester died, five years earlier, Mattie had decided she wanted to live as long as

she could, now that she was single again. And so she had
given up her beloved Salem Menthols. How could she have
known her big, grown daughters would go on ahead and kill
her with secondhand smoke? She had four hundred dollars
in her savings account. She would get Marlene to drive her
to Watertown and she would withdraw it. Marlene had the
smallest mouth of the three girls. It was *big*, but it was still
the *smallest*. The last time Sonny had needed money in a
hurry, Marlene had driven Mattie down to the bank, and as
far as Mattie could tell, Marlene had kept quiet about the
whole thing.

"What's the story?" Gracie was asking. "What in the
world is he up to?" Mattie stared at the television screen.
The picture had become a commercial for some kind
of deodorant. The room grew bluish-gray with cigarette
smoke. Mattie closed her eyes.

"Nobody has any idea what's going on inside his head,"
said Rita. She dropped her cigarette into the Coke can and
it sizzled loudly. "According to the police chief, they're
trying to set up communication with him."

"Well, good luck to them," said Marlene, "if they're
hoping to find out what's going on in Sonny Gifford's
head." Thunder exploded in the distance and Mattie heard
the grackles rise up outside in a great cluster of wings and
clucking sounds. She tried to think reasonably. Had she
brought in those sheets and pillowcases? They would be
drenched in no time. Now the television screen was filled
with actors who were afraid to lift their arms because they

hadn't used Sure deodorant. Mattie studied them carefully, wondering what they had done with Sonny and the pin-striped trailer.

"Don't this latest stunt take the sponge cake?" Rita asked again.

2

That was how Mattie Gifford received the news that her only boy, Sonny Gifford, had taken two hostages and was holed up with them in a trailer, down in Bangor, Maine, five hours south of Mattagash. It was later that day, on the regular Channel 4 News program at six o'clock, that more information was disclosed about the hostage incident. It was announced at the beginning of the show that a phone conversation with Sonny Gifford, who had been inside the trailer for over two hours, at Marigold Drive Trailer Park, would be aired for the first time. Then the station had gone to a commercial.

"That's what they call a *teaser*," Gracie said. She was doing her sit-ups in Mattie's living room, in front of the television set, because she hadn't had time to exercise before the urgent call from Rita arrived. Gracie had been saying all year long that she was going to take off twenty-five pounds before Christmas if she had to have a leg amputated in order to do so. Her only child, Roberta, had decided on a Christmas wedding, much to everyone's dismay. Folks in Mattagash, Maine, had seen plenty of Christmases come and go when Santa Claus couldn't find a rooftop on which to land his reindeer, thanks to a ton of fresh white snow. "We'll look cute wading about in high heels with the snow up to our asses," Marlene had complained the day she heard the news. But Roberta was eighteen years old, and although she had just graduated from high school with a crisp, new diploma, it seemed to Mattie that the space between her granddaughter's ears was bigger and lonelier than ever. "I wanna be different from everyone else," was what Roberta kept saying. "Oh, you're gonna be different all right," Gracie had agreed. "You'll probably be the only bride in Mattagash history who rides up to the altar on a snowmobile." Mattie had grown weary of hearing them argue.

"Fifty," Gracie said, and sat up, legs spread before her on the carpet. Mattie noticed weights of some kind strapped about her daughter's ankles. What would they think of next? Marlene had gone out for two pizzas from the new pub in St. Leonard and she had brought back bags of potato chips and pretzels, as well as a few packs of cigarettes. Now Mattie's coffee table was covered with plates of cold pizza crusts and half-drunk Cokes with cigarette stubs bobbing somewhere down inside of them. There was so much smoke in the tiny living room that it reminded Mattie of the picture puzzle she had done a year earlier, the one called *Fog in the Adirondacks*. The phone rang.

"One of you girls get that," said Mattie. That was the seventh or eighth time in less than an hour that someone had called. Twice, whoever was on the other end had simply hung up. Mattie supposed they had phoned just to see if she was still alive, or if she had dropped dead of a heart attack upon learning that Sonny had gone off his rocker in a big way. Only two of the other calls had been from neighbors one would expect to telephone in times of a crisis, offering help. Pauline Plunkett and Wilma Hart. The remaining calls had come from folks brimming over with curiosity, excitement lacing their words as they tried to sound genuinely concerned. Ruby Craft had actually hyperventilated. But then, Ruby had become what they call "hysterically pregnant" when a flyboy from Loring Air Force Base had refused to marry her. She had even worn a smock for four months and then put a crib on layaway before her mother slapped her out of it. "That flyboy ain't nothing but a fly-by-night," Ruby's mother had said.

"I hope this comes to some kind of a conclusion soon," Rita was now saying to Marlene. "I gotta go home and cook Henry and the kids their supper." Mattie scraped the cold crusts from one pizza plate off onto another, and again, and again, until one plate held all the crusts. She then stacked this plate onto the others and stood up.

"Oh, Mama, leave those plates be," said Gracie. "One of us will get them." Mattie found this statement of particular interest. After all, each of her daughters had watched as she cleaned up the plates and none had so much as lifted an eyebrow, much less a finger, to help. Mattie fanned the air about her head, circulating it. She opened the front door and thumped one of Gracie's shoes against it to keep it open.

"It gets any smokier in here," she said, "and the Mattagash Fire Department will pull up out front." She had had to disconnect her smoke detector, just a month after she had bought and installed it, because her girls smoked too damn much and were forever setting it off. This was something her homeowner's insurance company didn't need to know, but to Mattie it was a sad statement of parental life.

The newscaster's face was back full-screen as Mattie returned from the kitchen, where she'd left the dishes in the sink. The girls were making such a ruckus that she couldn't catch a word he was saying.

"Shush!" Mattie shouted, and finally she could hear the words coming from her television set. The picture had flashed to the trailer park they had shown earlier, a reporter standing on the road out in front, a microphone in her hand. Hoards of people could now be seen in the background, some leaning on cars and looking like nosy neighbors, others milling about with an air of news team importance. Bangor policemen were busy keeping the tiny crowd back. Mattie couldn't help but feel a stab of pride. When Sonny gave a party, he gave a party.

"Police Chief Patrick Melon conducted the conversation with Mr. Gifford less than an hour ago, Dan," the newswoman said. She looked to Mattie like some kind of peaked chihuahua.

"Donna, did Chief Melon say what state of mind Mr. Gifford is in?" the newsman back at the station asked. It looked to Mattie as though he might have a big wad of gum in his mouth. Maybe he chewed every time the camera switched to Donna, standing out in front of Marigold Drive Trailer Park.

"State of mind, my foot," said Rita. "What would Sonny be doing with a state of mind this late in his life?"

"As might be expected, Dan," the reporter answered, "the police are being very cautious at this time. As of yet, they have still made no contact with Mr. Gifford's ex-wife, the owner of this trailer." She waved a thin arm behind her, at the trailer in question. "Police Chief Melon has released part of the phone conversation he had just an hour ago with Mr. Gifford, which contains an explanation, albeit a bizarre one, as to the events leading up to this hostage action." The reporter's tiny nostrils flared, like the gills on Mattie's pet goldfish. *Dan and Donna*. It sounded like a dance team.

"Oh God, I'm gonna pee my pants," Marlene said. "This is too much excitement for me, at least in a single day."

"Don't this take the cake, though?" Rita wanted to know. And then Mattie heard Sonny's sweet voice, heard the voice of her baby boy coming from, of all places, the television. Her eyes watered.

"That's when the face of John Lennon appeared on

my television set during a show on starvation in Africa," Sonny's voice was saying, a tinny voice, being played off a tape. "And it was Mr. John Lennon himself who told me that the world's attention needed to focus upon them starving children. 'You're a sorry human bean, Sonny Gifford,' that's what the face told me. 'There you are, eating a large pizza, extra cheese, while much of the world's starving to death. Get your shit together, boy.'"

"You can't say *shit* on Channel Four, can you?" Gracie asked.

"I believe you can during emergency broadcasts," said Marlene.

"Quiet!" Mattie pointed to the television. The picture had frozen on the trailer, with its red line slicing it in two, a long, red vein. A silhouette had appeared in the window of the front door and Mattie wondered if it was Sonny, looking out at the eye of the world. The phone conversation was still running.

"What are your plans at this point, Mr. Gifford?" the police chief was asking. "Can't you let the women go so we can talk, just the two of us, man to man? Maybe we can even get this John Lennon on the phone." Inside Mattie's house her girls tittered.

"Where's that police chief been?" Marlene wanted to know.

"They got Johnny Cash on the phone to talk to Gary Gilmore, the night before he died," Gracie reminded everyone, an assurance that, socially, it was okay.

"Friend, you ain't been keeping up with your musical history." It was Sonny's voice. "Mr. Lennon was shot down by a low-life insect, just as the song says. But he appeared on my television screen long enough to tell me to make a little noise on behalf of the poor folks in this here world."

"Why not let the hostages go?" the police chief asked again. "What do those two women have to do with world hunger?"

"Well," said Sonny. Mattie leaned forward, toward the television, trying to peer into the house trailer on her screen, trying to see Sonny's handsome face. She had always been able to tell a lot about what was in her son's head when she could look into the blue pools of his eyes. "While I was listening to John Lennon talk about world hunger, the TV picture flicked to two women standing on a patio drinking wine coolers, with a great big dog looking on, so I took that as a sign. As you know, I got me two women in here, and the best I could find for a dog was one of them spindly assed poodles."

"But *why?*" asked Mattie. Her hands had begun to tremble. "*Why,* Sonny?" she asked the television screen.

"Since when did Sonny Gifford ever need a *why?*" Gracie wanted to know. "Since day one, Sonny's only been interested in the *when* and the *where.*" Gracie was flat on her back now, pretending to bicycle, her weighted legs making circles in the air. Mattie wished her daughter was on a *real* bike so that all the pedaling would take her out the door and back down the road to her own house. Better yet, Mattie wished Gracie was on one of those bicycles built for three. That way, she could take her two sisters with her. But everyone in Mattagash knew that Gracie was a woman destined to visit. "If Gracie had been born Indian," Sonny once noted, "they'd have named her Squaw Who Can't Find Her Tepee."

"Did Sonny tell you he'd bought a house trailer?" Rita asked. She was leaning forward on the hassock, peering at the TV. Mattie knew that Rita hated to learn interesting gossip from other folks, much less Channel 4.

"It's a pretty color, ain't it?" Marlene conceded.

"He always did have good taste," Mattie noted.

"Don't you two have ears?" Gracie asked. "That house trailer belongs to his estranged wife. He ain't got a bit of business in there. That's just the way Charlie acted when me and him got divorced, turning up whenever he pleased. Charlie and Sonny have one thing in common, if you ask me. Their thinking mechanism is dangling between their legs."

"Did they say the names of the hostages yet?" Rita asked. She was putting on her shoes, lacing them up.

"If Wolf Blitzer would shut up for a minute," said Mattie, nodding at Gracie, "maybe I could hear the television well enough to answer that." Donna was now saying that names of the hostages would be released when their families had been notified. The police chief was attempting another telephone conversation with Sonny. And it was hoped by the reporters that more background information would be unearthed on Sonny Gifford, the man. All that was known currently was what neighbors at the trailer park had to offer. With a promise to keep viewers updated as to the current hostage situation in Bangor, the station then went to a story about sewer leakage in Portland.

Mattie felt drained, as though someone had stood her on her head and poured her entire heart and soul out of her body. This was big, this newest adventure of Sonny's. And he'd be on his own this time.

"Well, it's just a matter of time now," said Rita, "and the jig will be up. Wait till they find out we're his family."

"You gonna start giving press conferences?" Marlene asked. "You been practicing all your life."

Rita stopped lacing and stared at her sister. "I hate to say this," she said anyway, "but there's a room in hell with your name on it." She picked up her purse, slung the strap over her shoulder. Her leather jacket squeaked when she moved.

"Nice talk for a member of the Born Again Club," said Marlene.

"A real *hot* room," Rita added. "A regular sauna." Mattie waved her hands before her face, the way she always did when her children were acting up, which they'd all been prone to do throughout their growing-up years. Although, listening to her daughters day after day, "growing-up years" hardly seemed the correct phrase. "Getting-bigger years" would be more like it.

"We gotta drive down there tonight," Mattie said. "We gotta let Sonny know that we'll help him."

"What do you mean, 'we'?" asked Marlene. "You got a mouse in your pocket?"

"This'll work out on its own, Mama," said Rita. "There's no need for us to turn up in Bangor and rile the waters even more. You know Sonny. He can't keep his mind on a task for very long. He'll be ready to come out by morning and it'll all be over. Besides, he's got a phone in there and he knows your number. He can call if he needs to." Mattie thought of Pauline Plunkett, with her tired face. Pauline would drive her. Out of the goodness of her heart, Pauline would do it. But Mattie couldn't add to Pauline's worries.

"Let's go," Gracie told Rita. "Marlene'll come with me so you two can't fight over religion. All I need to do is feed the cat and grab a couple things." She stored the ankle weights on the floor near Mattie's magazine rack.

"And *I* need to see that Henry and the boys can find something for supper," Rita said.

"Now, don't be dragging half the junk in your house over here," Marlene said. "All we really need is pajamas and cold cream, and Mama's got plenty of cold cream." Mattie was staring at the stored ankle weights and listening to this conversation. Her name had been invoked, so it must have something to do with her. But *pajamas? Cold cream?*

"I'll just see that Henry and the boys are okay with the buttons on my new microwave," said Rita, "and then I'll grab my old flannel nightgown and I'll be back in a jiffy." She went out and slammed the door to Mattie's house.

"What's this all about?" Mattie asked the two remaining

daughters. Marlene was waiting at the door while Gracie pulled jeans on over the purple tights she'd worn to do her exercises.

"We can't leave you alone here tonight, Mama," said Marlene. "Not with Sonny still holed up in that trailer."

"Yes you can," said Mattie. She'd just been thinking how nice it would be to have a little peace and quiet before she tried to sleep, a square of silence in which she could think this Sonny thing out. Having the girls around was like holding a cup of marbles up to your ears and shaking it.

"Now, Mama, think sensible," said Gracie. "When they find out who Sonny is, there's gonna be people calling us up nonstop and maybe even showing up on the front porch. How are *you* gonna handle that?" Mattie thought about this question.

"I guess the same way I handled that house fire when you four kids were just babies," Mattie told her daughter. "And I got you all out safe, in the middle of the night, mind you, and even come back inside and saved Grannie's old Bible."

"This ain't the same thing, Mama," said Marlene, shaking her head with impatience.

"Or the time Rita almost drowned in the river and I pulled her out and gave her mouth-to-mouth, even though I'd only seen it done on TV," said Mattie. "I just covered her mouth with my own and saved her life. I suspect that's the way I'll handle this latest thing."

"I got to admit *that* was a feat," said Marlene. "Covering

Rita's mouth would be like trying to put a piece of Scotch tape over the Grand Canyon."

"Now, Mama, that's nonsense," Gracie began, but Mattie stopped her.

"Or the time we were supposed to evacuate during that spring flood, and Lester was God only knows where and we were here alone, up on the top floor, waiting for the water to go back down. I'd say I handled that one pretty good." Marlene and Gracie glanced at each other, exchanged a look that indicated to Mattie that they knew everything and she knew very little.

"But, Mama, sweetie," said Gracie. "This is a whole lot different than a drowning, or a fire, or even a springtime flood. This is *television*, Mama." Mattie waited for a few seconds before she said anything. She tried hard to think of what it all meant, what the implications were in such a mess as Sonny was now wallowing. Would she need a new dress? Maybe she should have her hair done, some of those French curls that Lola Monihan liked to pile on the top of a client's head and lacquer with hair spray until they were as stiff as plastic flowers. Then Mattie hated herself for even thinking such vain thoughts when Sonny was in so much pain. And she knew darn well, just by the sound of Sonny's voice, that he was in *deep pain*. His heart was hurting him an awful lot. Maybe he did care about children starving. He always had the kindest thoughts about old people and animals. But something else was going on inside that son of hers. Something that no doubt had to do with this Sheila woman he had married, a woman with kids from another marriage, a woman Mattie had yet to meet. "I love this one, Mama," Sonny had told her over the phone just six months earlier, when he called to say that he and Sheila Bumphrey had gotten married. "This one's gonna be the last one," Sonny had predicted. He had never said such words before, and Mattie had no doubt that he meant them. She looked at Marlene, then at Gracie.

"If you stay here," Mattie said, "you'll need to go out on the porch to smoke. I mean it. That's just the way it'll have to be."

"For heaven's sake, you treat us like we're still in high school," Gracie protested.

"Well," said Mattie, "I wonder why."

3

When her four children had been at home, and Lester was still alive enough to chase women, Mattie had considered the house a tiny mushroom of a thing, too cramped and narrow to offer privacy. There was always the sound of someone's conversation in the air, the smell of someone's perfume or cologne, the sight of someone's shoes, or stockings, or schoolbooks scattered about on floors and chairs. There was even the indelicate smell of someone's private doings emanating from the closet-sized bathroom, mixing sometimes with the aroma of onions, or freshly baked cookies. But then, opening onto the kitchen as it did, the bathroom was only one of Lester's many architectural flops. Even the three bedrooms, meant to sleep a family of six, seemed more likely to have been designed to hold shelves of hatboxes, or Christmas decorations, a sewing machine, maybe. But Lester Gifford had always thought small, except when it came to female breasts. After Rita and Marlene and Gracie had married, Mattie had indeed turned their bedroom into a perfect little sewing room, and she had replaced the bed—which Gracie had paid for with potato harvest money and therefore taken with her—with a pullout sofa. When the girls had lived in it, it had been a room with wall-to-wall beds, what with the bunk beds in which Marlene and Rita had slept pushing up against Gracie's full-size. One of the girls could've put a twin bed in Sonny's room and slept there, where there would have been more space, but there seemed to be something socially wrong with this notion that only teenagers could understand. But they had survived those crowded, sardine years and then, one day, they were all gone, and Mattie was left with a house full of beds. She finally called up Rita one day, since she was the oldest, and offered to give her the bunk beds for her boys. "I'm gonna have a sewing room if it kills me," Mattie had told Rita. "Come get the beds if you want them." This had caused a commotion with Marlene, who felt *she* should have the bunk beds for *her* boys. Mattie was just about to take Lester's chain saw to the beds, then give one to each daughter, regardless of how lopsided they turned out, when she thought of her sister Elsa, who had so many big bedrooms and even more little grandchildren. That had shut the daughters up for good. Mattie hadn't seen either of them for two blissful weeks. But what she would remember more sharply about the bunk bed incident were the words she had used, idly, on the phone that day to Rita: *I'm gonna have a sewing room if it kills me.* As it turned out, it had killed Lester instead, his heart exploding in his

chest when he bent to lift up his end of the bunk beds,
Mattie hoisting the other end as Elsa waited outside in her
pickup truck, the tailgate down. All Mattie could do, as
she stood with the phone hugging her ear, waiting for the
Watertown Emergency number to answer and watching
Lester's contorted face, was to pray he would tell her he
was sorry, once and for all, sorry for the cheating, sorry
for the long evenings when she'd sat up alone in the dark,
waiting for him to come home, the sounds of their sleeping
children the only rattling noises in the tiny mushroom of
a house, a house made larger by Lester's absence. She had
stood there with the phone pressed to her ear as though it
were a plastic seashell, all the unhappy years of her marriage
echoing again in her eardrums, washing up in the coils of
her memory. But Lester had simply clutched his heart, that
organ he had given to so many women in his day, given it so
freely and so often that he had worn the sucker out. Mattie
had had a good mind to hang up the phone. "Let one of
your women call the ambulance for you and your used-up
old heart," she had wanted to say. But she could tell by the
gray color seeping into Lester Gifford's face, the slack way
in which his muscles had relaxed, the little string of drool
that was lacing down his chin, that his heart was making
its last big move. His heart was dancing its last tango. And
the house had become even larger once Lester danced on.

Now here it was full of daughters again, all chattering
and gossipy, like the grackles Mattie had watched that
morning under her clothesline. The girls had returned

with their arms filled with nightgowns and magazines and Marlene's VCR, in case anyone was up for a rental movie after the eleven o'clock news. But at eleven Donna, the small, tight-faced little reporter, had nothing new to tell her viewers. The news clip was a rerun. With no adrenaline pumping now to keep them awake, the girls decided to turn in. Gracie pulled the sofa bed out in the sewing room and claimed it as her territory.

"After all, this was my room last," she told her sisters, "for five whole years after you two left home." Mattie tried to imagine this. Rita and Marlene, once again sharing a room they had never learned to share as children, or as teenagers. In fact, those two had never learned to share *anything*. How many times in their growing-up years had they squabbled over which one would get those little onions in the bottom of the mixed pickles jar? Or which one would get those bright red cherries, scattered here and there among a can of fruit cocktail? It had gotten to the point where Mattie had to stop buying those products. And she had forbidden anyone in the family to purchase a single box of Cracker Jacks. God only knew what kind of war a *real* prize could create. Now Rita and Marlene would again be *sharing* a bed in Sonny's old room.

Mattie stood in the kitchen and listened to the same old tune that made up her daughters' voices, that continual whine about "Sonny this" and "Sonny that," a record stuck in time. She didn't like the idea of them being in there, enemies that they were of Sonny. The only times that room had been used in years was when Sonny turned up unannounced with a pillowcase full of dirty clothes. Or when a grandchild or two thought that staying at Grandma's house would be an adventure. Mowing the lawn once or twice, or washing a few pots and pans in the sink, had turned that adventure into hellish boredom. But Mattie didn't care. She hadn't fledged all four of her own chicks only to raise grandchicks. Now Rita and Marlene were camping in Sonny's room, inspecting the posters of scantily clad women he'd pinned to the wall, the Louis L'Amour paperbacks he kept stacked on the dresser, the baseball Sonny had caught that autumny day at Fenway Park. "Hit by none other than Mr. Rico Petrocelli himself," Sonny often noted. There were several colorful beer cans, the names of which were alien to Mattie, that had been collected by Sonny on a trip to Texas, during his first and last truck-driving experience. There were pictures of the dogs he had owned and loved in his boyhood days: Cody, his first German shepherd, and Tip-Top, one of the many German shepherds to follow, who had a round black spot on his head. And finally, some teddy bears Sonny had won at the Maine State Fair by throwing softballs at milk cans. And a deck of playing cards on which more young women sported an unspeakable amount of cleavage.

"I can't believe Mama keeps them posters up on the wall," Mattie heard Marlene say. "Not to mention these cards. Just take a look at the jack of diamonds, if you dare." Mattie was fixing herself a tall glass of vinegar and water, which was supposed to shrink her varicose veins. Ordinarily, she would have this drink with her supper, but she'd forgotten it, thanks to all the commotion on Channel 4. The spoon made loud clinking sounds as she stirred. She wanted to send a little Morse code into Sonny's bedroom. *Get the hell out of Sonny's stuff,* the spoon said. She *wanted* Sonny's stuff there, and that's why she left it just as he liked to find it.

"My taillights hadn't disappeared around the bend," Rita was now saying, "before Mama had all my stuff packed into boxes. But Sonny could've left a live alligator in here and she'd still be feeding it hamburger." Mattie let the spoon fall into the sink, a metallic *clunk.*

"I can take a hint, Mama," Rita shouted out. "But you know yourself it's true. While you were packing my stuff, the tin cans were still bouncing behind my wedding car."

Mattie took her glass of vinegar and water and went in to find her daughters. Gracie had now joined them, standing before a poster of Cindy Crawford.

"You'd think she'd be embarrassed," Gracie said. "It's bubbleheads like this who make it so hard on all us women."

Rita took one look at Mattie's glass and then threw her face into a twisted frown. "How can you drink that stuff?" she asked. "You're gonna turn into a walking douche bag."

"Thanks," said Mattie. This was nice talk from a born-again Christian. *B.A.* is how Rita referred to it. "It's true I ain't been to college like my sister Gracie," Rita liked to tell folks, "but I got my B.A. when I got born again." Rita's being born the first time had almost killed Mattie, a breach birth, and only a midwife to help out. But they had both lived, mother and child, sometimes even to regret it. Mattie was just glad she didn't have to be there with a towel on her forehead and old Mrs. Hart between her legs when Rita was born that second time. Once was enough, thank you very much.

"This sure brings back memories," said Marlene, "you know, when we were all home here, one big family." She picked up the Rico Petrocelli ball and rolled it a few times across the palm of her hand.

"Put that back," said Mattie. "It's very valuable."

"One big *dysfunctional* family," Gracie added. "By the way, the jack of diamonds is nothing. Have you seen the queen of hearts? She looks just like a young, naked Doris Day." Mattie took the playing cards from Gracie, opened Sonny's top dresser drawer, and dropped them inside.

"Dysfunctional family, pish posh," said Marlene. "You been taking too damn many college courses, Gracie, you know that? Who the hell ain't dysfunctional these days? When the Kennedys straighten out, then maybe the rest of us should worry."

"All *I* remember, personally," said Rita, "was the sheer hell of that last spring before I finally married Henry and got out of this nuthouse for good."

"The spring of 1970," said Marlene, "when Sonny was at his craziest." Mattie had moved to Sonny's bedroom window and lifted the curtain. How many times had she come in at night to tuck him in, only to find just the outline of him, the black outline of a boy against the window, his cowlick sticking up like a little periscope, his chin resting in his hands? "I'm looking for the Big Dipper," is what he told her on those starry nights, all those years ago.

"I can't see a single star out tonight," said Mattie, although she wasn't looking. She was staring instead at the ghostly reflection of her daughters in the glass and wishing talk about the stars would nudge them toward a new subject. She considered opening up the dresser drawer and giving them back the playing cards, just to shut them up. They hadn't even gotten to the queen of spades yet. Now, *that* one would give them considerable pause. At first, Mattie had thought that the face peering up at her over those immense, chocolate boobs was that of Pearl Bailey, in her younger years, before the wear of time cut her down. But it wasn't Pearl Bailey. It was just some poor misguided girl who probably needed to make a fast buck.

"He should've been taken to a shrink back in 1970," Gracie was saying, "when it was obvious that a couple of bricks had bounced off the wagon." Mattie peered out at the black heavens, past the phantom images of her daughters alive in the glass, and thought of Sonny in that house trailer down in Bangor, the one with the red pinstripe running through the middle of it.

"That was the spring we had what they call a *polterguest* living in this house," Mattie said, finally coming to her son's defense. She had been right. There were no stars anywhere in the dark sky over Mattagash.

"It's polter*geist*, Mama," said Gracie, "and you know damn well that was Sonny himself doing them things." Maybe Marlene was right. Maybe Gracie *had* taken too many college courses.

"It wasn't neither," said Mattie. "It was a *polterguest*."

"It was Sonny Gifford," said Marlene. "Pure and simple."

"You're the only one who never saw him, Mama," Rita added, "but the rest of us caught him in the act, throwing all them ashtrays up against the wall, slinging eggs on the floor."

"He was only a child," said Mattie. "He was only twelve years old."

"*Damien* was only a child," Rita reminded everyone. "I was lucky to get a date to come pick me up. Sonny was always sneaking out to let the air out of their tires. And I was even luckier to find a husband, considering the nuthouse those young men had to enter every time they took me out."

"I don't remember you dating much," said Marlene.

"Remember when Sonny put a box of toothpicks in my bed?" asked Gracie.

Mattie watched as the first drops of rain began to run against the window, thin varicose veins sliding down the pane. Did Sonny have clean underwear? she wondered, and then smiled. With two women hostages, Sonny would be waited on hand and foot. Women just couldn't help themselves when it came to Sonny Gifford. That was part of his deadly charm. Mattie imagined him seated just then before a full plate of good food, a boiled dinner, maybe, the New

England way, with plenty of ham and cabbage and carrots. She hoped at least one of Sonny's hostages was a good cook.

"I had as many dates as *you* did," Rita told Marlene.

"He should've gone to see a shrink back then," Gracie said again. "I can tell you, just from the psychology classes I've been taking as part of my requirements, that 1970 was the beginning of the end for Sonny Gifford and nobody did a thing about it. Now look what's happened." She pointed toward the living room, where Mattie's big television sat waiting for the next round of news about Sonny.

"I'm going to bed," Mattie said. In the hallway, she was overcome with a feeling of claustrophobia, the house having turned small again, the house having shrunk down to its original shoe size, what with all her daughters back under its rafters. *She had so many daughters she didn't know what to do.* Mattie put a hand to her forehead and felt cool sweat there. She could hear the sounds of her daughters turning down blankets, fluffing pillows, undoing jars of cold cream, slippers scuffing across the hardwood floors. The tiny bathroom would look like a trash bin by morning.

"He just wanted some attention from his big sisters," Mattie whispered. "Just like Cinderella did." She went on down the hallway, past the tiny kitchen where the luminous numbers of the stove's timer were casting blue streaks upon the teakettle, past the bathroom with its hummingbird night-light, the glowing red throat lighting up the basin and tub, to her own bedroom. At the door she paused and looked back to the living room, where the big television crouched in the shadowy beam of the porch light. Mattie could see its black, open face, and she felt as though she were looking into the mouth of a deep, dangerous cave. She listened a bit, pointing her ear toward the set, as though Sonny might say something to her, as though Sonny might throw his voice again across all those wires running between Mattagash and Bangor. *I'm just looking for the Big Dipper, Mama, that's all I'm doing in this house trailer.* But all Mattie could hear were bedsprings squeaking beneath the weight of her big, grown daughters, their bleeps of conversation rising and falling like the lament of some faraway truck as it climbs the hill, and a full steady rain bearing down on the roof of her house.

"Good night, Sonny," Mattie whispered down the hallway. Then she went into her own bedroom and closed the door.

4

Mattie woke to the sound of her phone ringing and discovered that it was Henry, wanting to know why Rita wasn't at home to fix him and the boys their breakfast. Mattie looked at the clock. Seven thirty. She had learned to sleep until eight once the kids were grown and out on their own. It had never mattered to Lester whether she rose at dawn to fix breakfast. For years, Lester's morning meal had been a cup of coffee and three aspirins, which he took whenever Mattie nudged him awake. You didn't need to be Julia Child to pull *that* off.

"Why can't you fix your own breakfast?" Mattie asked her son-in-law, remembering something Gracie had told her once, about men *pretending* they can't do certain things so that women will do them instead.

"Do I strike you as the Galloping Gourmet?" Henry asked. His voice was still gravelly with sleep. He had been laid off from the paper mill in St. Leonard the month before and had yet to find another job. "Besides, it ain't my fault Sonny's robbed a bank."

"Sonny ain't robbed no bank," said Mattie. "Is that what they're saying around Mattagash? Well, you can just tell the next big mouth who says that to go take a flying leap." She was sitting up in bed now, having been reminded that Sonny was holed up inside a house trailer in Bangor, like a sardine in a tin can. Unless there had been some new developments during the night. That's the term Gracie had used. "We'll just have to wait until there's some *new developments*," Gracie had said, before going into her old bedroom to unroll the sofa bed. Mattie wondered if Wolf Blitzer had ever slept on a sofa bed, maybe when he was over there in the heart of Desert Storm.

"I should've known Sonny was too lazy to rob a bank," Henry said. "And he never did learn how to use a gun." Mattie heard the sharp metallic click of a cigarette lighter snapping down on itself, and then Henry inhaling. Smoking first thing in the morning. Even when Mattie did smoke, she never lit up her first until after a couple cups of coffee and *Good Morning America*. "I got two kids sitting out there at the kitchen table about to starve to death," Henry added. "Would you please give my wife her car keys and send her home?"

"Can't them two big boys put bread into a toaster?" Mattie asked. "I know they take after *you*, Henry, but ain't they smart enough to open a can of cling peaches without spraining their wrists? Besides, them kids'll keel over from secondhand smoke before they starve to death. Your whole family is gonna have lungs that look like a pan of burnt biscuits if you people don't give up the cancer sticks." She had had a dream of Sonny, she just remembered, as bits and pieces of film ran again in her mind. He had turned up on the front porch, a pretty girl Mattie had never seen before hanging on to one of his arms. "How'd you like to meet Princess Di?" he'd asked. Mattie smiled in memory. That's what Sonny had said the night he took Dr. Pingrey's daughter to the dance in Watertown, when all three of his sisters had sworn she'd never go out with him. So Sonny had brought her home, just to show her off and to cause his sisters' mouths to drop open. *Ms. Pac-Men* is what Sonny called them. "Because when they're gossiping, their mouths look just like that little yellow Pac monster," he liked to tell Mattie, causing her to laugh. No, wait, Sonny had brought home *two* women in the dream, and neither of them was Dr. Pingrey's daughter. "Lookit what I found, Mama," he'd said, his crooked smile taking up one side of his handsome face. Only now, with Henry waiting on the other end of the line, did Mattie realize that she'd dreamed of his two hostages.

"One of them girls has long brown hair," Mattie whispered. She put a hand to her chest and felt her heart knocking away beneath her ribs. Her nightgown was like a soft, damp skin. She'd perspired heavily. So it hadn't been a good dream, after all. "Take them girls back to where you found them, son!" That's what Mattie had been shouting until Henry dialed her number and woke her up. Now she was almost thankful to her son-in-law. Of the three men who had wed her daughters, Henry had always been her favorite, it was true, and that was probably because he was the one who married Rita and took her out of the house before she drove Mattie crazy.

"Since Rita got that microwave," Henry was saying, "all I hear around this house is *beep, beep, beep*. You'd swear this was a Volkswagen dealership." He inhaled more smoke.

"Well, that's better than hearing nothing at all," said Mattie. "Grow up, Henry. Life's short enough as it is. Learn to fry your own bacon, sweetie. Make yourself a pancake now and then. It'll swell you with pride." She flopped the phone back onto its cradle and slid her legs over the side of her bed. *Sonny*. It was all back now, the reason that she should feel terrible and not good, not glad that the rain was over and sunshine was now blasting its way into her house, tearing up the curtains, splattering all the rugs. Not good that the smell of coffee and bacon would soon be filling the tiny kitchen, like sweet puffs of angel breath. Those smells would also rouse her daughters and they would rise like the zombies Mattie remembered from their high school days, rubbing their crusty eyes and reaching blindly for cups on the bottom shelf of the cupboard. *Sonny*. Had there been any new developments? Would they be *good* developments?

"Go home and fix your husband his breakfast, Rita," Mattie said loudly. "He's talking about finding himself a new woman." She banged on the door to Sonny's room. She had been tempted to tell her daughters that the old yellow bus was coming and they'd be late again for school. How many mornings had she played out that script in her life, waiting for that yellow squash of a bus to slide into the yard and toot its horn? More mornings than she cared to count.

"Tell him to put a couple slices of bread in the toaster, for crying out loud," was Rita's sleepy answer. "And to microwave some rolled oats. They're in that little package all ready to go." Mattie stared down at the doorknob, that silver fist that was supposed to be guarding Sonny's room, keeping out intruders. Why hadn't she just locked the damn door before the girls could hole up inside, the way Sonny had holed up in that trailer?

"Maybe Henry don't have the energy to work the microwave," Mattie said through the door. "Maybe he needs to eat first."

"Oh, Mama, listen at you," said Rita's drowsy voice. "What does Henry need energy for? He ain't got nowhere to go. And he sure as hell ain't looking for another woman. Henry's had it with women. He's said so a million times."

"Will you two shut up?" Mattie heard Marlene say. "Show a little respect for the dead." Bedsprings squeaked loudly and Mattie knew that Marlene was turning over on her side, hoping for a bit more sleep. Mattie had seen that trick, too, many times in her career as their mother. Well, let them sleep. At least they wouldn't be under her feet while she had her morning coffee.

In the tiny kitchen Mattie put her plate on the table first, then placed her favorite coffee mug beside it. *World's Greatest Grandma*, the mug declared. Mattie doubted this sincerely, but the mug had a deep, round body, able to hold a cup and a half of coffee. Two mugfuls always got her through the *Today* show. She put her frying pan on the stove, turned the burner on high, then went to the refrigerator for her pound of bacon. Four strips, side by side, no more, no less, and then it was time for the strawberry jam. When the bacon was half-cooked, she plopped two slices of bread into her toaster and lowered them. She could turn on the radio and tune in to the country station in Watertown. She did that many mornings when she was waiting for the *Today* show to come on. But what if the radio had some new developments about Sonny? She had ignored the television on her way to the kitchen, but now she found herself wanting desperately to turn it on. What if the news about Sonny was awful? She'd wait for her daughters to get up. She'd let *them* carry the burden, since they could do it so lightly.

"Da da da," Mattie hummed. "Da da da da dee dee dee." There was no melody that she recognized to her humming. Sonny and Lester had been the only musical units in the family. But she liked the full sound of her voice in the small kitchen. "Da da da dee dee dee ka-boom ka-boom ka-boom." And singing was one way to ward off bad luck. She flipped the bacon with her fork and watched as it bubbled and curled in the pan. When she heard the toast pop, she removed the bacon strip by strip, waiting for the grease to drain back into the pan as she laid each one out on her plate. Then she put one slice of toast on each side of the bacon, a little ritual of hers for years. "Call me superstitious," Mattie liked to say to her friends, "but at least call me." The truth was that her best friend, Ruthie Hart, had died of cancer just a year earlier and, therefore, never called anyone anymore. And her second best friend, Martha Monihan, had gone a little crazy when her husband's skidder rolled on him while he was cutting logs for the P. J. Irvine Company. Martha had taken to using a Ouija board to ask Thomas questions about car insurance and how to fix the leaky water pump, and what to tell that crazy young daughter of theirs who had come home Easter morning, three months after Thomas died, and announced that she was pregnant. The Ouija board was giving Martha all the answers she really wanted to hear, Mattie knew, but she didn't tell Martha this. It was only when Martha took to asking Lester Gifford questions that Mattie couldn't suffer her friend any longer. Trouble was, all the answers sounded just like things Lester would say. About Roberta's Christmas wedding, the Ouija board, speaking for Lester Gifford, had spelled out: LET HER FREEZE HER DAMN ASS OFF. Mattie could almost hear Lester's little intake of breath at the end of that sentence. "All right," Mattie had then said to Martha. "I'll play this silly game with you." Her fingers touching the pointer ever so lightly, she leaned in close, thought a bit, and then asked, WHY DID YOU CHEAT ON ME. That little pointer took off like a three-wheeler, spinning on its heels, darting from letter to letter, dragging Martha's and Mattie's fingers with it. That little pointer put the pedal to the metal, as they say. It was all Martha could do to keep track of the letters it was pointing out, but she did, writing them down with one hand. Martha wasn't one to miss a soap opera, much less a personal answer from beyond. NONE OF YOUR FUCKIN BUSINESS, said the Ouija board. That was enough for Mattie. She had stood up, pushed the little pointer off the board and onto the table, as though it were Lester's big fat tongue. "I listened to that enough in my marriage," Mattie said to Martha. "I don't need to listen to it from the grave." Martha had started to cry when she realized she'd spelled the word *fuckin*. "Never in my whole life have I used such foul language," Martha insisted, which Mattie knew was a crock. Lester Gifford had slept with Martha Monihan off and on for over thirty years. Mattie had no doubt that he'd told Martha what his usual response was when his wife asked where he'd been, why he'd been there. She had reached for the paper Martha was using to write messages on, messages from the spirit world. Mattie had a little spiritual message herself that she wanted to share with the living. DON'T CALL ME AGAIN, MARTHA MONIHAN was what Mattie wrote and shoved under Martha's beady eyes. This was a far cry from the "Call me superstitious, but at least call me" slogan Mattie had carried around Mattagash for a good number of years. So be it. Changes came about from the weirdest of circumstances. Now she almost wished she had a Ouija board. She could place her fingers lightly as butterflies upon that little pointer. "Any new developments?" she could ask it. "Any word on that sweet-talking, heartbreaking, good-looking, crazy son of mine?"

Mattie didn't even have a newspaper to read. The *Bangor Daily News* wouldn't arrive until the mailman came, just after lunchtime. So she rinsed her breakfast dishes and then sat staring at the television set for a full minute until she finally got up and turned it on. She dreaded the very action of bringing what might be disastrous news into her living room, bad news about her child. But nothing was being talked about that had to do with her son. Willard Scott was as jolly and annoying as ever. He wished someone in Idaho a very happy hundredth birthday. Mattie wondered if Sonny would live to be a hundred years old. After all, he had just turned thirty-six.

It was then that she slid the *Easter Rising* puzzle out from under the sofa and scanned the bluish pieces for that eyeball. Jesus looked as though he, too, had had a restless night. Some real bad dreams, about crosses, maybe, and friends who betray you. Mattie had managed to fit three or four blue pieces, what turned out to be parts of flower petals, and was back to looking for the missing eyeball when she heard one of her daughters lumbering down the hallway. The bathroom door slammed and Mattie could hear tap water running. She quickly slid *Easter Rising* back under the sofa, making sure the cardboard sheet wasn't protruding. Her daughters, especially Rita, had eyes like houseflies.

With Jesus tucked safely away, Mattie went into her little kitchen. If she let the girls make their own breakfasts, there would be grease splatters all over her stove, dirty dishes in the wrong basin of the sink, utensils stuck in places where she'd never find them, pancake batter all over her pot holders. Although Mattie doubted that today's woman knew what *batter* was, not unless you could whip it up in a microwave. That was one gift she'd made the girls take back to Service Merchandise, the microwave they'd chipped in and bought her for Mother's Day. "The electric burners on my stove are still pretty remarkable to me," Mattie had told them. "I don't have to cut and tote firewood to make them work. I don't have to tear the house down looking for a match. I ain't worried about a good strong wind coming along and putting them out. No, I'm still pretty amazed with my old stove, and if you don't mind, I'll keep it until the wonder of it wears off." They hadn't liked that response one bit. Marlene had gone so far as to call her mother old-fashioned, which was fine with Mattie. When it came to her *new-fashioned* daughters, she had no qualms whatsoever at being on the opposite side of the fence from them. She had tried at one period in her life, when her girls were still in high school, to determine what had gone wrong in the mother-daughter plan. Most of the women she had known had at least *one* good daughter out of the litter, one girl she could shop peacefully with, confide in truthfully, sit down and watch an old black-and-white movie with. But not *her* girls. And there didn't seem to be anything Mattie could do to turn the spinning ball of their relationship around. There weren't enough dresses she could iron, enough petticoats she could wash and then spread out like big white flowers to dry, not enough doughnuts she could bake to get a little appreciation from her daughters. And then one morning, she got up and looked at the three of them and it seemed as if surely some other woman had borne them, had nursed them, had wiped the snot from their noses, had braided all that snarly hair. How many ponytails had Mattie created in all those years of their growing up? How many bottles of baby aspirins had she pried open in the dark of night, how many little tangerine pills had she tapped into the palm of her hand? How many times had she leaned over in the shadows, her chest hurting, her breasts aching physically from the pain of Lester not being there, and how many times had she whispered, "There now, sweetie, Mama's here"? For a long time she blamed herself for taking a wrong turn somewhere on the parental path. There was probably a day, back in the history of her relationship with Rita, that Rita had back-talked, and it was *that* day that Mattie probably should've said, "Listen here, little girl. This is your mother standing before you. Shuffle me out a little respect or spend the rest of the weekend in that hatbox of a bedroom with both your door and your mouth shut tight." But she hadn't, and the snowball of misbehavior, that big cold avalanche of rudeness, had started its run downhill. Nowadays, it always surprised Mattie to find those three women in her house. Sometimes, in the middle of a holiday dinner, her mind wandering back to her own childhood of Thanksgivings and Santa Clauses, she would look up, startled to see three strangers breaking bread at her table. Only Sonny, only her boy, had been worth the pain of childbirth, worth the trouble of boyhood bandages and bloody noses and slingshots that sometimes broke a window. For every bandage there had been a bouquet of those blue flags from the swamp, for every broken window there had been a crayon picture, for every bloody nose, a soft hug about one of her legs while she stirred a pot on the stove. Even as a grown man, he still did this, still crept up behind her and encircled her with his strong arms, a son showing his mother some affection. She should've had all boys.

Mattie reached for the receiver of the wall phone in the kitchen. She squinted at the names on the piece of cardboard she had taped next to the phone, and then dialed Pauline Plunkett's number. It had only rung twice when she heard scuffling behind her, slippers scraping across the floor.

"Anything new from Butch Cassidy?" Marlene asked, tottering in the doorway of the kitchen. Mattie put the phone back onto its cradle. Her percolator had just stopped its rhythmic perking and had quieted.

"Nothing," said Mattie. "But the local news ain't on until six o'clock tonight. Unless they have another news bulletin."

"Why don't you get yourself a Mr. Coffee?" Marlene asked. She groped a hand about on the bottom shelf of the cupboard and it emerged with a cup. "It'll save you loads of time." Mattie thought about this. It took her maybe thirty seconds to ready her percolator, forty-five seconds if she had a bit of trouble finding the strainer. Yes, she supposed a Mr. Coffee could add eons of valuable time to her morning breakfast experience, could broaden her life in many ways. Pity for her that she would miss it.

"I want to go to Bangor," said Mattie. "And I want *you* to drive me, Marlene, because as far as I know, you ain't breathed a word about that money I sent Sonny the time you drove me to Watertown to take it out of the bank. That's been one of the pleasant surprises of my life, and I wouldn't mind enjoying a second one. What do you say?" Marlene quit drinking her coffee to stare fully into Mattie's eyes. Then she ran a sleepy hand through a head of drowsy hair, yawned, and stretched an arm up behind her neck. Mattie would like to believe that this was Marlene's morning stance, but she'd seen her do the same thing at noon and at supper time. She'd seen her do it just before bedtime. She had the three laziest girls in Mattagash, Maine, and there was no doubt about it.

"You need to head straight for Plan B, Mama," said Marlene. "Because Plan A sucks. There's no way in hell I'm getting caught up in Sonny's latest shenanigans. It's bad enough folks here in Mattagash know I'm his sister, but I have no intentions of letting the state of Maine know it." Mattie put a plate on the table in front of Marlene, four strips of bacon and a fried egg. She took the newly popped toast from the toaster.

"You shouldn't fry things anymore, Mama," said Marlene, poking at the egg with her fork. "You should watch your intake of fat. Why don't you at least get yourself some of that low cholesterol spray?"

"I used the bacon grease to fry the egg," said Mattie.

"I know, but that's not smart," Marlene announced.

"I don't suppose that pepperoni pizza you ate last night was the mark of a genius," said Mattie, "but you ate it anyway." She saw Marlene frown, shake her head a bit, the way all three daughters liked to do in sync whenever Mattie said something that displeased them.

"I only had two pieces," said Marlene. "It's not my fault that Rita got regular pizza instead of picking up some Weight Watcher's." She ate around the yolk of her egg, leaving it lie like a yellow sun on her plate.

"Will you drive me?" asked Mattie. "I'll spit in the pan and fry you a brand-new egg. What do you say to that?" Marlene went to the percolator and poured herself a second cup of coffee. At the kitchen door, she paused to look back at Mattie, who was standing by the stove with an egg in her hand.

"You're getting as bad as Sonny, you know that?" Marlene asked. "I swear he inherits his craziness from you." She went on down the hall and disappeared again into her old bedroom. Mattie heard the bedsprings squeak. Marlene flopping back down. Having breakfast had obviously exhausted her.

Mattie knelt again in front of the sofa and pulled *Easter Rising* out of its hiding place, lifted the cardboard sheet up onto the coffee table. She stared at the pieces of puzzle, hoping to concentrate on finding the eye. But it was true.

Sonny *did* take after her. And the girls took after their father, Lester. They even walked like him, with a tendency to lean too much to the right, a bit short-legged on that side. Mattie wouldn't have been at all surprised to wake up one morning and find that her daughters had all grown mustaches, the way Lester liked to keep his, full all the way up to his nose, his upper lip disappeared. And if the girls were all to go bald one day, as Lester had gone bald, the top of his head coming at the last of it to shine like a pinkish-colored hen egg, well, then, it would be further evidence that they were his girls. *He inherits his craziness from you*, Marlene had said. This had given Mattie great pause over the years, this notion, even though Marlene had been the only daughter to mention it. And that was just because Marlene was the smartest one. Had the other two made the connection earlier, they'd have been waving flags in Mattie's face about it. The truth was that their grandmother, Mattie's own mother, hadn't died of stomach cancer down in Bangor, as Mattie had always told them. Only a handful of people knew the truth, knew that Maybeline had awakened one night, took a butcher knife out of a kitchen drawer, and started up the stairs with it raised high in her hand. "Because God told me the time has come to kill my babies," she'd informed her husband as he struggled to wrest the knife from her hand. Mattie had been eight years old, the eldest child, and she had cowered at the top of the stairs, staring down at the strange sight of her parents wrestling for a butcher knife, her mother dressed in her Sunday finest, her father in his underwear. And then she had gone to calm the other children, the four other lambs who had wakened in the shadows of night to strange noises, never knowing they'd just been saved from a motherly slaughter. They had whisked Maybeline to Bangor that very night, her family telling the townsfolk— telling even Mattie, who knew better, who had *heard*—that the problem was a rare disorder that would be treated by specialists unknown in Watertown. Finally, two years later Maybeline had died, sitting in her bed and peering through the bars of her hospital window as though they were the rails of a baby's crib. Mattagash was told stomach cancer. But Maybeline's sisters, Mattie's aunts, whispered of suicide when they came to tend the children, to help Mattie with the washings, to bake fruit pies and plain white cakes. And since grown-up words like *suicide* and *adultery* are such ponderous, heavy words, Mattie sat cross-legged on the floor of the kitchen and waited for them to drop down to her ears, which they did. She heard all, and she carried all in her heart for years. The sisters seemed to feel that something called *adultery* had driven Maybeline to attempt unforgivable things. Maybe it had, maybe it hadn't. No one wanted to own up to even a sprinkle of insanity in those days. When her father finally told her that her mother had died and would not be coming home, Mattie had gone up to her bedroom, pried open the window, and tossed the valentine she'd made for Maybeline out to the northeasterly winds. And the winds had carried the valentine, as though it were

Mattie's own red heart, up into the air on fingers of breeze, had rocked it sweetly, then dashed it to earth behind a swell of chokecherry bushes. *Happy Valentine's Day to my mother. A mother's heart is always true, even if her heart is blue.* Mattie's first and last attempt at poetry. A real Shakespeare down the drain. And it wasn't until that word *adultery* came to have its own personal meaning for her that Mattie began to reconsider her mother's life. When Lester had his first flings but still kept that glint in his eye which suggested his Casanova days were far from over, Mattie came to feel a genuine pity for her mother, and for the innocent babies she had wanted to murder. If God was gonna tell Maybeline to kill someone, Mattie found herself thinking as the years of her own life unwound, then it should've been her husband. But she knew God wouldn't do that. When it came down to brass tacks, God was just another man.

5

The next tidings about Sonny came with the *Bangor Daily News*, delivered after lunch by old Simon Craft, the mailman. Mattie watched through the curtains as Simon fidgeted about in his mail car, hoping she would come out to fetch her mail so that he could harvest some news from her. Simon didn't just deliver *mail*. He delivered gossip. And he seemed to think the letters he carried were for *him*, too, and not just those names on the envelopes. Gracie once said that Simon Craft thought he was mailman by "divine right," but Mattie didn't know what that meant. She only knew that she had no intention of being cornered at her mailbox by Simon Craft on such a newsworthy day. After sorting his meager handful of envelopes a dozen times and staring forlornly at the house, Simon finally left his and Mattie's personal mail in the mailbox and drove away in a spurt of road dust. Now Mattie could finally read her newspaper in peace, around on the back porch, where the girls wouldn't be peering like monkeys over her shoulder.

Sonny had made the front page. After all, a hostage incident in Bangor, Maine, was almost as rare as one of those comets that spin past the earth once in a great while. But since not much was known about the situation, the story was short. BANGOR MAN TAKES HOSTAGES, it announced, along with a brief sketching of events. Nothing new, Mattie realized as she read. There was a description from witnesses at the Bangor Savings and Loan. Two women, still unnamed until their families were notified, had been standing in line at the bank when Sonny appeared out of nowhere and pointed a gun at them. They were told to go with him and no one would be harmed. One of the witnesses, an elderly retired game warden, didn't believe the gun Sonny was holding was a real gun. "It looked like a black water pistol to me," this witness said. The poodle, which had also been taken, belonged to one of the hostages. She had been holding the dog in her arms while she stood in line at the bank. Then Sonny and his captives had driven away in his blue pickup, to Marigold Drive Trailer Park, to a house trailer that belonged to his estranged wife, Sheila Bumphrey Gifford, who could not be reached for comment. When the newspaper went to press, police were in the process of setting up communication with Mr. Gifford. There was a good photo of the trailer. And there was also a description of Sonny, given by a Marigold Drive neighbor. "He was a one-man party in full swing," the neighbor said.

Mattie closed the paper and put it on the porch next to her chair. There was nothing she could do, nothing at that point in time, anyway. So she turned her attention to the mountain ridge across the road, hoping it would clear her head. The ridge had grown into a beauteous thing, green now with summer. Mattie thought she had lost it forever, but it had managed to bounce back after that outbreak of spruce budworms, years earlier, and now it rolled along the horizon like a mossy log. When autumn came, her favorite time of year, the tamarack's needles would turn yellow as hay, golden almost, a show-off among the conifers. And then those spots of birches would rattle their yellow leaves, if you were close enough to listen. Then the oak, one of the last trees to turn, would follow suit, its leaves running to brown in those mornings of bright sun. Finally, the aspen, its leaves like dark yellow fruit. When autumn came, surely this trouble with Sonny would be over, and Mattie and Elmer could take that walk along the ridge that they'd been planning for years. Maybe Sonny could come with them. They would make a little fire, using birch bark for kindling so that the natural oils would send up a black tunnel of smoke. And then they would boil tea in an empty Crisco lard can, after Elmer added a little handle made out of haywire. There was no better tea than the kind boiled outside, in autumn, then drunk outside, under that fall rainbow of dying leaves.

"Mama, get in here!" Gracie opened the door to say. "They just interrupted *One Life to Live* for a special bulletin."

The crowd was now larger. Mattie saw a van in the picture with *WNPT News, Portland, Maine* written on the side.

Donna, that same little chihuahua reporter, was peering intently at the camera. Mattie was taken aback, as though Donna were peering at *her*. "There she is, everybody," Mattie expected Donna to announce. "There's his *mother*." But that wasn't the case.

"This is an update of the hostage situation that has taken place at Marigold Drive Trailer Park, here in Bangor," Donna said. Rita laughed at this.

"Where are the marigolds?" she wanted to know. "I don't see any *marigolds*." Gracie swatted Rita's arm, and she quieted down to listen.

"Sonny Gifford," Donna was saying, "who took two women hostage yesterday afternoon from the Bangor Savings and Loan is still barricaded inside this house trailer. Now that the families of the hostages have been notified, we're able to release their names. Vera Temple, a salesclerk at Mr. Paperback here in Bangor, and Stephanie Bouchard, a student at the University of Maine, have been identified as the two women being held inside this house trailer against their will." The camera had been panning the length of the trailer, slowly following the red pinstripe. Now it found the child's sand pail and shovel and zoomed in to freeze on the toy.

"I wish they wouldn't do stuff like that," said Rita. "It only makes things worse. Sonny ain't even got any kids."

"If this was a novel, that'd be called *foreshadowing*," Gracie announced. Rita rolled her eyes upward.

"Hush," said Mattie. It had always bothered her that

Sonny had married a woman with two children from another marriage. It wasn't that Mattie hated youngsters or anything like that. It was just that fatherhood didn't seem a likely notion for Sonny to entertain just yet, even if he was thirty-six. Sonny still had a bit of stretching out to do in the area of growing up. The camera was back on Donna's face, the trailer peeping out behind her head in the background.

"Yesterday, in a telephone conversation, Mr. Gifford told police that the face of former Beatle John Lennon appeared on his television screen and advised him to take a stand against world hunger. According to Mr. Gifford, he decided to apprehend the two women and Stephanie Bouchard's dog after Mr. Lennon's face faded into a wine cooler commercial. In a conversation this morning with Bangor Chief of Police Patrick Melon, we were able to learn that Mr. Gifford's actions may very well be intended to garner attention from his estranged wife, Sheila Bumphrey Gifford. Here, now, is part of that taped conversation."

Mattie pressed forward and so did her girls, their three rear ends barely touching the edge of the sofa. She could hear her heart beating out, could feel the quick thump of it in her chest. There had always been something she had done in the past, some word she had chosen to say, that had reversed the spin of Sonny's actions. There had even been that time she'd made the plate of peanut butter fudge and taken it over to the principal's office. He was that fat one they had hired from downstate, a Mr. Prentice, or something like that. And she had waited until Mr. Prentice bit deep into his second chunk of fudge before she said, "I ain't really with the PTA committee like I said. I'm Sonny Gifford's mother and I come to talk about that broken gym window." But now what? That's what her heart kept thumping out in its little Morse code, beneath her dress, beneath the cameo brooch she'd pinned to her lapel that very morning, her good luck brooch. *Now what?* her heart wanted to know.

"And I just want to add this one thing, Mr. Melon," said Sonny's voice. "If you get the chance to track down Sheila Bumphrey Gifford, my future ex-wife, will you tell her that I ain't ever loved another woman in my whole life like I love her? And I wish her lots of luck with her new beau. Now all I want is my dog, which she's gone ahead and hidden somewhere. You tell her that if you can find her. But I doubt you will, Mr. Melon, because the"—*beep beep*—"has gone to Atlantic City with some"—*beep beep beep*—"who don't give a"—*beep*—"about her and the kids." Mattie let out her breath. She knew it. She had known it from the start. Sonny was hurting over a woman, maybe for the first time ever, and now, not knowing what to do, he'd gone and gotten himself into a mess bigger and deeper than any plate of fudge could ever get him out of.

"I don't blame her one little bit for leaving him," said Gracie. "Look at how I had to go ahead and kick Charlie out. If men can't learn to talk to women, to just sit quiet and listen to what they have to say without—"

"Shut up, Gracie," said Mattie.

"—interrupting," said Gracie, "then how are men and women—"

"So she run off to Atlantic City with another man," Marlene said dramatically. "I can't say I blame her."

"—gonna learn to communicate?" Gracie was finally done.

"Who said men and women have to communicate?" Rita wanted to know. "Who started that rubbish, anyway? The only communicating I do with Henry is when I put his lunch pail in his hands in the morning, and when I take it out of his hands at night. At least when he had a job, we communicated real well."

"I said *shut up*," Mattie insisted. Donna's face was again filling up the screen.

"Chief Melon is hopeful that his department will be able to locate Mrs. Gifford," Donna was saying, "and that perhaps this terrifying situation can be peacefully resolved." After promising to be back with the six o'clock news, Donna disappeared and *One Life to Live* returned. Mattie watched the actors bouncing about on the screen and said nothing. Her girls, however, had a lot to say. Now they were involved in an argument as to whether or not it would be wise to drive their mother to Bangor.

"She *is* his mother," Marlene was saying. "How would you feel if it was Willard? What would you do if that was *your* kid?"

"*I'd* pretend it wasn't," said Rita. Mattie thought about this. It wasn't very likely that Rita could pretend Willard wasn't hers, what with him being the only kid at Mattagash High School who was almost six foot three. A good portion of Henry's family had been long on length and short on brains. And, as if there had to be some architectural support for all that body length, all of Henry's family—and it seemed this was true of Willard in particular—had the biggest kneecaps you'd ever lay your eyes on. There were times when Mattie saw Willard lumbering about in cutoff jeans at some family picnic and it always looked at first as though some prankster had superglued two softballs to her grandson's knee joints. And then there was that vicious case of his crossed eyes. Gracie once commented that both of Willard's eyes looked out of the same hole, but they were eyes passed down to him from Lester's mother's side. Everyone always said that the Harts were so cross-eyed that it was a wonder they didn't burn the house down, considering they still heated it with that old wood furnace. At least, everybody said that *until* the Harts burned their house down. And then Willard had that lisp, and that bad habit of twitching his left eye and his right shoulder when he got nervous. And there was that front tooth that got knocked out in a basketball game last season, which Henry and Rita couldn't afford to fix just yet, what with Henry being laid off at the mill. Still, this all could've been chalked up to bad luck on the part of nature, until Willard witnessed that crazy rock group down at the Bangor Auditorium, the one with all the different colored hair, and went ahead without Rita's permission and dyed his hair bright orange. When Rita tried to dye it back to its natural shit-brown color, Willard had emerged with the most peculiar shade of green hair this side of Hollywood and Vine. Not even considering the fact that Willard spit at the end of almost every sentence, just as if those little balls of foam were periods he was carefully placing there, not even considering that, Mattie felt quite sure that Rita could not pretend that Willard wasn't hers. Not in Mattagash, Maine, anyway. Maybe in Hong Kong, or right smack dab in the heart of New York City's craziest street. But Rita would definitely have to own up to Willard in Mattagash, Maine.

"Just what good do you think driving Mama down to Bangor is gonna do?" Rita asked Marlene.

"Think about it, Marlene," said Gracie. "Can you see Mama in front of a television camera? And you know that's what will happen if we take her down there to talk to Sonny." Mattie ignored this insult. How did Gracie know what would happen if someone decided to put her mother's face on television? Maybe some big Hollywood producer would give Mattie her own show. Distressed mothers from all over the country could call in and share their parental horror stories. Jeffrey Dahmer's mother. Son of Sam's mother. Mothers whose children are involved in drugs and gangs. Madonna's stepmother.

The phone rang. Gracie beat Marlene to it, just as she had always done in the old high school days.

"I swear you were born with roller skates instead of feet," Marlene told Gracie.

"It's for you, Mama," Gracie shouted. "It's Milly, calling from the store." Mattie gave up the antics of the actors and actresses on television, all that foolish kissing and conniving, and came to the phone.

"Don't tell her anything," Gracie whispered. "You know what a gossip bag she is."

Mattie was confused. "Don't tell her *what?*" she asked. "It's all over the television, for crying out loud. At least he ain't robbed a bank. And robbing a bank is a lot worse." She took the receiver from Gracie and covered the speaker part with her hand.

"Oh, I beg to differ," said Rita. "Taking human beings against their will into a house trailer is a lot worse than robbing a bank."

"Taking human beings into a house trailer *of their own free will* is a lot worse than robbing a bank," said Marlene. Mattie had uncovered the phone in order to speak, but now she covered it up again with the meaty part of her palm. It was obvious that Winken, Blinken, and Nod had no intentions of coming ashore yet.

"You know, Marlene, I ain't stupid," Rita said. "You're making remarks like that about house trailers only because me and Henry and the boys live in one."

Marlene patiently considered this. "No, I ain't," she said, and Mattie knew darn well she was lying. "It's just that you never know when a house trailer might decide to go wheels up."

"Be quiet," Mattie warned them. It was bad enough

that her only boy was being watched on the news by all of Mattagash. But did they have to hear her three daughters warring it out in her living room?

"By the way," Gracie asked. "How *do* Henry and Willard and Josh manage to fit into them low-ceiling little rooms? Don't they bump their heads?" Marlene tittered, an irritating sound even if you liked her. Rita's face was becoming nearly transparent. Mattie could see anger rising to the surface of the skin, like something in a pond that has sunk below the water and is just beginning to emerge again.

"Henry and Willard and Josh fit wherever I tell them to," Rita said. "Which is a talent you obviously never learned at college, Gracie. I don't suppose Charlie has to worry about bumping his head on Sally Fennelson's trailer ceiling, considering how much time he spends all curled up in her bed." It was Gracie's turn to fill up with anger, her eyes going all gauzy and her left eyebrow beginning to twitch above her eye like a thin brown fish.

"Just for the record," Gracie screamed, "*I* was the one who left Charlie! I threw his ass out!"

"Who said anything about who left who?" Rita asked.

"I think house trailers can shape your personality," Marlene said thoughtfully. "They can make you think small for your whole life. I don't think many successful people grew up in house trailers. Someone should do a study on that."

Now Rita was furious. "Then your precious husband, Wesley Stubbs, must have been *conceived* in one. Everybody in Mattagash knows that Wesley spends more time in front of the television than a turtle spends in its shell."

"Hang on a minute, will you, Milly?" Mattie said into the receiver. "I'll be right with you." Then she tucked the receiver under the pit of her arm, where nothing could seep through to Milly's anxious ears, not even the stench of body sweat. "I said to shut up, and I mean it," Mattie told the girls. "If you intend to stay here in my house, you'll keep your big mouths closed. I'm within an inch of tossing all three of you out into the front yard, along with them big chunky pocketbooks. It's bad enough I had to listen to this bedlam while you were all in high school and I was still legally responsible for you. But I ain't anymore. And I'm telling you to park your lips."

Marlene grabbed her half pack of cigarettes from off the kitchen table and went out the back door, letting the screen slam with a thud. Gracie picked up the crossword page from the *Bangor Daily News* and disappeared into her old bedroom. Mattie heard the springs of the sofa bed squeak. With the other two women gone, Rita became instantly confidential. But Mattie was ready for it, knew just what to expect. At a pit stop somewhere along the years of her growing up, Rita had gotten it into her head that being the oldest child meant something.

"If you ask me," Rita whispered, "them two could stand a lesson in manners."

"I said *shut up*," Mattie repeated. "And I meant *shut up*."

"Oh, good Lord, Mama," said Rita, waving a hand. Mattie met Rita's eyes, poured herself deep into them, a constant stare, until Rita was reasonably sure that her mother was furious.

"Now I intend to take this call," Mattie said softly, "from another bigmouthed Mattagash female, and I intend to do it in peace. So how's about you go out to the front yard, Rita, and talk to St. Francis of Assisi?"

"I *will* say this," said Rita, gathering up her own crumply pack of cigarettes. "I agree with Gracie and Marlene about *one* thing. You're gonna go off your rocker over this if you ain't careful, Mama. You're gonna go to *you know where* in a handbasket."

The front door slammed with such force that Mattie feared a window might shatter. But then, Rita had always had lots in common with jets breaking the sound barrier. Mattie waited for a few seconds, breathed in the sweet notes of silence, and then she unburied the receiver from her armpit. She had no doubt that Milly was still in there, down in the coils and wires, waiting for her own breath of clean air. Gossips could hold their breath forever. Gossips would one day inherit the entire earth, just like those hard-shelled insects Mattie had seen on *Nova*, insects immune to *everything*.

"Now then, Milly," Mattie said nicely into the phone. "What's on your mind?" Milly acted as if being kept waiting for five minutes on the end of a receiver, kept dangling like a fish on a line, was second nature to her.

"I just wanted to let you know that a reporter from the *Bangor Daily* has been nosing around the store," said Milly.

"He's been asking all kinds of questions about Sonny. But everyone down here has been filling him full of lies. You should've heard the story Donnie Henderson told him, that Sonny was adopted by older folks who found him floating in the Mattagash River in a potato basket. And they raised him up until they died. Donnie even sent them out to the Catholic graveyard to find Ronald and Louise Gifford's graves. Now, you know as well as I do that Ronald and Louise never had a single child between them. I don't think the state of Maine would've let them two have a *cat*. But that reporter even took photographs. Rosemary Craft saw him down there in the pines, among the tombstones, snapping away on one knee."

Mattie had let this stream of words come and go, had been swept along in the images of what was being said: a nosy reporter from Bangor, a potato basket, sweet old simpleminded Ronald Gifford with his slow walk, Louise Gifford's big garden of colored flowers, Donnie Henderson's mischievous face. It was Donnie Henderson who had told some journalist at *Downeast* magazine that all of Mattagash was descended from three sisters from Watertown who had canoed up to Mattagash looking for husbands. And that poor journalist had gone ahead and written it down, without ever once checking it out. It was true, as Donnie often noted, that once you cross the Aroostook County line, heading south in Maine, the fewer mountains and the less gray matter you were likely to encounter. Folks farther south tended to believe almost anything you told them. Not like Mattagashers. You could tell a Mattagasher that blue was blue and he still wouldn't believe you. Right away he'd suspect you were up to something. And maybe Sonny didn't have a glut of friends in Bangor, hanging out at the house trailer to show their support, but there were plenty of folks willing to go to bat for him in Mattagash.

"What else did he want to know?" Mattie asked.

"Well, mostly, he was looking for Sonny's relations," said Milly, "until he met up with Donnie. I suspect you'll read about Sonny's adoption in the papers tomorrow." Mattie felt fatigue slipping in, claiming her mind, and fatigue was a bad thing this early in the game. If only those big, loud girls would go home, she might be able to get a logical thought to float into her head, a suggestion pertaining to Sonny's newest adventure.

She had just hung up the phone when it rang again. It was probably Milly, phoning back to say that little green aliens were now asking questions about Sonny, wanting to know which planet he'd been born on. Mattie heard the sofa bed squeak in Gracie's room.

"I'll get it," Mattie called out. "It's only Milly phoning back." No answer came from behind Gracie's door, which was just fine with Mattie. She imagined Gracie's lip hanging like a flap down from her mouth. Gracie had been the best pouter of all three girls. Mattie picked up the phone and, suddenly, the receiver pressed against her face, she knew. She knew and she could say nothing.

"Mama?" Sonny's sweet voice asked. "Are you there? How's my favorite girlfriend doing?" Mattie reeled an inch or so backward, as though a hand had come out of the phone and pushed her, the push of birth, the same little push you'd probably feel in death.

"Son, what have you gone and done?" Mattie asked, her voice a low whisper, so afraid one of her daughters might hear. "Sonny, what's gonna happen to you *now?*"

"I'm gonna be just fine, Mama," said Sonny. "Vera and Steph have been taking real good care of me. I'm sorry this got on the news. I never thought of that." No, of course, he never thought of *that.*

"Let them women go, Sonny," said Mattie. "Let them go right this minute. Open that trailer door while I'm still on this phone and turn them loose. It's your only chance. This is serious business, son." She had canted her head toward the front door, where she could see Rita pacing back and forth on the porch, smoking a cigarette.

"Don't you worry none, Mama," said Sonny. "I'll get this straightened out. Me and the girls here were just discussing how to go about it." The line cracked and Mattie could hear what sounded like mice feet running about.

"Is this line being tapped, Sonny? Is that what I hear?" Mattie waited, her breath curled and silent in her throat, afraid she might miss the reply.

"I know they tapped *my* line," said Sonny, "but this is Sheila's business line, for her Avon customers, and it's under her former married name. I don't think they know about it. I ain't dealing with Sherlock Holmes here, Mama. The chief of police thinks John Lennon is still alive. I don't believe they looked to see if there was more than one line. But just in case, I probably won't be calling you again. And, Mama?"

"Yes, Sonny?"

"I don't want you to come driving down here thinking you can help me. I want you to promise me that. You can't do a single thing down here. You stay right where you are, with a nice big puzzle and a hot cup of tea. Will you promise me, Mama?"

"I promise," Mattie said. The line crackled and she felt as if lightning might come out in a ball of fire. She looked toward the window and saw Rita flick her cigarette butt out into the flowers around the St. Francis birdbath.

"Baby," said Mattie to her only boy. "Sweetie pie, you gotta straighten this out while there's still time." She knew Rita would fill up the front door at any minute. Rita would roll into the scene like an unwanted snowball. Then what would those big awful daughters have to say? That Sonny had called his mama for help? That Sonny was nothing but a no-good mama's boy? But he wasn't calling for any help at all. He was calling to tell Mattie that he was all right, that he was in the middle of the pond but he was swimming like hell for shore. Sonny Gifford seemed prepared to get out of this one by himself. Sonny and *the girls*. They'd be on his side by now, no doubt about that. That scrawny little poodle was probably fetching Sonny his slippers and a rolled-up newspaper.

"Mama?" said Sonny. Mattie saw Rita's shape move past the front windows on the porch, headed directly for the door.

"What is it, Sonny? What is it, sweetheart?"

"I don't want you to worry a nickel over this. You hear me? You worried enough in your life. And I bet them sisters of mine, them three Pac Monsters, are going at you tooth and nail. You keep your door locked, Mama, you hear me? You know darn well they're gonna come down on you like cops on a doughnut if you let them."

"Sonny," Mattie said. But no other words rose up in her throat. There was nothing she could say. A sense of motherly helplessness overtook her. She felt tears forming.

"Now, it's just a matter of time until they find this other line," said Sonny, "so I won't be phoning you no more. But I want you to give your best dress to the dry cleaner's truck and then put your teeth to soak. The minute I get to Mattagash, I'm taking my favorite girlfriend dancing." Mattie smiled. Sonny knew darn well how proud she was that her teeth were all still her own, especially since that awful dentist down in Bixley had plucked out most of the teeth belonging to Mattie's generation. Some people would do anything for a buck. Sonny wasn't like that, though, and this was what Mattie wished the whole world knew about her son. He was good and kind, the sort of kid who steered his bicycle around snakes crossing the road when other boys rode right over the bodies. If there had been a traffic light in Mattagash, Sonny would've spent each afternoon down there helping old ladies cross the street. If there had been an animal shelter, he'd have passed his idle hours finding homes for cats and dogs. He dragged home every stray animal he ever saw as it was. And all during his three bumpy years of high school, Sonny sent valentines to every single homely girl in Mattagash, girls who didn't have a prayer of getting one otherwise. And he always signed them "A Secret Admirer" so that no one would know. Mattie even helped him lick the stamps one year. This was her boy. She saw the front doorknob turning, imagined Rita's chubby fingers on the other side of the knob.

"I love you, Sonny Gifford," Mattie whispered, and she hoped Sonny heard her, hoped the words were loud enough. "I'm putting my teeth to soak."

"I love you, too, Mama," Sonny was saying as Mattie saw one of her own fingers reach down to the cradle and disconnect her son, cut the cord, the way the doctor had done thirty-six years ago. Now Sonny Gifford was in some kind of limbo, way down there in Bangor, Maine, where Mattie could never reach him, where other women would now have to help him.

6

From the road, it looked as though Elmer Fennelson had put in another doozy of a garden. Mattie stood in front of Elmer's mailbox and gazed across the rows and rows of what would be wonderful vegetables come late summer. She had needed to get out of the house, to replay Sonny's words in her head, someplace where the girls couldn't look into her eyes and read her thoughts. It would be another two hours until the six o'clock news was on. And it was possible that Elmer would be out on his porch and would invite her up for a cup of tea. They could sit and complain about the changes that had swept them along since they were children, changes in the landscape, changes in the faces they met each day in Mattagash, changes in the weather. Everyone knew the winters were nothing like they used to be. And neither were the people. There was once a time when Mattagash folks considered it high entertainment to sit on summer porches, the workday done, the men home from the woods. And some kid would make a little fire with kindling and wood chips in the bottom of a discarded water pail. Then he'd cover the fire with green grass to make it smoke, and that smoke would fight off the blackflies and mosquitoes. And with evening drawing itself in close, Mattagashers told the stories that had passed around town for generations, stories that were tattered as old coats. And in the winter, a hardwood fire in the cookstove was the magnet folks drew up to in someone's kitchen, as they listened to the summer stories being told again, this time a little better than the previous telling, a little more cheese in the beginnings, a little more spice in the endings. Old stories. Stories Mattie's father had heard as a boy. Stories Elmer's mother thought old in *her* day. But in the here and now, all Mattagash women tended to do was watch TV and jump up and down to exercise videos. They didn't even have to drive to Watertown to shop for odds and ends anymore. They could order off those crazy shopping networks. Mattie remembered the first time she ever saw a human being running when there didn't seem to be a good reason for it. "Why is Marilou Fennelson running along the road?" Mattie had asked Gracie as they drove past in Gracie's car. There didn't seem to be a house fire. There wasn't a black bear chasing Marilou. Her husband, Stewart, wasn't running after her with a garter snake or anything. "Exercise," Gracie had muttered. Mattie had turned and looked back at Marilou for a long, long time. Exercise. "But what's she running *for?*" Mattie was still asking Gracie long after Marilou had disappeared behind a turn in the road. Then, suddenly, a whole lot of people were running and jogging and walking and bouncing all over the place. All things Mattie's generation had done during the course of a regular workday.

The door to Elmer's mailbox was open, so Mattie closed it before some bird with notions of having more babies starting filling the box up with grass and twigs, some bird ready to raise its second brood of the year. She was hoping that Elmer might have been working on something in his garage, or in his garden, or sitting on his porch keeping a vigil on his hummingbird feeder. Mattie didn't want to knock on the door in case she might disturb him. She knew Elmer liked to read the Bible now and then as his day unfolded. He was always finding something in the Good Book to pertain to modern life. If Elmer had been on his porch, Mattie could have ambled across his lawn, climbed the four or five steps to the spare rocker, and the two could have taken the opportunity to gripe about the river of time that had washed through their lives, a river that had swept them up against their will, had tumbled them along as toddlers and had tossed them to shore as old-timers. But Elmer was nowhere to be seen. Nor was his dog, Skunk, with the narrow white stripe running halfway down his back. Chances were that Elmer and Skunk had gone for a little ride, maybe out on the back mountain now that the wild cherry trees had long ago dropped their fuzzy flowers and were covered with tiny red cherries.

Elmer's garden was going to be more than a doozy. As she walked, Mattie could see row after planted row of Elmer's work unfurl before her eyes. She had no doubt that Martha Monihan, whose house sat on the little knoll across the road from Elmer's, had torn herself away from her Ouija board to spy through the crack in her curtains. Mattie could almost feel the weight of Martha's big, brown, cocker spaniel eyes—*Craft* eyes, which was what Martha was before marrying Thomas Monihan—burning little eyeholes into her back. No doubt Martha was wondering why Mattie wasn't down in Bangor with a megaphone stuck to her face, trying to talk her only son into coming out of a pin-striped house trailer with his two hostages. And this was probably true of Dorrie Mullins and Lola Monihan. Mattie could see Dorrie's big Jeep Cherokee driven snugly up to Lola's front door. Lola lived just beyond Martha Monihan's house, well within spying distance of Elmer's garden and yard. Mattie knew that Dorrie and Lola, who had been a couple years ahead of Rita at school, had dedicated their lives to snooping and gossiping. *Scandalmongers*, Sonny called them. It was common knowledge that Lola considered this daily activity as a kind of full-time job. And her territory expanded mightily when she bought herself a satellite dish, the first ever in Mattagash. Now the names of movie stars were turning up in Lola's conversations as often as Mattagashers. Sometimes Lola would say, "Well, look what happened to *Burt*," and you wouldn't know if she meant Burt Gifford or Burt Reynolds. Sonny had once said that Lola could probably list the cost of installing the huge window and the satellite dish as a deduction on her yearly taxes. "As a business expense,"

Sonny had noted. "Just like them Hollywood gossip colum-
nists do." Mattie wouldn't be surprised if one day a giant
telescope, like the one they have out in California to look
at planets and stars, appeared on the top of Lola's house,
next to her chimney. Today, however, all was still behind
the curtains. Lola and Dorrie were probably glued to the
television set, a barrel of nachos between them.

Mattie took one last surveillance of Elmer's new garden
before turning back toward home. It was laid out with exact
care, all perfectly even rows. And six beds! What was a
bachelor like Elmer going to do with all those cucumbers?
Well, Mattie knew now where the cucumbers for her
mustard pickles would be coming from. She even wondered
if Elmer might have planted a few extra beds after learning
that Mattie had decided not to sow her usual garden. It was
almost common knowledge that Elmer Fennelson had what
is known as "a crush" on Mattie. Although *crush* sounded
painful. Downright deadly. In Mattie's day it was known
as "being sweet on someone." But that was just another
reminder that the world was no longer such a merciful place
in which to live, such a friendly place. It was a planet where
folks no longer got sweet on a lover. They crushed them
instead. Elmer Fennelson had been sweet on Mattie since
the day they started kindergarten together. And Elmer had
kept his crush intact, kept it at a safe distance, like something he carried in his pocket, even after Mattie had gone
ahead and married Lester Gifford on that fiery August day
almost fifty years earlier. Two things had happened during

that hot month of August, when it seemed that the dog days would never end. When it seemed that the Mattagash River was simply going to suck its way down into riverbed mud and never appear again. No one could remember it ever being so hot so far north. Old-timers made mention of a memory when they were young-timers, when even the farm animals had suffered sunstrokes. Two memorable things had happened that hot, dragging month of August in 1945: The U.S. of A. had bombed the bejesus out of two cities way over in Japan, somewhere in the Pacific Ocean. Mattie supposed that it was still raining debris out of the Japanese sky by the time the second thing happened. That was when she had stood stiff and still as a pole in Mattagash's Catholic church to marry Lester Gifford. And all the time the priest was talking, all the time she could smell Lester sweating beside her in the deep heat of August, the wet aroma of her future husband, Mattie had said over and over again, "I will be happy. I will be happy. I will be happy." But when she turned around as a married woman, her back to the priest, and looked down the aisle to the open door through which she would walk into a shower of rice and happy faces, she knew she was looking straight into the mouth of a brightly lighted cave, a tunnel of luminous despair. And she walked toward the light, just like people are told to do when they're dying. *Go to the light.* Mattie had walked toward the stifling August sun, where she could see hands reaching out to her, the older married folks who had gone on ahead down the marital path. *Go to the light.* Folks who were there to show

Mattie the way. But Mattie sensed even then, as she felt her feet moving her body down the aisle, next to Lester, who seemed to be a stream of sweat in his itchy suit, that all those nice, kind folks had lied to her. Not one of them had leaned forward, a pale face arriving out of the sunlight, not one of them had shouted, "Turn back, honey, before it's too late. This bright light ain't nothing but a fireball from hell."

Elmer Fennelson had even turned up for the wedding. Sweat was running in everyone's eyes by the time the preacher pronounced Mattie and Lester man and wife. Dresses and shirts had stuck to shoulder blades, leaving a darkened spot on each and every back, like wounds drenched in blood. Curls had gone straight, unable to hold such heavy balls of perspiration. Men flaunted dark rings under their arms, wet half-moons. Babies were too fatigued to cry. They burped, and sucked on bottles, and passed wind, and every now and then a baby's rattle dropped to the floor in an eruption of noise, causing jittery old Mrs. Bell, a Holy Roller, to cry out, "Praise Jesus!" Heat rose in ringlets from the road outside, which Mattie could see through the little window beyond where the organ player sat fidgeting with the sheet music. Mattie could see the road lying out there like a dare. "Run," the road was crying out, amidst all that rising heat vapor. Amidst the smell of baby vomit. Mattie could hear it hissing. "Throw off them pointy-heeled shoes and run like hell." And in the heart of all that excitement, in the core of that episode in time, she had turned to catch Elmer Fennelson's two sad eyes.

And that's when she knew for sure she was making a grisly mistake. It was true that Elmer was no Clark Gable and Lester Gifford was the spitting image. It was true that Elmer had been born with the yoke of shyness about his neck so that it was almost impossible for him to talk to clerks and salespersons and long-distance operators. But he and Mattie talked together just fine. And while catching a glimpse of Elmer's back and narrow buttocks as he ambled down some road, or pumped gasoline into his old Plymouth, had never made butterflies swarm about in her interior, Mattie couldn't help but remember something Grannie had told her about love. And it was true that the first time Mattie saw Lester Gifford as a possible suitor, the day he came home from the army in his dress uniform, walking with a stiff leg from the shrapnel he took over in France, so many butterflies opened their wings in her stomach that she vomited a half bottle of Moxie out behind the Mattagash Filling Station and felt quite sure that it was the true mark of love. Still. Love shouldn't make you sick, it took Mattie years to realize. It should make you smile. And seeing Elmer Fennelson standing off in the shadows of her wedding to Lester, Mattie had come to know a truth about life a little too late, Grannie's truth. "I'll tell you the key to a happy marriage and a successful life," Grannie had said. "You gotta marry your best friend. And you better love your job, no matter what it is." And Mattie knew right there, in the heat of her heated marriage to Lester, that he wasn't going to be her best friend. She had seen Lester eyeing Eliza Fennelson, who was strapped out in a sexy dress and perched in the front row, even as he slipped the ring onto Mattie's finger. Lester wasn't going to be her best friend. He wasn't even going to be around enough to be her *enemy*. And Mattie's *job* would involve the art of finding out where Lester might be. That's what Mattie had seen in Elmer's eyes, in the eyes of her best friend as he lurked about at the back of the church, taking up just enough space to accommodate his big feet. Elmer Fennelson never wanted more than what was his, and he applied that philosophy to foot space as well as everything else he encountered in life. Folks referred to this habit of his as "hanging back." Mattie supposed he had come to the wedding just in case she passed out in the shower of excitement pouring down on her, or needed a hand descending the church steps in those god-awful high-heeled shoes, things she had never again placed upon her defenseless feet. But Lester's arm had been there that day, to help steady his wife, to open the door of the 1941 gray Pontiac for her. And for a while there, amidst all that rice flying like grainy snow against her warm face, amidst all those well-wishers pressing their hot lips upon her, Mattie forgot what she saw in the shadows inside the church, what was lying in the garden beds of Elmer's eyes. She saw only the halo around Lester's handsome head, that burnishing sheen of a soldier, come home from fighting Hitler, come back alive from battling with the Hun. She saw the shiny chrome of the Pontiac, the newest car in Mattagash, and it was a light that blinded her for almost ten years. Yet during

all those blind days, those sightless months and unseeing
years, it was Elmer Fennelson who came by to start the water
pump for her, to drive a sick child to the doctor, to coax
up the car engine on a cold December morning. And where
was her best friend? Where was her husband in all those blind
years during which Elmer had become her Seeing Eye dog?
Who knew? Who the hell knew?

When Mattie finally stepped up onto her own porch, after
snapping off a few dandelion heads from around the front
steps, she could hear music blasting away. Inside, Gracie
was "Sweating to the Oldies" with Richard Simmons, her
ankle weights jumping up and down with her.

"Come on, Mama," Gracie panted. "Come work out to
these old songs."

"Are you crazy?" asked Mattie. "I got underwear older
than them songs. Besides, that boy gives me the creeps."

"Richard?" Gracie asked. She seemed astonished. Mattie
turned the volume down on the VHS tape. Her teeth were
beginning to rattle. "I thought everyone *loved* Richard."
Gracie did a little dance, what looked to Mattie like a
drunken version of the Charleston.

"I'd take a poll in a lumber camp, if I were you," Mattie
advised.

"Well," Gracie puffed, arms and legs flailing, her words
now jumping up and down with her. "I for one would be

thrilled if Richard was to turn up at my house, in that cute little blue convertible of his."

"And that's another thing," said Mattie. "What kind of life is there to tracking down fat people and snooping in their refrigerator?"

"Oh, Richard don't look in anyone's refrigerator," said Marlene, who had appeared in the living room doorway. She had a towel wrapped about her head and was wearing a bathrobe. More hot water money down the drain, that's what Marlene represented to Mattie. "All he does is sit on a fat person's sofa and cry with them. He's saved thousands of lives. Where do you get the notions you get, Mama? That's what I'd like to know."

"She watches too many of them so-called news shows," said Gracie. "This Diamond Ring" had come on, a song Mattie remembered from her daughters' high school days, and now Gracie seemed to be prancing, a Clydesdale with silver fetlocks. Mattie decided to ignore them both. If Richard Simmons wanted to wade through the old magazines and loaded ashtrays and dirty dishes at Gracie's house, so be it. Just wait until he opened the refrigerator door over *there*. That'd teach him to keep his little poodle nose out of other people's business. Besides, it was Charlie's dumping her for Sally Fennelson that inspired Gracie to lose those fifty pounds that had sneaked up about her buttocks and thighs over the years of her marriage. And it was sheer despair that had tossed her toward women's studies courses at the university. Richard Simmons had little to do with it.

Mattie went into the kitchen, caught up the teakettle on her way to the sink, and filled it with water. She didn't want tea, but her geraniums needed a drink and a teakettle's spout was long and perfect for watering plants.

"Besides," Mattie heard Gracie saying to Marlene, "Richard only visits real *fat* women. I just got this ten to lose."

"Wait until 'Wipe Out' starts playing," Marlene warned. "It'll make that ten pounds feel like forty."

Mattie let the geraniums drink until water appeared above the soil, as well as in the little catch dish that sat beneath the pot.

"Good heavens," said Mattie. "I'm gonna drown you poor things if I don't start concentrating on what I'm doing." But she could still hear Sonny's voice, that soft curl in every word he chose, the whisper of a large laugh just lying between the lines. What was gonna happen to her son?

At six o'clock, Donna, the reporter, opened the *Channel 4 News* with a teaser promising that even newer developments were ahead with Sonny Gifford, who was still holed up in his estranged wife's house trailer. Mattie noticed that there were more cameras than ever milling about the street in front of the trailer, more people trying to look important.

"What does *estranged* mean?" Mattie asked any of her daughters.

"It means she can't wait to get legally divorced," Gracie explained. "Believe me, I been there."

"Separated, Mama," said Marlene. "It means they're

separated but ain't divorced yet." Mattie nodded. It was all so *strange* these days, anyway. Marriages weren't taken any more seriously than signing up for a night class, or putting a winter coat on layaway. It wasn't long term, like the old days. In the old days, marriages were like wars. You were in for the duration. But what could Mattie say against the new way? She knew damn well that if someone had waved a divorce in her face back when she first caught Lester Gifford in bed with another woman, a Mattagash woman at that, she'd have snapped that paper up in a minute. But no one got a divorce back then. A few people chose not to live together, but they stayed married. What was a Mattagash woman going to do with a bevy of little children, little ducks, tagging along behind her and no way to feed them? There weren't any jobs in Mattagash back then for women. There weren't any *now*. Now Gracie was taking all those courses at the college in order to construct a new life for herself, and Charlie was paying her alimony. Mattie wondered what Lester would've said about alimony. If she hadn't had that falling-out with Martha, she could go on over some afternoon and ask Lester that very question through the miracles of the Ouija board. WOULD YOU HAVE GIVEN ME ALIMONY MONEY IF I'D DIVORCED YOU? YOO-HOO, LESTER GIFFORD? YOU THERE, OR DO YOU HAVE SOME LITTLE ANGEL PRESSED TO HER BACK ON A SOFT CLOUD SOMEWHERE, HER LITTLE WINGS PRIED WIDE OPEN?

After the commercial, Donna was back, her eyes bright with excitement as she recounted the events of the past twenty-seven hours: John Lennon's appearance on Sonny's TV, the wine cooler commercial, the line of people at the bank, the controversy over whether Sonny carried a real gun, the dog, the whole shebang.

"And now, Dan," Donna said, staring the camera straight in its eye, "there have been more developments in this very unusual story." Mattie kept her attention on the trailer, which sat above Donna's right shoulder. A dozen or so policemen stood guard along a yellow plastic ribbon, which was now encircling the trailer's front lawn, and that's where the newspeople had been herded, like obedient cattle. "According to Police Chief Melon," Donna continued, "Mr. Gifford has demanded that he speak directly to the press." Dan's voice flooded the picture now, as though he were a kindly god.

"And is Chief Melon willing to go along with this, Donna?" he asked. Donna's face scrunched up with deep concern.

"Dan, we believe that the chief of police is willing to do just about anything to see this unfortunate incident resolved peacefully, with both women safely out of the trailer and Mr. Gifford taken into custody and then perhaps held for psychiatric observation."

"It's about time," said Rita.

"Why are the police letting him talk to newspeople, anyway?" Marlene wanted to know. Mattie smiled. She'd bet a million dollars if she had it that Sonny had refused to talk privately over the phone and had insisted on some attention being paid to him. How else could he let Sheila Bumphrey Gifford know his heart was breaking? How else could he let her see his handsome face again, let her remember just what she was giving up?

Now a policeman was lifting the ribbon so that Donna and what appeared to be a few other reporters could duck under. Donna began a brisk walk across the lawn, headed toward the trailer, her cameraman trailing behind like a well-trained dog. Mattie could see that four of the police-men had positioned themselves about the tiny front porch. Another seemed to be talking to the window of the trailer's door. His hands were motioning, his head occasionally nodding. He turned to face the crowd.

"Don't go up on the porch," Mattie could hear the policeman warning the press.

"No one but press is allowed in the yard," a booming voice declared from offscreen. Donna was saying something about family members having come by to ask about their loved ones. Now, with a gesture of importance, she pushed her way into the group of other reporters. The cameraman followed as the camera noted the three small steps leading up to the front porch. Then the eye of the camera zoomed in and waited on the screened window of the door. The policeman made a gesture.

"It looks as if we're ready to begin, Dan," Donna said. Microphones surged upward in the air. Mattie counted seven. And then she saw Sonny's perfect silhouette on the other side of his estranged wife's screen door. He looked taller than she remembered him, but that might have been the netting of the screen working up a trick, or a shadow that changed the outlook of things. All that really mattered was that he seemed okay, talking above the pain of his broken heart.

"I'm gonna lift this screen," Sonny was saying, "but you cops make sure you don't try something you saw on TV last week. Remember I got a gun in here and it's pointed at two innocent females." The screen slid up out of sight, like an eyelid disappearing, and then there was Sonny's handsome face as he squinted out into the eye of the camera. He was prettier than any movie star Mattie had ever seen, and that included Gary Cooper, whose picture she had kept over her teenaged bed until she married Lester.

"He's got himself a nice tan," said Mattie. "Funny how you girls always burned but Sonny could get himself a tan while standing on his head."

"He's stupid enough to stand on his head to get a tan," said Rita. "I'll give him that much."

"He probably worked on his pickup one afternoon when the sun was out," Gracie said. "I doubt he's been working in construction, or a real job."

"Mr. Gifford," Donna's voice said from offscreen. Her hand was still in the picture, holding her microphone. Mattie could see other microphones appearing near Donna's own. "Can you give us a statement as to why you've taken these two women hostage?" Sonny thought a bit about this. Donna waited.

"The way I see it," Sonny said, and then paused. Rita and Gracie sighed in chorus, but Mattie smiled. Even as a child, Sonny had had a flair about him, a penchant for a little drama. He knew how to work an audience, and that's why he'd always had so many girlfriends. And now the whole state of Maine was waiting to hear his answer. Maybe even other parts of America, too, judging from the number of microphones. Sonny cleared his throat again and then spat a little jet of spittle out through his teeth, spat it down toward his feet. It disappeared like a tiny comet trailing foam.

"Gross," said Rita.

"Billy Plunkett taught him how to do that," Gracie said. "One day on the school bus. There was spit all over the floor of the bus. Patty Fennelson slipped and fell."

"Clam up!" said Mattie.

"The way I see it," Sonny was saying now. A thick silence engulfed Mattie and the girls. They bent forward, perching birds, and waited. "The way I see it," Sonny said again, "this is one small step for Sonny Gifford, but one giant leap for welfare recipients everywhere."

"What is it that you expect the city of Bangor to do for welfare recipients, Mr. Gifford?" Donna asked. "Or is this a statement which you're directing all the way toward Washington, to President Clinton, perhaps?" Sonny seemed to like the notion of that. He smiled broadly.

"I can't believe they're interviewing him like he's important," said Rita, "instead of the petty criminal he in fact is," Mattie kicked the toe of Rita's sneaker, a command to silence.

"I ain't quite had the opportunity to figure out what Mr. Lennon was trying to tell me," Sonny answered truthfully. This was another fine point which Mattie had always appreciated in her boy. There might be a side to Sonny that would eat the Lord's Last Supper, thinking it was cooked for *him*, and then ask Jesus for a doggie bag. But, regardless of what his sisters declared, the boy hardly ever lied. "When I figure it all out, I'll let you know. In the meantime, I'll be needing some supplies sent in, not to mention a few cans of dog food. And this may be a bit delicate for some of your listeners," Sonny added, "but one of my guests—and I won't say which one so as not to embarrass her publicly—will need a box of them little tampon things." Someone tittered loudly behind Donna's shoulder, and Mattie realized it must have been the cameraman. Donna turned and looked sharply beyond the camera, a quick warning.

"Mr. Gifford, do you have any intention at this time of releasing your hostages?" a man standing next to Donna asked. He had the air about him of a big-city television reporter. Bigger-city-than-Bangor television. Sonny ignored the man's question. But that was Sonny. He'd never bow to social pressure.

"Mr. Gifford?" another reporter called out. This was a woman with a long, narrow face and curly brown hair. "Mr. Gifford, if you had to describe yourself in one sentence,

what would it be?" Sonny cocked his head, his profile tip-
ping on its side just a bit.

"You might say that I'm Mattagash, Maine's biggest
underachiever," Sonny announced.

"He said a mouthful there," said Marlene. Sometimes
Mattie wished Sonny wouldn't be so darn friendly with
strangers, especially if they had microphones in their hands.

"I was born on the Ides of March," Sonny continued.
"You ever heard of them?"

"I thought he was born March fifteenth," said Rita.

More questions were thrown at Sonny, words all welded
together in the excitement of competition. He finally held
up his hand, silencing them.

"Now," said Sonny, "if you'll excuse me for interrupting your questions, someone wants to say hello." He
disappeared from the window. Reporters scrambled about
near the porch. Microphones bounced around in the air.
Photographers pushed into the picture suddenly and onto
Mattie's television screen.

"He's gonna let one of the hostages say hello," Gracie
whispered. Mattie could almost feel the waves of tension
washing all the way up from Bangor, drowning everyone
who sat watching in Mattagash, Maine. She imagined her
neighbors, up and down the twisty Mattagash road that followed the twisty Mattagash River, could hear their intakes
of breath being sucked up into their chests, could imagine
their eyes burning holes into a few dozen television screens.
Sonny was back at the window with the poodle in his arms.

"Oh God!" shouted Rita. "We'll be the laughingstock of town!" Sonny looked into the camera and smiled his Sonny smile.

"This here is one of them little dogs of the French persuasion," Sonny said. He held the thin-nosed poodle up for all to see. The poodle glared out at the cameras and the people scattering about. Sonny raised its right paw and waved at the world. Mattie watched as the poodle turned toward Sonny and began licking, struggling to get closer to his face. She'd said it a million times, and she'd say it again: When it came to old people, little kids, and animals, no one was better than Sonny Gifford. It was that *in-between group* that always gave Sonny trouble.

"I got news for you, sister mine," said Gracie. "We're *already* the laughingstock."

"And could you send in one of them rawhide chew bones?" Sonny was asking. "The small size?"

7

Why ain't you doing a puzzle tonight, Mama?" Marlene asked. Rita and Gracie had driven home in their separate automobiles to take inventory of what was happening in their own houses. Rita had suspected for some time now that Willard was smoking pot, ever since he died his hair orange. "It just don't strike me as the act of a straight-thinking child," Rita had noted. Of course, ever since Willard had been a baby, he had never struck Mattie as a "straight-thinking child." But that was Rita's business. Mattie had her own motherly woes. So did Gracie, who was convinced that Roberta was sneaking her fiancé up to her bedroom for a little premarital romp.

"Not in my house," Gracie had said of the romp.

"Not in my *lifetime*," Rita had said of Willard's suspected marijuana use.

Then, like two policemen, they had climbed into their vehicles and barreled toward their possible emergencies. Mattie wished they'd just stay in those houses, where they belonged. She wasn't an invalid, for crying out loud. She wasn't even *old* when you thought about it. She was sixty-six. The world was full of people that age and older who were running countries, heading up major corporations, inventing things. There was a grandmother in her late fifties who had even given birth. Mattie wasn't old by many standards, but she *felt* old. She sometimes woke up in the core of the night to troubling tickles, little aches roaming up and down her legs, her varicose veins pumping away. And the skin of her neck! When did it happen that she leaned in close to the mirror one morning a couple of years ago and was absolutely staggered to find a whole parcel of fat dangling from beneath her chin, like the crop of a chicken. She hated to touch it when she washed her neck, all those mornings after Lester had died. It was as if he was laughing at her somewhere, watching that bag quiver beneath her chin and knowing full well he was the one who gave it to her. Knowing full well that bag was loaded with every lie he'd ever told her, every dream she'd ever left behind, back in her youth, back in those high-heeled shoes she'd worn to her wedding and then never again. Married life with Lester had hurt the minute she walked toward it that Augusty day in church, hurt bodily. And she had had a chance. The minister had said so. If anyone has any cause that these two people not be joined together, say so now. But only the corns on her feet cried out, and all the rest, all those traitors, had stood with dead tongues in their mouths and said nothing.

Marlene had turned the television set off, finally, and now Mattie sat in her rocker, rereading that day's paper.

"Has Henry called you?" Marlene asked. She had set up the ironing board in the kitchen, in order to iron a blouse, and now the room was filled with the fresh smell of pressed cotton. The starchy aroma reminded Mattie of all those shirts, the blue cotton shirts Lester had loved dearly in his lifetime, blue that showcased his flirty brown eyes. She wondered how many of them she had smoothed and steamed to perfection. She wondered how many of them Martha Monihan had unbuttoned.

"Why would Henry call *me?*" Mattie asked. "He's married to Rita." She was studying the photograph of the house trailer in the *Bangor Daily News*: Then she reread the paragraph describing Sonny's personality, his general outlook and philosophy on life, given by the neighbor. "He's a one-man party in full swing," the neighbor said. Mattie supposed that until they tracked down Sonny's *estranged* wife, this Sheila Bumphrey woman, no one in Bangor would be able to offer reporters much more information on Sonny than that he was a "one-man party" originally from Mattagash, Maine. And maybe even Sheila didn't know much more than that, depending on what Sonny had told her. Mattie could say one thing for most Mattagashers: They might be spiteful and mean among themselves, but they rarely turned in one of their own, especially if it was to some government group. Mattagashers were suspicious of the government and any organization that reeked of union. Newspaper and television people were no exception. Their pushiness put them on the outs immediately. Sonny's identity was safe for the moment.

"I ask because Henry called here today while you were out walking," said Marlene. "He wants to talk to you about something."

Mattie folded the paper so as not to crease the picture and laid it on the floor beside her rocker. She would wait until the girls weren't looking and she'd take her scissors and snip out the article on Sonny.

"Henry needs to find the blueprints to his life," said Mattie. "That's all that's wrong with him."

"Henry Plunkett's problem," said Marlene, "is that he can never decide which side of the road he wants to drive on, his side or Rita's side. He's been straddling the white line since they got married." She flipped over the blouse she was ironing so that she could press the back of the collar. Steam hissed out of the holes in the iron. "The government ought to give him a pension for his years of service to Rita."

"Don't be putting your sister down when she's not here to defend herself," said Mattie. "And thank God that she ain't. All I need tonight, after reading about Sonny in the paper, is another fight between you two."

"Rita says Henry worries too much about money," said Marlene.

"And Henry says Rita worries too much about Willard," said Mattie. "So there you have it."

"I can't say I blame her for worrying about Willard,"

Marlene said. "Everybody in town knows that Willard's book of Green Stamps is only half-full."

"Raising a child ain't easy, Marlene," said Mattie. "You should know that, what with the trouble you've had with Steven." Marlene started to protest, but Mattie held up a hand. "I know, I know," said Mattie. "You say that teacher had no business leaving the keys in her car in the first place. I heard it a million times. But what it all boils down to is the same thing. It wasn't easy being a mother years ago, and now it's worse. Now we got things like drugs and green hair dye out there on the market."

"Willard dyed his hair *orange,*" said Marlene. "It's *green* because Rita's trying to get it back to its natural color."

"Whatever," said Mattie. "It ain't easy. I got my own child troubles, so I'm one who can talk."

"Are you still wanting to go down to Bangor?" Marlene asked. "Not that I've changed my mind about taking you. I'm just curious." Mattie already knew that. So were her two sisters curious. They were curious as cats, the three of them.

"Sure, I still want to go," Mattie lied. "Why wouldn't I want to go? That's my son in that trailer. If only I'd learned to drive a car back when I was a girl, I'd go ahead and drive on down there. But a lot of women in my generation never learned to drive. You didn't need a driver's license to get around a kitchen." She began to rock, a slow, mellow rocking, and the kind of motion that puts babies to sleep.

"Well, I'm sorry," said Marlene. She had fitted the blouse about the back of a chair so that it wouldn't wrinkle, and now she was ironing a cotton skirt. "And I suppose I'll end up going to my grave filled with guilt if this Sonny thing has a bad ending, but, Mama, I can't let them television people make fools out of all of us. Imagine what would happen if they found out Sonny's mother was in the crowd. And they would, you know. That's what you'd be going down there for, to talk Sonny out of that trailer. No, I'm sorry. Someone has to look out for your best interests and Sonny ain't the one to do it." She waved a hand in the air, as if to say she was finished with the whole thing. Mattie felt anger rising in her blood, in her face, up the backs of her arms, her neck. She had to pucker her mouth to keep it shut, to keep it from saying, *"Oh yeah, Miss Know-It-All? Well, listen to this news bulletin. Listen to this 'cause it ain't no teaser. Sonny himself called and told me not to come down or I'd be hiring someone right now to take me. Your very own brother made that decision because he felt it'd be best for me to stay put. Sonny Gifford's calling the shots this time out of the chute, so you girls, you Pac Monsters, can just keep your noses out of it. And when it's over, Sonny and me are gonna celebrate. My teeth are soaking as I speak."* But she said nothing. She rose, left the rocker swaying behind her, and went on out to the porch.

"I'm sorry," Marlene was saying above the hiss of the iron, "but that's just how I feel about it." Mattie let the screen door slam.

Out on the porch a cool breeze was swaying the hanging plants. With darkness moving in swiftly, the St. Francis of Assisi birdbath was now just a silhouette on the front lawn, the way Sonny was lately, from behind his trailer window, the outline of better days. Mattie could see a rosy glow above the top of Pauline Plunkett's garage, evidence that Pauline was burning trash in the big rusted drum that sat out there by the swing set. Or she was roasting hot dogs with the kids now that summer had surely come. How Pauline found time to do things with her children was a wonderment to Mattie, but the family always seemed to be involved in some activity during the moments when Pauline wasn't in the cafeteria at school, or peddling Avon up and down the Mattagash road.

Mattie was just about to inspect the hanging plants for dead leaves when she saw movement at the upper end of her porch, a hand rise in the shadowy night, and then the orange glow of a cigarette tip. Mattie put her own hand up to her mouth.

"Who is it?" she asked. Maybe Elmer Fennelson had taken an evening walk and felt like chatting a bit. After all, Mattie hadn't seen him in almost three days, and that wasn't like Elmer.

"It's Henry," a dull voice said, and then the cigarette tip glowed orange again. Mattie could see now that it was, indeed, her son-in-law Henry Plunkett, Pauline's brother, sitting there on her evening porch, his back leaning against her house.

"And here I thought those three girls would be the reason my poor old heart finally blew up," said Mattie, "and instead I find you out here, Henry, like some kind of outhouse hound. Why ain't you home? That's where Rita is, believe it or not." Henry flicked his cigarette out into the night. It rolled like an orange comet, spinning, and then disappeared beyond the birdbath.

"I'll expect you to find that butt as you're leaving," Mattie said, "and take it with you. That ain't no parking lot, Henry. It's my front lawn." Henry unrolled the two legs he had pulled up to his body, stretched them out good. Mattie could see that he was wearing his mill boots, the big heavy brown ones that protected his toes with a steel tip.

"I gotta talk to you about something," said Henry. He sounded almost like the boy Mattie remembered from his childhood, the first Mattagash youngster to attempt a *Grit* newspaper route in Mattagash and St. Leonard. Henry Plunkett had wanted the baseball mitt that *Grit* promised for so many newspapers sold. But his sales had slipped, and so did his dream of the baseball mitt. But Henry had always been the kind of kid to give something a try. And most times he had succeeded. But the *man* hadn't been quite so successful, what with marrying Rita and now losing his job at the mill.

"What's the matter?" Mattie asked. She had come to the edge of the porch where Henry sat and, with a noticeable grunt, had lowered herself down to a sitting position.

"You don't move as easy as you used to," said Henry. "Now would be the perfect time for me to raid your garden." Mattie smiled. It was true that Henry and two other boys had once sneaked into her garden, when they were nine or ten years old, and attempted to make off with an armload of cucumbers and a pocketful of pea pods. Spying them, Mattie had leaped from the back porch and broken into an easy stride right at their heels.

"I'd say I caught up to you back then in about thirty seconds," Mattie said, thinking. "What would you say?"

"Oh," said Henry. "I remember you being a little faster than that." She had waltzed all three of them back to the porch, where they emptied their hands and pockets. And for the rest of the day, rather than having Mattie tell their parents about the theft, they had weeded and watered the immense garden.

"Well, you can steal all you want out of my garden this year," said Mattie. "Just help yourself."

"I gotta find me some work to do," Henry said quickly, ending this talk about childhood thievery and gardens. Mattie fell into pace with him, knowing he had a hard time sticking words to his emotions, as most Mattagash men did. Although Sonny wasn't one of them. Sonny was a born talker, even if most of what came out of his mouth was sweet talk.

"I know you, Henry Plunkett," said Mattie. "And I know Pauline and the rest of your family. You're a family of workers. I know this ain't been easy on you." Henry took a toothpick out of his pocket and stuck it in one corner of his mouth. The toothpick jerked as he slowly chewed on it. Henry and his toothpicks. Mattie even bought him four boxes for a dollar one Christmas. She wrapped them all up in shiny red paper and stuck a big gold bow on the top. It was supposed to be a joke, but Henry was moved by the gift. "This is great," he had said, almost tearfully. "We're always out at the house and Rita never remembers to buy any." He had even carried a box around in his pocket, as though it were a pack of cigarettes.

"I picked this up in Watertown today," Henry said, and took something out of his shirt pocket. It was a brochure, which he handed to Mattie. She could tell by looking at it that Henry had already folded and unfolded it many times. "You, Too, Can Sell Life Insurance," the heading promised in dark letters. An 800 number would put any interested parties in touch with an agent representing Mutual Liberty Insurance. On-the-job training would take eight weeks.

"I already dialed that 800 number," said Henry. "The closest agent is in Caribou. I'd have all the area north of Caribou to myself." Mattie said nothing. Henry selling life insurance. Sonny holed up in a pin-striped trailer. What next? She handed the brochure back, treating it with a certain respect.

"What's Rita say about this?" Mattie asked.

"Rita says I couldn't sell whores in a lumber camp," said Henry. Mattie nodded sympathetically. It was true. Henry *couldn't* sell whores in a lumber camp. Henry couldn't even sell *Grit*.

"Well, I wouldn't go jumping to a conclusion if I were you," Mattie said finally. "There's no telling when the mill is gonna start hiring again. And where would you be if the foreman called to say so? Running around in a suit and tie somewhere north of Caribou? How'd we ever track you down, sweetie, if you were out selling life insurance to the multitude?" Henry sighed and pushed a big hand, a big Plunkett hand, through his wiry hair. He was a tired man. The mill job aside, just living with Rita could age a human.

"You know as well as I do that there ain't no multitude north of Caribou," said Henry. "That's another drawback for me selling insurance. That and the fact that I'll have to move away from Mattagash."

"And then there's the biggest drawback of all," Mattie reminded him.

"What's that?" Henry asked.

"This time Rita's right, Henry. Selling's your short suit." Henry said nothing for a time. He cleared his throat once, then twice. The toothpick began to work frantically.

"I guess I'm gonna have to reconsider all this," said Henry, "now that *you've* added your two cents."

"I had no intentions of putting up any money," said Mattie. "It was *you* asked *me*. And I can't lie to you, sweetheart. I just don't see you going door to door with a briefcase full of papers and forms and talking about beneficiaries. That just ain't you, Henry."

Henry kicked one boot against another and then reversed the action. Mattie could hear nighthawks circling about in the dusk overhead, searching out the early-evening insects. Gracie told her once that scientists had examined the stomach contents of nighthawks and discovered that one had eaten more than five hundred mosquitoes, another more than two thousand flying ants. This put the nighthawk high up on Mattie's list of important birds. Now she could see them, filling up the overhead sky with their easy wing strokes, then shifting gears quickly into rapid winging.

"There ain't nothing to do in Mattagash if you ain't working in the woods," said Henry. "And no one's hiring. So what am I supposed to do?"

"You ain't nearly as bad off as you think," Mattie told him. "You ain't as bad off as Pauline, with them five little kids, and Frank riddled with cancer. Now, *that's* a tough ride. But you, Henry, you got yourself two growed boys who can find part-time work in Watertown, that is if Willard dyes his hair some color that befits an earthling."

"His hair is kind of a grassy color right now," said Henry. "Rita's still working on it."

"You got yourself a mobile home that's all paid for," Mattie continued. "You don't need a pickup truck *and* that big Buick that Rita's running around in, burning up tire rubber. Get rid of one or the other, Henry. And tell Rita she can't buy no more clothes or Avon makeup until you're back on your feet." Henry scoffed at this last remark, the notion of Rita without her eyeliner, her eyebrow pencils, her gobs of creams, her lipsticks of every color, her eye shadows to match all her sweaters and blouses, summer and winter shades of liquid makeup.

"That'd be like telling a porcupine to give up its quills," Henry said. It was Mattie's turn to scoff.

"You know she'll have to defy you in some way," Mattie argued. "And she'll do it by buying her makeup. Let her. Let her think she won that round of the battle. Pauline needs the extra money from them Avon products, so you'll be helping your sister in a roundabout way. You're getting enough unemployment benefits that you can survive if you tighten your belts over there just a bit. And before you know it, things'll get better at the mill." Henry said nothing for a long time. He sat looking up at the sky, as though he, too, saw the nighthawks circling up there, gulping up their quota of bugs.

"Is Sonny out of jail yet?" Henry wanted to know. Mattie sighed.

"Henry, do you and Rita *ever* talk? Do you ever turn on the television, sweetheart, and listen to the news? What planet do you live on, Henry Plunkett? Sonny's not in jail. He's in a house trailer. Don't ask me why because I'm not in the mood." Marlene opened the front door.

"Mama?" she said. "You out here?" Mattie and Henry said nothing, their bodies blending into the shadows at the upper end of the porch. "Mama?" There was a stroke of silence as Marlene peered through the night, out at the St. Francis of Assisi birdbath, then down the road to Pauline's house, where all the windows were shining with a bright yellow warmth. "Crazy old woman," Marlene muttered and closed the door with a thud. Mattie giggled. She couldn't help herself. There was something especially gleeful in catching her daughters with their true colors flying like flags. That all three hoped to headline in Mattie's Last Will and Testament was an unspoken fact that floated like a bat over their heads. A vampire bat. How many times had they tried, alone or as a team, to edge Mattie toward talk of a will? "It'll all just go to lawyers if you die without one," Gracie had noted sadly. Well, there were days when Mattie would rather lawyers get what little she had to leave behind. Henry stirred in the dark beside her, stood up, and stretched.

"Wasn't that a lovely sound?" Mattie asked him. "The music of my daughter's voice?"

"Why don't you send the three of them home?" Henry asked. He selected a fresh toothpick from his pocket. "I never understood why a strong woman like you lets the three of them get away with so much."

Mattie's eyes could no longer see the nighthawks. They had blended into the twilight sky, disappeared except for the nasal-sounding *pee-ik, pee-ah.*

"I wasn't a good mother to them," Mattie finally answered. "That's why."

"You wasn't a bad one, either," said Henry.

"Not being a bad mother ain't much better than not being a good one," said Mattie. "I don't know why that's true, but it is." Henry adjusted his toothpick.

"You ever hit one of them?" he asked.

"No," said Mattie. "Maybe I should've."

"You ever leave them alone when they was little?"

Mattie shook her head. "No," she said.

"Was their supper always waiting for them when they come home from school?"

"I spent a few days in bed with pneumonia," said Mattie. "But I got Eleanor Ryan to come cook for us."

"Them girls ever look in their closets and not have clean clothes to wear?" Henry kept on.

"They always had clean clothes," Mattie conceded. "Clean and *ironed* clothes."

"You ever steal money from them?"

"You know better than that."

"Then I think you been a pretty damn good mother, old girl. Even if you are crazy, like Marlene says." With that, Henry Plunkett ambled off across Mattie's lawn. Just before he reached the St. Francis of Assisi birdbath, he stopped, looked toward the western sky.

"Speaking of planets," said Henry, "that there's Venus." He pointed at a huge, sparkling ornament in the sky, what Mattie thought to be a brilliant star. "And that there," he said as he spun around and pointed to the south, "is Jupiter. You can see four moons with a steady pair of binoculars." He put the life insurance brochure in his hip pocket and went on.

"Mind my birdbath," Mattie warned.

"Birds taking a bath," Henry muttered as he sidestepped St. Francis.

"Henry?" Mattie asked. He stopped and turned. The

light from the living room window caught his weary face in its beam. "I been thinking, Henry. Maybe you *could* sell whores in a lumber camp." Henry smiled. Then he disappeared into the shadows of night. Mattie heard his boot heels hit the tar. Overhead, the soft music of the swooping nighthawks, *pee-ik, pee-ah*, was still playing. Mattie looked up at the Mattagash sky where Jupiter and Venus were peering down at her, two bright eyes. Then she watched the orange glow of Henry's cigarette bouncing about in the dark until it disappeared.

8

Mattie had put on her nightgown and slippers and was sitting at the kitchen table with her puzzle when Rita drove up to the door in her big Buick. Marlene and Gracie were in the bathroom brushing their teeth and plastering their faces with cold cream. Mattie had decided that if she waited for her daughters to leave before she took the *Easter Rising* puzzle out again, she'd never get it finished. Besides, there was something in what Henry Plunkett, her son-in-law, had said that gave her a bit of a boost. Maybe she hadn't been the best mother, but she hadn't been the worst, as Henry had mentioned. And while it was common knowledge that Mattie Gifford worshiped her boy, Sonny, it didn't seem that any of her daughters stopped long enough to consider that maybe their own mother didn't think the world of them, too. That maybe their own mother would have preferred to have Pauline as a daughter. Ignorance was bliss, so Mattie pulled the puzzle out, took all the little plastic bowls she kept the separated pieces in, and dumped them on the table. She was looking for the blue eyeball when Rita came in and threw her purse on the table, scattering the reds of the clothing Jesus was wearing.

"You ain't gonna believe what Henry Plunkett come home and said to me," Rita announced. Mattie pushed a finger through the blue pieces, passing over sky, and flower petal, and background water to search for the eye piece.

"No," she said, as it was obvious that Rita was waiting. "I probably won't believe it."

"He told me we gotta tighten our belts," said Rita. She was getting herself a pop from the fridge. "He said the kids need to look for a summer job in Watertown and that I can't buy no more clothes and makeup until he's working again. And listen to the clincher." She had opened her pop with a loud *fizz* and now she paused to take a big drink of it.

"What's the clincher?" Mattie asked. She opened her eyeglasses case and took out her reading glasses, and now they rode low on the bridge of her nose. Rita was at the wall phone, her finger running down Mattie's cardboard sheet of frequently called numbers.

"He says we can't afford two car payments," said Rita, "and that the Buick goes. He's at home making up a 'For Sale' sign now."

"You *don't* need two automobiles," said Mattie. She put her finger on a brownish piece that was hiding among the blue pieces, scooted it back into the right pile, where it belonged, the earth of the Holy Land.

"You always take his side on everything," said Rita. "I

suppose if Henry come and told you he wanted to move to Caribou and sell life insurance, you'd tell him it was a good idea?" She had found the number she wanted and now she was punching out the digits angrily.

"I don't see anything wrong with Henry selling life insurance in Caribou," said Mattie. She fitted a piece of blue flower into its rightful spot. She still couldn't find the darn eyeball. "Henry'd look good in a suit, carrying a big shiny briefcase full of important papers. I can see him now."

"Henry couldn't sell whores in a lumber camp," said Rita. "Pauline? Pauline, it's Rita. I hope I didn't wake you up, but I'm all out of blush and eye shadow and I need to place an order pronto." Marlene and Gracie came out of the bathroom looking like they'd had a flour fight.

"You're almost out of cold cream, Mama," Marlene announced. Her two blue eyes peered from her white face like glassy buttons. Jesus should be so lucky.

"And order me a tube of lipstick, something *red*," Rita said into the phone. She plunked the receiver back onto the cradle. "That'll show him," she said. Mattie could feel Gracie peering over her shoulder at the puzzle pieces.

"That looks like the piece of shawl that's missing," said Gracie, and pointed a fingernail at a bright red chunk of puzzle.

"If I want help, I'll ask for it," Mattie said calmly. "I ain't color-blind." She studied the blue pile from over the tops of her glasses, the heap of potential flowers.

"I suppose we should stay up for the eleven o'clock

news," Marlene said, "in case our crazy brother has something new to say."

"I'm gonna look cute rattling around in that damn pickup," said Rita.

"What's the matter with *you*?" Gracie asked.

"Never mind," said Rita. Now Marlene's white face was peering over Mattie's shoulder at the puzzle pieces. Would they ever go home, back to where they belonged?

"Remember the Christmas we worked nonstop to put that picture of the Last Supper together?" Rita asked. "We were gonna glue it and then give it to Mama to hang on the wall?" Mattie pretended not to hear, but Marlene and Gracie nodded.

"And all we needed was one piece to finish it," Marlene added, "the brown piece that was Judas's money bag." Mattie remembered the incident painfully. That had been the very day she'd scooted the whole puzzle into her woodstove after the argument over Judas's religious leanings took place.

"Speaking of money bags," said Mattie, "did I hear you just place an Avon order, Rita? I thought you told me Henry said to tighten your belt." But it didn't work. Rita was off and running, Sonny's shortcomings too enjoyable a feast for her to walk away from the table.

"We thought we'd lost that piece for good," Rita plowed on.

"What's Henry gonna say about another makeup order?" Mattie wondered aloud.

"We vacuumed the whole house and then I even emptied

them damn vacuum bags and searched through all that mess," said Marlene.

"Remember how we thought the dog had chewed it up?" Rita wanted to know. Her sisters nodded. "And the whole time we searched for it, Sonny was sitting at the kitchen table watching us, drinking a can of beer and watching."

"Look, there's the piece of shawl I been hunting for," Mattie announced. "Now if I could just find that blasted eyeball."

"Sonny had that piece in his pocket," Rita said. "It wasn't until Mama did the wash the next Monday and was cleaning his pockets that it fell out on the floor. Do you remember that, Mama?" Mattie was still staring at the puzzle, pretending to be unconcerned, all during this current persecution of Sonny, but she was listening to every word. If only Gracie hadn't been visiting that day, sitting at the kitchen table with a bottle of pop and gossiping up the whole town, Mattie would've been the only one to lay eyes on that brown piece of puzzle. But it seemed as though the minute Mattie got her old wringer washer out into the middle of the floor, one of the daughters dropped off a kid, or came to borrow a stick of margarine, or stopped by to look under the cake plate lid. "What do you suppose *this* is?" Mattie had asked. She had wanted to get Gracie's mind off Sonny *that* day, too, because Gracie had started in again on why did Mattie still do Sonny's wash. "But Sonny's a man," Mattie had said. "What's a man know about bleach?" Gracie had shaken her head. "Oh, but they can learn, Mama.

We're finding out all kinds of things about men these days, things they been pretending they can't do for years. It's all out of the bag now. Let Sonny do his own wash." This was a few years before Gracie would come to take those women's studies courses and learn that men weren't good for *anything*, much less doing the laundry. Women like Gracie had been gearing up for such nonsense all their lives. So Mattie had gone ahead and pulled the pockets of Sonny's jeans inside out to check for quarters, or those matchbook covers he was forever writing a girl's phone number on, and that's when the piece of puzzle fell out. "What's this here?" Mattie had asked, hoping Gracie would forget all about men trying to get the stains out of their Fruit of the Looms. Hoping Gracie would just shut up and leave Mattie to her wash. Mattie had held up the little brown piece of puzzle, only to hear Gracie gasp. Mattie had thought about that day over the years, thought about how Sonny chose that money bag piece, chose the thirteen pieces of silver to carry around in his own pocket. It didn't hurt a person to want to be rich, did it? When a child is poor and has to live in a country with people who are rich, what does it do to that child's mind? Those were the kinds of questions Mattie wished those women's magazines Gracie loved would ask, followed by the answers, instead of whether or not men were capable of using Downy fabric softener in an intelligent manner. And yet what had she done? She had held that piece of puzzle up, under the glare of the kitchen light, under the glare of Gracie's pointed little nose. And, Judas that she was, she had betrayed Sonny in doing so, had sold him for a few seconds of peace and quiet.

"Well, I gotta go put on my pj's and cold cream," said Rita. She plunked her pop bottle down on the counter, grabbed her purse off the kitchen table, and disappeared into the little bathroom.

"Why is she gonna have to ride around in the pickup?" Marlene asked.

Mattie shrugged. "Beats me," she said.

"That looks like a piece of his sandal," said Marlene, pointing at the brown pile.

"And I think that might be the yellow center in that flower in the corner," said Gracie.

Mattie stood and began replacing the piles into their plastic bowls.

"Well, if you didn't want any help, why didn't you say so?" Marlene asked. "Honestly, Mama, you can be so childish in your old age."

Mattie piled the bowls onto the puzzle itself and lifted the sheet. She carried it gently to the sofa, knelt on the floor, and then scooted it underneath and out of sight.

"I don't expect to come into this house one day soon and find that some elf has pulled this puzzle out to work on it," she said. She put her glasses back in their case on the kitchen table and went down the hall to her bedroom.

"Have you ever?" she heard Gracie ask Marlene.

The eleven o'clock news had carried just a recap of Sonny Gifford's hostage-taking adventures. The girls were disappointed that nothing new had been offered concerning their brother's shenanigans, no Sheila Bumphrey Gifford to turn up and deliver her own part in the movie. After they went to bed, Mattie crept back out to the living room and turned the television on, put the sound down. She would be able to see the set if she left her bedroom door open. Turning if off, leaving it black and quiet, seemed almost like abandoning Sonny in some way. And he had always been so afraid of the dark. Now, with the television's round eye alert and watching, Mattie would be closer to her boy. She had said her prayers and then stood in the darkness at her window, looking out at the starry Mattagash night. This was a habit she had picked up during those years of Lester's cheating, when only the sounds of the sleeping children and the ticking clock had kept her company. By the time she no longer cared where Lester Gifford might be, or who he might be with, Mattie had acquired the habit of spying on the quiet of the night. It was at moments like this that she could almost hear her neighbors, asleep and dreaming in their beds, their dogs snoring on all those front porches, their kids twitching with little nightmares. It was as if Mattagash itself was a big old clock that had run down for the night, its heartbeat still and steady until someone got up early and wound it all up again by being the first one to start a car, or a pickup, or a skidder. And then the mechanism of the clock would commence again, all whirring and ticking and tocking, folks eating and cutting wood and washing dishes and reading newspapers. Only at night, when the clock was still, could Mattie think of her neighbors with a kind of sisterly love. Even knowing that Lester was out there, dozing in one of those beds, his sleeping mouth popping little Os as he slept, even that knowledge didn't bother her after a time. She heard a dog take up a rapid series of barks and wondered if it was Skunk, wondered where the hell Elmer Fennelson had been. She couldn't remember a time in her whole life when she hadn't seen Elmer for three days. And this was a time when she needed him most. Sonny and Elmer had been great friends down through the years. Elmer had been much kinder to Sonny than his own father had.

Mattie couldn't sleep. She tried first on her stomach, then her left side, then her right. The little aches were back again in her calves, tiny fingers of electricity. Maybe she should take up walking, like Gracie was pestering her to do. Maybe she should have her varicose veins cut and pulled out, as if they were old shoelaces you could throw away. It wasn't a pretty thought, but Dorrie Fennelson had had it done. Dorrie even went through every detail of the operation for anyone who cared to listen. "They cut you here and here," Dorrie liked to say, her dress pulled up and her meaty calf exposed to her audience. "And then they just pull them suckers out."

Mattie finally tossed off her comforter, for it felt too weighty on her skin. She lay on her back and pulled the top sheet up to her chin. And that's when the memories started to arrive, those thoughts about Sonny's upbringing that had plagued her for years. Was there such a thing as loving a child too much? Could too much affection kill or cripple a boy? Could too much devotion be a dangerous weight for a young man to carry? His sisters said he was lazy and good for nothing, but every time Mattie saw that Atlas person in those muscle-building ads, all she could say was, "There's Sonny. Holding up the whole weight of the world and no one realizing it." Memories floated down from off her bedroom ceiling, her personal thoughts that had wafted up there over the years and then bounced like balloons unable to get free. It was while lying on her back in bed, over all those lonesome years, that Mattie did her best thinking. Thoughts of Sonny. How to get Sonny out of trouble, how to set a fire beneath Sonny's pants—which is what Lester said he needed—without burning the boy in the process. Now she remembered a time when Sonny's fifth-grade teacher called her in for a little chat. At least that's what the teacher had labeled it. "I'm worried about Sonny," she told Mattie. "Can you come in for *a little chat?*" The little chat had gone on for well over an hour, with the teacher finally digging out pictures Sonny had drawn. "He mostly draws lighthouses on lonely islands, or silos standing in the middle of fields, beneath zigzags of lightning," the teacher said, showing Mattie one lighthouse after another, putting silo after silo into her hand. In most of the lighthouse pictures, shark fins cut through the dark waters. "Ain't that something," Mattie noted with pride. "Sonny ain't ever been to the ocean. I bet the others kids are drawing pictures of the river. Sonny's got an imagination that won't stop. Now, where'd he ever see a silo?" But the teacher didn't view it that way. "It worries me," she said. "And when we draw pictures of our family, this is what Sonny draws." Then she handed Mattie a picture of a tiny house with five people all piled into one room. Well, that was Lester's architectural spruce goose all right. In another room was a small stick character, all by itself. Above its head was written *Sonny*, with an arrow running down to point Sonny out. He'd even drawn in his cowlick. Sonny hiding out in one small room by himself. Well, that made good sense to Mattie. That's all she ever wanted in that crazy shoe of a house, too, a little peace and relaxation. "I'd say this is a picture of some good logic," Mattie said, handing the drawing back to the teacher. "Me and Sonny are of like minds. We both appreciate time alone to think." And that had ended the little chat. Now Mattie thought about that drawing of Sonny's family, with Sonny holed up alone in one room of the house, *barricaded*. And it seemed so prophetic to her now that she felt hysteria rise up in her chest and flood her very ability to breathe. *Sonny barricaded against the world.* It was true. It seemed that Sonny, for all of his life, had been pedaling a bicycle that took him nowhere, like the invisible bike Gracie pedaled during her exercises. Sonny's legs might have been turning, but his body didn't seem to ever get somewhere important. Or if it did, he always managed to turn a corner just before the final destination, like the time he *almost* got a job with

Maine Parks and Recreation, like the time he *almost* signed up for continuing education classes, like the time he *almost* went into business with his cousin Milton, who now owned Gifford Auto Repair and was doing very well for himself. No, there was something in Sonny Gifford's cards that made the ace of hearts jump out of a royal straight flush so that the ace of clubs could jump in.

And then, with balloons coming off the ceiling every-where she turned her eyes, Mattie remembered that cold winter when Sonny had painted an entire scene that Jack Frost had left behind on the windowpane. He had taken his watercolors and turned Jack's white trees into beautiful sweeping green ones, above brown-bark trunks. Right on the window glass, those flowery swirls of frost had become red and yellow and blue blossoms, magnificent things in the heart of a winter's day. And then Sonny had bordered the whole scene with a fernlike border of brilliant green. "Come see what Sonny done!" Rita had burst into the kitchen and announced. Mattie had opened the door to Sonny's bedroom and just stood there in her slippers and stared, so stunned was she to see this magnificent scene. She should have punished him, there was no doubt about that, because he knew better than to paint on any of the walls or furniture. She never did tell him to leave the windows alone, however, and she retained this thought as she stood with her mouth open and let her eye trace the swooping lines, drink in all the mischievous color. She had had no idea, none whatsoever, that Sonny Gifford was

capable of such artwork. And her heart swelled with pride
to learn of it now. "You ain't mad, Mama?" he had asked.
"No, I ain't mad, son," Mattie told him. That was when
Rita and Marlene and Gracie flew into the room, like little
snowbirds, and stopped dead in their tracks before Sonny's
masterpiece. "Ain't you gonna punish him, Mama?" Those
were the very words out of Rita's and Marlene's mouths, at
the same time, little stereos, as they stood there breathless
and winded. "You gonna punish him good, Mama?" they
wanted to know. Mattie had simply pushed them out of
the bedroom, had closed the door on Sonny and his work.
God and all his angels knew that when the sun hit that
masterpiece, it was gonna be the most colored mess of shit
you ever laid your eyes on, but for a while, for an hour or
two, she and Sonny could look at it in peace, could imagine
it was a place where they both lived, happily, maybe even
ever after. "If *we* painted on the window," Rita had noted,
her lip flopping downward like the tongue of a shoe, "you'd
have a fit." Mattie could merely nod. Maybe she had never
been in a fancy museum in her life, but she knew art when
she saw it. And Sonny had created *art*. If the girls had
painted on the window, it would've been garbage. When
had the battle started between Mattie and the girls, with
Sonny caught in the middle? Between her and Lester, with
Sonny caught in that same damaging hub? When did they
trap themselves into their jobs of attacking Sonny? When
did she, his mother, take up her career of defending him?
Because now it had come to seem to Mattie that they were

all hostages, she and her daughters, Lester, all of Mattagash. They were hostage to one way of life or another, one crazy notion or another that they'd each hung on to all their lives. It was the individual ear of corn dangling in front of each of them that led them onward, led them blindly up the path to the Protestant graveyard on the hill overlooking the Mattagash River, or onward to the Catholic graveyard down by that clutch of pine trees near the old meadow. The girls were hostage to hating Sonny, mindful of his every mistake. And Mattie was hostage to loving him, despite the wildest blunder he ever made. Keeping this thought in mind, Sonny suddenly seemed to be the only one who was free, the one who never opened the door expected of him, too interested was he in the shiny knobs on all those other doors. And here Mattie was, holed up in her own little house, holed up while her daughters kept on trying to brainwash her about Sonny, changing her mind almost, *talking talking talking* at her until there was no place left in her head to think.

That night, Mattie slept with the television on, its round eye open all night, like it was one of Sonny's own eyes, staring down the hall at her while she slept.

9

By the next morning, which had broken to a heavy rainfall, Sonny was again decorating the front page of the *Bangor Daily News*. Pauline Plunkett had called from Watertown to tell Mattie so.

"The paper's already out down here," Pauline said. "Want me to bring you a copy? That way, you won't have to wait for Simon to fill you in. I'll just put it in your mailbox and toot."

"Don't toot more than once," Mattie told her. "I got three big babies asleep in this house."

And so, Mattie got her paper long before the other rural subscribers along Simon Craft's gossipy mail route. She stared at the clear, crisp shot of Sonny's handsome face hovering in the door of the house trailer, the poodle in his arms waving a paw at the public. A bold, black heading rode above Sonny's picture: HOSTAGE-TAKER WOOS PRESS. Mattie stared at her son's face for a long time as she drank her morning coffee. She hadn't bothered with the bacon and toast, her stomach still too agitated from a fitful night's sleep. And now, with rain battering the roof of the little house, she sat bleary-eyed and looked at the picture. The story itself was so much longer and newsier than the day before that it had to be continued on page six. Milly had been telling the truth about that reporter nosing about the store. Now everyone in Maine would read that Sonny Gifford had been an adopted child. His parents, Ronald and Louise Gifford, were both deceased. Mattie could thank Donnie Henderson for his help in hiding the truth from those newspaper people. Donnie had always been a good friend to Sonny Gifford. And it was Sonny Gifford who saw to it that Donnie got the second best-looking girl at every dance those two turned up, at every bar they raised a beer. It was a simple fact of nature that people like Donnie just seemed to fall into step behind people like Sonny.

On page six Mattie was surprised to find a second photograph, this one of Ronald and Louise's shared gravestone, the one with the big GIFFORD above both their names and birth-death dates. She peered deeper at the picture. Someone ought to go out there, to the Catholic graveyard, and mow around that gravestone now that summer had arrived and the grass was sprouting in every which direction. She wondered what poor old Ronald Gifford would think if Martha Monihan let him know, via the Ouija board, that he had finally made the hallowed pages of the *Bangor Daily News*.

There was no mention of Sonny being found in a

biblical potato basket. Even a reporter must sometimes know when his leg is being pulled. The rest of the story was mostly a recap: Sonny Gifford, estranged husband of Sheila Bumphrey Gifford, was holed up with two hostages, Stephanie Bouchard and Vera Temple, in a house trailer in Bangor, Maine, because John Lennon's face had appeared to him on his television set. And, oh yes, Stephanie Bouchard's poodle was named Winston, according to a statement made to police by the Bouchard family. Winston Bouchard was also a hostage of sorts, although it looked to Mattie that, in Sonny's arms, Winston was having the time of his life. The article went on to praise the local Bangor Police Department for bending to Sonny's demands that he speak directly to the press. The department was hard at work, according to Chief Melon. "We're doing everything possible to avert any kind of tragedy," he assured readers. "What we want is to get those women out safely. And we want to do so without anyone getting hurt, including Mr. Gifford." Mattie read on. The police department was hoping to bring in a hostage expert from Boston, someone to reason with Sonny, she supposed. Wait until the girls read about this.

While rain beat furiously against the windows and on the shingles of the roof, Mattie admired the picture of her son in the *Bangor Daily News*. She could see Lester's eyes nestled there on his face, beautiful chestnut eyes with dark, curving lashes. She could see Lester's nose, the straight bridge, the perfect tip. Lester's full lips, the dimpled chin, the dark, silky hair, hair beautiful and soft enough to be a woman's. The only thing Lester Gifford left to his son, he left by accident, and that was his own good looks. Because whether you liked him or not, Lester Gifford, in his prime, had been the best-looking man to ever traipse through the female bedrooms of Mattagash, Maine. But sometimes good looks were like too much money in a dull town. They got you into more trouble than you'd find yourself in if you'd been born a little higher up on the ugly tree. And Sonny was no exception. How could anyone expect Sonny to settle down with one girl and raise a family when women as far away as Bangor were throwing themselves at his feet? And then along comes this Bumphrey woman, with two little ragamuffin children from a failed marriage. Something about her had caused Sonny Gifford to go a little love crazy for the first time in his life. And how could it be any other way? Sonny had had no experience in any kind of female rejection. On the pond of love, he was a sitting duck.

The phone rang, causing Mattie to jump with the *Bangor Daily* in her hand. She tucked the paper under the seat cushion of her chair and then quickly grabbed the phone in the midst of its second ring. She didn't want the girls to stir any earlier than necessary. It was Cecilia Hart, pretending to talk about the weather, which was still thundering down rain. Then Cecilia went on to discuss the new section of road the state was finally putting in, at the turn where the Mattagash River was eating into the riverbank. Then she mentioned that her Skin So Soft, the large size, was back-ordered, and she hoped Pauline got it to her before the summer mosquitoes carried her off. Ha-ha.

"It's still cool in the evenings," Cecilia announced, as though this was something Mattie didn't know. "And I suppose the mosquitoes hate the cool weather as much as we do." She shuffled out another unnatural laugh. Mattie merely grunted a swift response. What would Cecilia know about mosquito likes and dislikes? She spent most of her time curled up on her couch, in front of the television. After her big family of children chipped in together and got her that satellite dish for Mother's Day, Cecilia was hardly ever seen at Mattagash functions. Which was fine with Mattie.

"Well," said Mattie, "I got a baker sheet of biscuits in the oven. I'd better go see about them, Cecilia." And that's when the truth about the phone call presented itself, a truth Mattie had suspected the minute she heard Cecilia's voice.

"Oh, by the way," Cecilia finally asked, as if offhanded. "Where's Sonny these days?" Mattie could feel her face and neck growing warm with indignation as these words settled in. Why couldn't most Mattagash women just come on out and say what they wanted to say? Why all the sniffing around first, like dogs at fire hydrants? Mattie waited for a few seconds before she said anything. She could hear Cecilia's feathery breath on the telephone line, coming in excited puffs as she waited for Mattie's answer.

"I would've thought that you'd know all about where Sonny is, Cecilia," said Mattie, finally. "What with that big spacecraft you got sitting in the field below your house. How many stations do you get on that dish? Enough to keep you up on news in China, I'd think."

"Well," said Cecilia, who had never been one for a good comeback. So Mattie didn't wait for one.

"You know damn well where Sonny is, Cecilia Hart. He's in a trailer down in Bangor with a long red pinstripe running through its middle, with two women and a poodle. Is that enough detail for you? Now, where's *your* son? You remember Reginald, don't you? The son who run off with that crowd of gay hippies from Quebec City? If I was *you*, Cecilia Hart, *that's* the mystery I'd be working on this early on a Wednesday morning, and I'd never mind about Sonny Gifford." Just before Mattie slammed down the phone, she heard Cecilia say, "Well," one more time.

She had no sooner gotten off the line with Cecilia, when Theresa Craft called, all the way from Connecticut. Theresa had been good friends with Sonny back in school. And then, like a lot of other Mattagashers, she had gone off to Connecticut to work, had married a Polish man down there. Now her name was Theresa *Something-Polish*, as Rita liked to say. It started with a *K* was all Mattie could remember and was long enough to cover the body of a pulp truck. And it ended in *ski*. Rita once joked about it. "Do you know why so many Polish names end in *ski?*" Rita had asked when she heard of Theresa's new name. "Because Polacks can't spell *toboggan.*" Sonny had considered this, in Sonny's slow and thoughtful way. "How *do* you spell *toboggan*, Rita?" he'd asked his sister, who was finally forced to try. She left out a *g* and then ended the whole thing in *on*, instead of *an*. "Oh, never mind, for crying out loud," Rita had finally said, flustered. "It was just a joke." Sonny considered this, too. "You ain't a Polack, are you, Rita? Was you adopted, by any chance?" Well, lessons lay in the strangest of places, it was true. And Sonny seemed destined, his role in life, to deliver most of those lessons to his sisters.

"I hear Sonny's holed up in a camper somewhere on a lake," Theresa's voice was saying, tinny and long distance. "What the hell's going on, Mattie?" Mattie heard angry voices in the background. It sounded like shouting.

"What the hell's going on down *there?*" Mattie asked.

"My teenagers are in a fight again over the car," said Theresa. "Can you believe I got kids that old, Mattie?" And then she laughed, that sweet, musical laugh that was Theresa's own. She was another of Sonny's old girlfriends who couldn't seem to get him out of her system. Sonny remained friends with everybody who ever loved him. This may have been another accidental gift Lester had left him.

"At least it ain't reached Connecticut yet," said Mattie. "I expect it will."

"What's going on?" Theresa asked again. So Mattie told her what little she knew, because it seemed as if no one, including Sonny, had figured out what John Lennon had to do with it all, or what kind of a statement Sonny was hoping to make by taking hostages. And then Mattie threw in the part about Sheila Bumphrey Gifford, and the sandpiles with the miniature shovels, sitting there in the sandbox in all those television shots.

"She's gone to Atlantic City with her new beau," Mattie had finished.

"Oops," said Theresa. "Sounds to me like the charming Mr. Gifford has finally met his match. Love has reached him at last." Mattie agreed. The noise of the squabbling teenagers had finally receded in the background.

"Should I come up to Bangor, Mattie?" Theresa wanted to know. "Is there anything at all I can do? I mean, you and I know Sonny wouldn't hurt a flea, but the Bangor police don't know that. I'd hate to see this take a nasty turn." Mattie felt relief rushing in. It was good to have someone to talk to, and with Pauline so busy with her kids and husband and Avon orders, Mattie had almost been tempted to swallow her pride and go back into Martha Plunkett's house. Maybe Lester could advise her again through the miracles of the Ouija board. YOO-HOO, LESTER, IT'S ME AGAIN. GUESS WHAT? SOMEONE NAMED SHEILA LIT A FIRE UNDER SONNY'S PANTS AND NOW HE'S HOLED UP IN A MOBILE HOME WITH TWO WOMEN AND A DOG. WHAT DO YOU THINK? IS IT FINALLY TIME FOR THAT FATHER-SON CHAT?

"I'm worried, too," said Mattie. "But Sonny called me yesterday and told me to stay put. He said he had it all under control. I think the minute this Sheila woman turns up and gives him her undivided attention, Sonny's gonna set them women and that dog free. In the meantime, all I can do is keep my fingers crossed. I'll let you know, Theresa, the minute I hear something new." She hung up the phone and wished Theresa was there at the kitchen table, a cup of tea in front of her, helping Mattie look for the blue piece of eyeball. Mattie had always liked the girlfriends in Sonny Gifford's life. So why did she have such a heavy heart over this Sheila Bumphrey?

She thought the knock at the door might be Elmer, appearing like Lazarus after nearly three days of being dead. But Mattie opened the door to see Roberta, her granddaughter, Gracie's only child. Out in the driveway, behind Robbie's shoulder, a little red car was sparkling with raindrops. Gracie's wheels. Gracie had complained the evening before that Robbie borrowed the car too much. Next to Rita's big Buick, the little red car looked like a cowering potato bug. Mattie could see that the rain had let up and was now dripping slowly from the eaves of the roof. Good. Later, after a little *picture puzzle addiction*, she would take a brisk walk over to see if Elmer's pickup was back in the yard, Skunk returned to his porch rug.

"Grandma?" Roberta asked, her small, blue eyes on the St. Francis of Assisi birdbath. She had clunked up onto the porch in shoes with heels so tall she may as well have been wearing stilts. And the heels were big and square as door stoppers. *Combat boots*, she called them. What would make fairly intelligent children act the way they all seemed to be acting? Television, that was what. "Can you spare a few minutes? I got something I want to talk to you about."

Mattie came out onto the porch and shut the door behind her softly. It was almost ten o'clock, but the Gabor sisters were still in bed. No need to stir them up any earlier than necessary.

"Your mother's still asleep," Mattie explained.

"What else is new?" Roberta wanted to know. "Ever since she started college, she's been acting like a teenager."

"What's bothering you, sweetie?" Mattie asked. "And what in the world have you got on?" She was looking at Roberta's T-shirt, one of those tie-dye jobs, splashes of red and yellow and blue and green all spread out, as if someone crashed into a rainbow doing ninety miles an hour. "I thought that stuff went the way of the dinosaur. And what's gonna happen if you fall off them shoes? You're sure to break an ankle." Mattie motioned to Roberta to step down from the porch so they could take a walk over to where the garden would be, if she'd planted one. She had had a vision of one or all of the girls with their ears and eyes glued to the window. And judging from Roberta's sad face, this was a private problem. They stood where the sweet peas used to spiral their way up the fence. Mattie waited.

"Gracie don't want me to get married," Roberta said. Ever since Gracie had started college, she had decided it was best for Roberta to call her by her first name. "So I can maintain my own identity," Gracie had explained to everyone.

"And why's that?" Mattie asked, although she knew. Roberta was only eighteen, and Peter Laforest only twenty. Children. Babes in a northern Maine woods. "Because you want to get married at Christmas? I can't say I blame her for that, Robbie. Who knows how much it might snow on Christmas Day. I remember one Christmas, back when the kids were little, that we didn't budge from our yard for a week. It was a darn good thing I did my shopping early that year. The only drawback was that your poor grandfather had to spend the holidays with his family." Roberta smiled, but Mattie could see she was in no mood for humor.

"I'm pregnant," Roberta said, with great punch, as though those words were the answer to some math problem, words she'd no doubt been practicing saying all the way down the road to her grandmother's house. "I just picked Christmas Day to throw Mama—*Gracie*—off. If I'd said we were getting married right away, she'd have figured it out."

"Oh, dear heavens," said Mattie. "You know what's gonna hit the fan in a big way. The same way them colors are spread out all over your T-shirt." Roberta tried to force another tight smile, then gave up. Mattie took her hand.

"What's done is done, sweetie," said Mattie. "I wish it had happened different for you. I wish you'd lived up a portion of your life first, like I never did. Like your mother never did. But it didn't happen that way. So there. Let's go on to the next square."

Roberta sighed. "Which is?" she asked.

"Which is telling your mama."

"Jesus," said Roberta.

"At least don't swear," said Mattie. "It's too late to tell you not to do that other thing." Roberta smiled this time.

"That's better," said Mattie. "I like to see my only grand-daughter smiling." Roberta's eyes filled instantly with tears.

"What am I gonna do?" she asked. "I know you got enough on your mind right now, what with Uncle Sonny on Channel 4."

"Do you love this boy?" Mattie asked. Roberta nodded. And Mattie had to admit that Peter did, indeed, seem like a decent little fellow, even if he was hiding half the time behind a flimsy excuse for a mustache, a few straggling brownish hairs clinging to his upper lip like pencil marks. But no matter. He'd have a real manly mustache in a few years and muscle on those long, thin arms. He'd be okay, with a few years of living under his belt. There were worse things than being young and foolish, Mattie supposed, although she didn't know what. Unless it was being *old* and foolish. But it was the former two traits that had led her to the altar with Lester Gifford. But Lester Gifford was no Peter Laforest. Peter Laforest had been known to bring Roberta roses when it wasn't even Valentine's Day. And besides, what could Gracie say about her own choice in a mate? Charlie Craft, her ex-husband and Roberta's father, thought he was secretly living with Sally Fennelson, but all of Mattagash knew it. You couldn't ride by Sally's house trailer at night without seeing big, tall Charlie inside, his head canted forward so that it wouldn't scrape the ceiling.

"Peter's gonna buy us a new mobile home," said Roberta. "Maybe like the one Uncle Sonny's holed up in, with a nice pinstripe and all. We only need another thousand dollars for the down payment, and Peter'll have that in a couple months. He's driving skidder, you know, for the P. J. Irvine Company." It was Mattie's turn to nod.

"Well, then," said Mattie. "Sounds to me like you got yourselves a plan." She turned and looked back at the little house Lester Gifford had built, a house she had worn for forty-nine years, as though it were a good warm coat. It might have been small, but it had kept her from the wind and rain and snow and sun all those years, without much more complaint than a broken cellar step, a few rotted shingles, a cry for paint every decade. And it had been a warm sturdy nest for four little babies. Life would have been easier if it had been a bigger nest, true, but it hadn't been. There were tragic things in life, but a new mobile home wasn't one of them.

"The problem is how to tell Gracie," said Roberta.

"Let me think about it," said Mattie. "We gotta handle this with kid gloves." Roberta swayed a bit on her big clunker shoes, then caught her balance.

"She ain't gonna understand," said Roberta. "Not like you, Grandma. She's headset on me going to college. And all I want to do is get married and have myself a family." Mattie kicked at a clump of soddy ground, probably where she'd tossed a pile of weeds while gardening last summer.

"Understanding and approving are two different things, Robbie. Don't mix them up." Mattie thought she heard a cupboard door slam in the kitchen. It would look suspicious to be seen out at the garden at ten o'clock in the morning with Roberta, especially when there *wasn't* any garden.

"I just want to be happy," said Roberta, as though that weren't asking for much in a big wide world of such *unhappiness*.

"I can tell you the secret to a happy marriage and a successful life in just a few words," Mattie told Roberta. "It's a secret my own grannie told me, but it didn't do me a whit of good because I had nothing but wind between my ears in them days. Now I'm passing that advice on to you, just like it's a piece of china for your trousseau. You do with it what you think is best. You gotta marry your best friend. That's the most important part. And you gotta love your job, no matter what it is. If you want to be a housewife or a schoolteacher, then you go on ahead and be the best damn housewife or schoolteacher you can ever imagine. But if you want to be something else, I'd suggest you take your best friend and hightail it out of Mattagash, Maine."

10

It had seemed as if one day Mattie was living a quiet life in Mattagash, Maine, discussing the ravages of time with her dear old friend Elmer Fennelson and tending to a yearly garden. Then, for no reason, she had decided not to plant a garden for the first time in thirty-four years. Next, Elmer and his dog, Skunk, had disappeared, as if into one of those black holes scientists talked about on television, thanks to that big Hubble telescope, an apparatus Lola Monihan would dearly love to own. And then Sonny Gifford, her only boy, had turned up on Channel 4. Now it seemed Sonny was everywhere. Theresa had called to say that she'd seen a news clip on CNN, way down there in Connecticut. And now Mattie could almost feel the air around Mattagash growing tense, the way it does before a storm, or a big woods fire, or a flood. Something was breaking, like the ice in the spring river. Something was on the wing. And it all had to do with Sonny Gifford barricading himself in a trailer with two women and a dog. No, it was more than just that. It was

Sonny the actor, the best-looking man in Mattagash since his father, Lester Gifford, had made his exit. It was Sonny *courting* those damn news teams, as though the eyes of those cameras were the dark, loving eyes of *women*. Sonny's own charm was now creating quite a stir, and Mattie was forced to sit back and watch it all unfold on television.

Rita and Gracie had driven up to Lola's to see what kind of news that big satellite dish was bringing to Mattagash, Maine, now that Theresa Something-Polish had let them know that CNN was carrying the story. Mattie preferred to stay at home and listen to what Channel 4 had to say, which was plenty for her. A special report at two o'clock had carried the story again, with a promise of live coverage just ahead. Marlene and Mattie had waited patiently in front of the television as the hands of the kitchen clock moved closer and closer to three thirty, when Sonny would make his second appearance. Mattie was glad the other two girls were gone. Marlene was a better person without them, softer, less judgmental. But she was still *Marlene*.

The special report would carry another live interview with Sonny Gifford, or so Donna told her Channel 4 listeners. She was back, with her little chihuahua face, giving another rundown on what had happened: Sonny, John Lennon, the bank, the mystery of the gun, the women, the dog, the house trailer. Was there anyone left in Maine who *didn't* know the particulars of the event? Mattie guessed that maybe there was. Or that Channel 4 had to believe that there was. She personally wanted something new to

chew on, something that might move them all to a conclusion, once and for all. But it seemed that while the police
were sorting out how to get Sonny to give up the hostages
without any lives being taken, the news media was suddenly
interested in Sonny Gifford, *the man*. Sonny had informed
the chief of police, however, that he would now conduct all
interviews with the press from behind the screened window
of the trailer.

"Sonny Gifford has told Chief Melon that he's concerned for his safety, Dan," Donna explained to the camera.
"From now on, he'll not be lifting the window screen, as he
did yesterday."

"Why is he suddenly concerned, Donna?" Dan asked.
The picture on the screen flicked to Dan, tapping a pencil
upon the surface of his news desk and looking most concerned himself. Then it flashed back to Donna, at Marigold
Drive Trailer Park.

"Well, Dan," said Donna. Why did news reporters keep
repeating each other's names? "The general consensus
among reporters here is that Mr. Gifford isn't armed, at
least not with a real weapon. During the excitement, it's
very possible that the women went with Mr. Gifford without getting a good look at the gun." Donna waited. Dan's
face was back.

"Then why is the chief of police waiting, Donna, if
he believes Mr. Gifford is unarmed?" Now Dan waited,
although it seemed to Mattie that he already knew the
answer. Who wouldn't know?

"It's just too dangerous, Dan," said Donna. "And, of course, there's no way of knowing if there might have been a weapon already inside the trailer."

"Nonsense," said Mattie. "Sonny hates guns." It was his love of animals that held him back, even as a child, while other boys were shooting sparrows out of trees, and ambushing rabbits and squirrels.

Donna had turned to the swelling crowd behind her, for the live interview was beginning, and she obviously had questions of her own to ask Sonny Gifford.

"Sonny only wanted to get his face on TV," said Marlene. "You know it, Mama, and I know it. We both know it." Mattie ignored her. Instead, she watched as the reporters scrambled for positions near the trailer's porch.

"No one is allowed on the porch itself!" a policeman shouted at a man who had started up the steps of the trailer with a microphone in his hand. Now Donna pushed her way through the crowd, toward the window of the trailer, her cameraman trailing behind her with a jerky picture. Then Mattie heard Sonny's voice, and she was instantly swept into the wake of her son's newest adventure. She felt as if she were lingering there in Bangor, in the summer sunshine, at Donna's spindly side.

"One of these fine hostage women is standing right here beside me," Sonny's voice announced. "So don't anyone do anything foolish." As far as Mattie could tell, there was only one silhouette, and it appeared to be Sonny's, tall and nice-shouldered. And it certainly had Sonny's voice.

"Sonny?" one reporter asked from behind a microphone thrust toward the window. "Have you ever been in trouble with the law before?" Sonny's silhouette moved slowly behind the screen. He seemed to be giving the question particular concern.

"This ought to be good," Marlene declared.

"Only once," said Sonny. "Not stopping for a light." Mattie heard Marlene snort.

"Not stopping for a red light?" the reporter asked. He frantically scrawled words onto a tablet he carried in his hand. Sonny cleared his throat. His shadowy face moved closer to the window.

"Actually," said Sonny, "it was a *blue* light, and it was attached to the top of Sheriff Dan Wicker's patrol car." Mattie imagined that Sonny's face had probably produced that famous grin—she could almost see it through the mesh of the screen—because a mass of grins now exploded among the gathered reporters. How many times had Mattie seen him able to do that, able to entertain the multitude with his charm, entertain them as surely as if he had divided bread and fish to feed their starving souls? That was Sonny Gifford. That was her baby.

"Sonny?" Donna now asked the window. Mattie noticed that Donna's attitude had changed from just the day before. She'd gone from *Mr. Gifford* to *Sonny*, wrapping that *Sonny* in a bunch of sugar. And she had her hair done up in a sweet bun. If it weren't for her little dog face, she'd have gone and made herself pretty, and Mattie wondered if it was for Sonny. She'd seen a million women do just that. And it wasn't as if Sonny wasn't working his own kind of magic. Mattie could see him lingering there in the window, as if it was some balcony in a play or something, running his hand up through his hair. His silhouette was even more effective, mysterious. Sonny was doing okay in his being holed up. He was still wooing the girls. Bless him. That's why his sisters hated him so. He represented every good-looking, good-talking, good-loving man who'd ever broken their hearts. And the girls would be the first to say that there'd been a slew of such men to walk through their lives.

"Can we talk to the hostages?" Donna wanted to know, her little pooch face all scrunched up in thought. "And do you have any plans to release them?" Sonny cleared his throat again, the way he always did as a youngster when he didn't want to deal with a pressing issue. Mattie could read her child, her boy Sonny, as if he were a set of traffic signs. Sonny was going to ignore this question, no doubt about it in Mattie's mind.

"I appreciate everyone's interest and all," Sonny was now saying to the reporters. "And I enjoy talking to you fine folks. But from now on I won't be available between the hours of four and five p.m., except on weekends." A chorus of whys? rang out from reporters as more microphones were readied and cameramen fought for positions around the trailer's porch.

"Because *Star Trek* reruns are on," Sonny explained. "Sorry if that causes you any inconvenience. Other than that, I'm yours." A silhouette of Sonny's arm rose into the air, the hand canted back toward his face. Mattie assumed Sonny was looking at his watch. "Almost time for Captain Kirk," he told his audience, "so ask your questions now."

"Ain't this just about the most embarrassing thing that's happened to us yet?" Marlene insisted.

"Not really," said Mattie. It might've been the most public thing that had ever happened, but it was far from the most embarrassing. Rita camping out on that Watertown basketball player's front lawn, in her prom dress and long white gloves, was a dead ringer for first place. Rita had somehow, somewhere along the way, made a miscalculation about life and love. It had appeared in Rita's mind that if she gave some man her virginity—as though it were like one of those gifts you give to men, a necktie, or cuff links, or a subscription to *Sports Illustrated*—then he was obligated to marry her. The basketball player had seen it all in a different light. He had taken his necktie, his cuff links, and his subscription to *Sports Illustrated*, and he had run like hell for the road. It was his mother who phoned the police to have Rita removed from around the zinnias and box elders. Years later, Rita would misremember the whole event, as was Rita's greatest talent. The basketball player had loved her dearly, pined to marry her, and been kept away by his family. Romeo and Juliet in Mattagash and Watertown.

"No," Mattie said again, "I'd say this hostage incident is way down on the list of embarrassing family milestones."

And Lester Gifford, eating up his social hours with everyone and anyone other than his wife and children should at least *place*.

"Try to imagine Lola Craft Monihan and Dorrie Fennelson and all of Mattagash watching this," Marlene was now saying. "I bet satellite dishes are spinning all over town."

"Let them spin," Mattie said. "Nobody ever said Sonny was boring."

"I've been told by a childhood friend of yours up in Mattagash," the same reporter continued, "a Mr. Donnie Henderson, that you've been keeping a Great Americans list for years now." Microphones again appeared from all angles of the screen, microphones that seemed to exist without people. Mattie heard Sonny laugh a short laugh, saw his silhouette nod from behind the screen.

"You tell Donnie Henderson to get himself down to Bangor more often," Sonny scolded.

"Can you tell us the names on your list, Sonny?" someone else wondered.

"Are there any women on the list?" Donna wanted to know. Sonny nodded again.

"Jackie Kennedy," he said, "because there ain't a lot of folks I know, men or women, who wouldn't duck down in the car if a bullet was fired in their general direction. But Jackie climbed right out onto the trunk. I tell you, that girl had spunk."

"As if Jackie Kennedy would've given Sonny the time of day," said Marlene. She bit anxiously at a fingernail.

"She might've," Mattie said. "After all, she *married* that short-legged little Greek."

"And then there's Sheila Bumphrey Gifford," Sonny continued, "my soon-to-be ex from right here in Bangor, Maine. And that pretty well rounds out the women on my Great Americans list. But I'm willing to expand." Mattie twitched on the sofa and leaned nearer to the television. Marlene's stomach had started to growl and it was annoying Mattie greatly.

"Who else is on the list?" a faceless voice asked.

"You remind them Bangor cops that I got me a gun held on these innocent women," Sonny suddenly announced. "I'd hate for anyone to take a shot at me while I'm standing here conversing with you nice folks."

"He ain't got no gun," said Mattie. "I can tell by his voice that he's lying. I could always tell, you know."

"Well," said Marlene. "With Sonny you had plenty of opportunity to practice."

"Who else is on the Great Americans list?" the voice repeated. Sonny's hand moved up behind the screen to scratch his head. There were a few seconds of silence.

"Scottie on *Star Trek*, for one," Sonny finally answered.

"And why is that?" a thin-faced, thin-haired man wanted to know.

"Because he's always beaming everybody up and never complaining about it," said Sonny. "That's the mark of a true gentleman. And now, speaking of Scottie." He tapped at his watch again.

"Ronny," said a newswoman Mattie hadn't seen before. She seemed to have just arrived on the scene. She looked far more important than the other reporters, who fell back to let her move in closer to the window. Mattie wondered if Barbara Walters might show up. She had always liked Barbara, even thought she took after her, lookswise. "Can you tell us why you've taken these hostages?" this new woman asked. "What were the exact words you believe John Lennon spoke to you, Ronny?" She was good, all right, with little time for questions about Great Americans lists. She seemed intent to get to the heart of the hostage matter, which Mattie thought was a healthy idea.

"Don't she look like a constipated rabbit?" Marlene asked as she rounded up a fistful of chips.

"It's *Sonny*, ma'am," the voice behind the screen kindly corrected her. "I was named after the legendary country musician Sonny James, a great American and one hell of a tearful singer. He's also on my list."

"See?" said Marlene. "He's still the liar he always was. You of all people, Mama, know darn well he wasn't named after Sonny James, or Sonny Bono, or any other Sonny. Now can you admit he's a liar?" Mattie tried not to think of Sonny's comment to the newswoman. He hadn't been named after Sonny James. He had not. But what did it hurt if he wanted folks to think he had? The truth was that she and Lester had argued so long and so hard over what to name their son that they never got around to agreeing on anything. Lester had been all in favor of Lester Junior, but

Mattie felt that if she named her son after his father, he would inherit all that was bad about Lester. Sonny would go through life a tagged child, and then a marked man. As it turned out, it had probably hurt him worse that they just let the issue ride. "Son Gifford" is all it ever said on his birth certificate. *Son Gifford*. And it seemed that, as the years passed, Sonny had come to feel that he'd been cheated out of a name, a birthright of sorts. One time Mattie had found him sitting on the front steps, staring at the harvest moon, a big boy by this time. "What about Thomas?" Sonny had asked her. "Wouldn't Thomas be a nice name for me, Mama?"

"Will you be stating your demands soon, Mr. Gifford?" the thin-faced, thin-haired man asked. Mattie smiled. They were calling her son *mister*. And it seemed as though the important-acting woman had steered them all toward some important-sounding questions. That's probably why that important-acting woman got to be so important in the first place. Her presence had changed the atmosphere of the live press conference. A buzzing rose up from the journalists, everyone wanting to ask their own important question, it seemed to Mattie. Voices cried out about demands not met, hostage conditions, background traumas. Someone representing animal rights inquired about the poodle's well-being.

"All I've got to say at this point, just for the record," Mattie heard Sonny finally say, "is that if I don't walk out of this house trailer alive, I want Preston Gifford, another great American, to have my pickup truck, which is parked right there in the driveway." A hand motioned from behind the screen. "And which I notice is being leaned up against by you news folk, and if you don't mind, I'd appreciate it if you could lean on trees and such instead. Them cameras can cut a mean swath across a paint job." Donna was shunted aside suddenly by a burly newsman. She was losing Sonny, Mattie could tell, and she had had him first, before this other woman even knew about him. Before anyone else cared about him.

"If your demands aren't met, Sonny," the man wanted to know, "what do you plan to do with your hostages?" More microphones were thrust in for the answer.

"And I want my cousin Maynard to have my chain saw," said Sonny, ignoring the question. Another newsman wondered if the state of affairs in Serbia and Haiti, followed by the despair in Rwanda, had had anything to do with Sonny's actions.

"Is that what John Lennon meant when he told you to stand up for the unfortunate people of the world?" the reporter wondered. Sonny seemed to like that question and fielded it from out of the mass coming at him.

"I got nothing but good wishes for all them people, all over the world," Sonny announced dramatically. "Now, that's all I have to say at this point in time, for I must boldly go where no man has ever gone before." His silhouette disappeared and microphones receded. People scrambled about in the front yard. Policemen began herding them away from the trailer. Only Donna and the important-looking woman remained in place, their faces still aimed at the window.

"Oh, another thing," said Sonny, his outline reappearing. A chorus of voices rang out from the newspeople as they hurried to reassemble. A huge bouquet of microphones appeared immediately, sprouting from several directions, parts of arms and hands holding them firmly. "I would also like to tell Sheila Bumphrey Gifford, from right here in Bangor, Maine, the United States of America, but now on vacation somewhere in Atlantic City with a no-good bum, that I would appreciate it if she would return my dog, Humphrey, or tell me where she hid him. And all I can say at this point is that he'd better not be in Atlantic City with that"—*beep beep beep beep beep*. Then he was gone. Mattie winced. And Henry thought Rita's microwave did an abnormal amount of *beeping*. But at least now Mattie was one hundred percent certain. With no amount of fallback experience when it came to womanly rejection, Sonny had gone off the limb in a big way to get some attention from his philandering wife.

"Humphrey Bumphrey Gifford?" Marlene asked. She had started on another fingernail. Mattie wondered what her new daughter-in-law looked like. She hoped one of the newspeople would find the time to scrounge up a picture. The Bangor police chief, Chief Melon, was now being interviewed. He had been in touch with Sonny by phone and he felt quite certain, wanted to assure everyone, that the incident would be cleared up soon, with no harm befalling anyone. They were still trying to find Sheila Bumphrey Gifford, and now that CNN was airing the story, they hoped that Ms. Bumphrey Gifford would learn of the events taking place in her house trailer. Bangor police would begin an immediate search for Humphrey the dog. Anything to calm Mr. Gifford down and get him to release the women and himself without further trouble. It seemed to Mattie that Chief Melon had figured out what was wrong with Sonny, too. She imagined Sheila Bumphrey Gifford, in bed in some seedy motel room in Atlantic City, her hair sweaty and ruffled from rolling in the sack with her new beau, the kids asleep on another bed, new shovels and sand pails lying quietly on the motel's frayed rug.

Marlene turned off the television set. Mattie shivered. Something was bothering her. Her motherly instinct was kicking at her insides with a fateful thump. Her heart had begun pounding briskly, all on its own, without any permission from her mind.

"Well, I gotta go home and see if Steven and Lyle have torn down the house yet," Marlene announced. She stood quickly, and Mattie felt the sofa readjust itself beneath her. "Wesley lets them do as they please when I ain't home. And the last thing I need is for one of them to grow up and be like his uncle Sonny. See you tonight." Mattie had to ignore the motherly insult, for Marlene was gone in a slam of door, followed by an engine spurting to life, and then tires eating up gravel to get to the road. Then, silence, sweet and long and drifting like a cloud all around Mattie's head and ears.

Peace. Tranquillity. The things it now seemed Mattie would never have again, not unless she died and they carted her off to the Catholic graveyard, down by that clutch of pine trees near the old meadow, with only the wind for company.

The picture puzzle of Jesus might stave off that feeling of dread that was tapping its finger on her back. Mattie pulled the cardboard sheet out from under the sofa and placed it gently on the kitchen table. Then she arranged all the bowls with their separated colors in easy-to-grab spots. But all she could do with the puzzle was stare down at it, dazed, dumbfounded as an ox, unable to lift her finger to a single piece of holy earth, of flower, of blessed, blessed sky. It seemed to be telling her something, the scattered puzzle, revealing to her a secret about life, about *her* life, about her life *with Sonny*. It was as if maybe the chips and fragments of Sonny's existence were like a big picture puzzle, one that Mattie couldn't put together, like that one puzzle she'd bought and failed to solve, the only one since her addiction began. It had twenty-five hundred pieces, and half of them black sky except for an orange of a moon hanging over a desert at night. You could count the clues in that huge picture, those good solid objects to aid you, on one hand. So Mattie had eventually given up, had scooted all the pieces back into the box they came in and filed it away on the top shelf of her closet, feeling embarrassment that, after forty years of unwavering experience, she'd finally met her match. And now Sonny was like that puzzle. Sonny was like *The Desert with Night Moon*.

11

There was something about afternoons on any given day that brought a sadness into Mattie's heart. She had had a whole lot of years to consider the whys of such a thing and she had decided this: Life had shoveled up its most smelly stuff during some of the most beautiful winter, spring, summer, and autumn afternoons that northern Maine had to offer. She had caught Lester Gifford with his Fruit of the Looms about his ankles in Eliza Fennelson's bedroom on a spring day in April of 1954. She was eight months along with Gracie at the time. She had already lost three babies, all miscarriages which she would learn later were due to the fact that she didn't have in her O negative blood something that was called an RH factor. She would learn this years later, long after all the other *negative* traits of her life had already surfaced. But she still didn't know it the day she walked—*tiptoed* was a more truthful word—into Eliza Fennelson's house, on that day in late April when you could hear snow melting and dripping from the eaves of all the

Mattagash houses, when the warblers had begun returning from the south and were firmly perched in all the trees and singing the new hits of 1954, when the wild cherry trees were thinking about sprouting fuzzy white flowers. All she knew was that she had miscarried three babies, and that was a funny word, *miscarried*, as though she had *dropped* them. And then she'd gone on to have two girls, Rita and Marlene, babies who'd been born anemic but at least healthy enough to live and grow. And she was carrying a third, eight months into lugging that stomach around in front of her, when Martha Monihan stopped by the little mushroom of a house and bothered to tell her a great big Mattagash secret. It seems Lester Gifford was at that very moment in bed with Eliza Fennelson, who was an out-of-state woman, brought to Mattagash by her husband, Pete Fennelson, who had met her while he was stationed down in Fort Dix, New Jersey. Martha Monihan told Mattie this with big tears rimming her eyes. And Mattie thanked her for having the nerve to come forward—*thanked* her, good, kind friend that she was. It would be another five years, after Sonny was finally born and toddling about in his diaper, that Mattie would learn the whole truth from Eliza Fennelson, who had found Jesus in a real big way shortly after Mattie found *her* in bed with Lester. There had been a lot of hide-and-seek going on in those days. And since not even good-looking, sweet-talking Lester Gifford was a match for Jesus, Eliza gave her heart to God and wanted to clear her conscience. Mattie had always found it interesting how folks who find God seem to have a need to do that, to drop off all their dirty baggage on the very folks who'd had to put up with it in the first place. But there came Eliza Fennelson up the road one day. Mattie had just given Sonny his bottle and put him down for his nap. She could still remember how his head of curls fell against the pillow, his little red lips doing some imaginary sucking as he slept. October 1959, one of the most beautiful autumn afternoons she would ever remember. Or maybe she remembered it only because those other details had unfurled in her mind like red and orange leaves. But it *had* been beautiful. The maple trees on the mountain behind the house had burst to scarlet blotches on the horizon. Goldenrod stood yellowish brown in the fields. And the Mattagash River curled like a long, blue dream that day, not a cloud in the sky that rode above it. And here came Eliza Fennelson, clutching her little black Bible in her hands, shaking and perspiring. Mattie let her in. The past was past. Lester had cleaned up his act. He had sworn to this on his mother's grave. And then Eliza was sitting at the kitchen table apologizing, sorting through her dirty, sinful laundry so that she could float on up to heaven one day without so much as a feather of guilt to hold her down. Mattie forgave her. That's what she'd come to hear, *forgiveness*. The way the Fuller Brush man comes around to hear you say you need some furniture polish. Or the man from the bank comes around to hear you promise you'll put that check in the mail. Or the apple man comes by to hear you say you'll buy a crate of apples. Mattie told Eliza Fennelson what she'd come to hear.

But then Eliza said something Mattie hadn't expected, something you'd never have to worry about hearing from the Fuller Brush man, or the man from the bank, or the apple man. Men usually didn't have time for things other than business, anyway. "Now that you've forgiven me," Eliza had cried out that day in the autumn-warm kitchen, that day the last of the river roses ate their way up the banks like a dull red fire. "Now that you've forgiven me, I can go ahead and forgive Martha Monihan for telling you. After all, Lester broke Martha's heart in two when he took up with me." Mattie had realized that her head was bobbing, pretending she already knew all about Lester and Martha, pretending it didn't matter a whit. And it's a curious thing about people who find God. They can't seem to leave well enough alone after that. They go out looking for poor innocent folks to take to heaven with them, folks who don't even want to go. "You're a saint, Mattie Gifford," Eliza had gone on to say. "Everyone in Mattagash says so, what with Lester and Martha sleeping together all these years. What with Lester sleeping with all those other women in Mattagash who ain't given up their hearts to Jesus." It's a curious thing when the day comes that you realize you've been living your tiny life in a big fish bowl and didn't even know it. When you realize that most of the smiles you've encountered on your neighbors faces weren't real smiles, but things pasted there to hide the truth of life from you. You start remembering that quilting party when so-and-so had laughed a little too hard at some joke that was being told about a cheating husband. Or that Sunday picnic, years earlier, when you yourself had made a statement about fidelity, and its importance, and all your listeners fell silent as stones. And eventually you get around to disbelieving everything you've ever done and seen and felt. You go into your miniature house as if it's some kind of hard, safe shell and you watch your neighbors from a distance. That day, a day Mattie always referred to as revealing more of *the RH factor,* had been October 15, 1959. She had never once suspected Martha Monihan, not once, not in all those years of knowing her, of having her sit at the kitchen table and nibble on fresh string beans from the garden, of sitting down in Martha's living room to play a game of Charlemagne with Lester and Martha's husband, Tom. Never. Not once. Lester had sworn on his mother's grave that he'd never cheat again. So much for Lester. So much for his dead mother and her grave. And that's when life had begun revealing itself to Mattie as the strangest, most mixed-up notion anyone had ever come up with yet. October 15, 1959. And Martha Monihan had been Mattie's best friend since 1937, since the day that Mattie picked her up from the mud puddle where Thomas Monihan had pushed her. She was Martha Craft in those days, skinny-legged, space-toothed, curly-haired. But she eventually grew up to be Mattie's best friend and to marry Thomas Monihan. Mattie could've left Rita looking after Sonny that day in 1959. She could've waited for her to get off the yellow squash of a Mattagash school bus to babysit. *Could've.* And if Rita was home to babysit, then Mattie should've gone on down the road to confront Martha Monihan. *Should've.* And just when Martha had leaned back against her kitchen sink, her hands finding the cotton of her apron so that they could wipe themselves dry, or her hands pushing back the strands of that still-curly hair, Mattie would've said, "I ought to put you back in the mud, Martha Craft, right where I found you back in 1937." *Should've. Could've. Would've.* Those words were no better than the whores Lester had been sleeping with all those years behind Mattie's back. So Mattie didn't do any of that stuff. Instead, she let Martha's round Craft eyes, big cocker spaniel eyes, look into hers every time they met, whether it was over a bowl of homemade ice cream or while they were standing watching their kids play baseball, or even at someone's wake, as they both stared straight ahead at the coffin and thought about the spidery webs of lies spun by the living. And Mattie made little comments, when gossip arose about other women, comments like "That woman has to face her maker one day, and He knows who she's been sleeping with behind her husband's back." And once, when they sat beside each other in Martha's living room, watching a soap opera in which a woman slept with her friend's husband, Mattie had shook her head sadly. "I'm so lucky I don't know anyone as low as that," Mattie had said. "There's no one that low in Mattagash, Maine, that's one thing for sure." And the years had melted away like that. The years had turned from the fifties into the sixties, and the sixties had become the seventies, and the seventies went on to develop into the eighties, and then Lester Gifford's heart took it upon itself to explode and Lester vanished from the two-lane roads of Mattagash, Maine, vanished from the white sheets on all those female beds, sheets that smelled like they'd been drying a whole day in the Mattagash river breezes. Lester disappeared. August 12, 1989, one of the prettiest summer afternoons you were ever privileged to see in northern Maine, was the day they put him into the old-settler earth forever. And what Mattie felt on that day, as she watched Martha Monihan come dizzily into the tiny Catholic church, the only one there wearing black, like she was some kind of widow or something, the only thing Mattie could feel was pity. After all, it was *Martha's* heart that had ached and throbbed and yearned for Lester all those long years of sunrises and sunsets, of flash floods and rains and fires eating up the timberlands, of babies being born and old-timers dying, of PTA meetings and basketball games and softball tournaments, of all those horseshoes tossed on the Fourth of July, all those fireflies burning up the summer nights, the millions and millions of snowflakes that had fluttered over Mattagash, the cuts and bruises that had appeared, then disappeared on the feet and elbows of children, the sandwiches thrown together for all those school lunch pails, the cucumber seeds that had been pried into the earth in all those gardens, the pillowcases washed, the letters written and mailed out to the world, the monthly blood that had flowed from all those women, the cans of peaches opened, the loaves of bread baked, the doughnuts eaten. Martha Monihan had craved Lester Gifford through all of that. And for thirty years Mattie had watched it unfold, with a genuine smile pasted to her face, instead of one of those fake ones. Even after the cancer took Eliza Fennelson up to heaven, light as a feather. And now, in 1994, with Lester dead and gone almost five years, Martha was still after him, through the Ouija board this time. Chasing Mattie's husband when he was alive was one thing, but chasing him long after he went into his grave was another. And that's why Mattie had walked out on Martha's Ouija board session. Enough was enough. Even the marriage vows said "until death do us part." So there they were, in the present, Martha left with her Ouija board and Mattie with what she called the RH factor and the afternoon blues.

When you got right down to the nitty-gritty, though, the afternoon blues were still better than having the girls all pile back into the little hubcap of a house. But that's just what they did.

"Pauline dropped off my Avon order," said Gracie. She was back in her exercise outfit, long purple leggings and white turned-down socks. She reminded Mattie of a colt horse, prancing about the springtime fields.

"She dropped mine off, too," said Rita. "I dare Henry Plunkett to say a single word about my ordering that perfume. Besides, I ordered it back in May."

"She finally brought me my Skin So Soft," said Marlene. And then, remembering, she giggled. "Pauline says she's got to teach her daughter Sonya the facts of life. Sonya got up this morning and asked if babies get delivered by Avon."

The girls laughed in tune. Mattie was surprised to hear them harmonizing on something.

"You need to sit right down the moment they ask the first question," said Gracie, "and tell them everything." Gracie had that look on her face again, that psychology class, women's studies glare that just defied anyone to argue the point with her. Mattie decided she would.

"I don't think you should tell a child too much too soon," Mattie pointed out. Marlene shook her head.

"I wouldn't say you were the best when it come to telling us about the birds and the bees, Mama," Marlene said. "When you were expecting Gracie, I asked you why your belly was so big, and you told me you'd swallowed a watermelon seed."

"I was so young and stupid in them days," said Mattie, "I probably believed that myself."

"To this day I can't eat watermelon," Marlene added.

Mattie knew the talk couldn't possibly stay away from Sonny. Even if he *wasn't* holed up in a house trailer with two women and a dog, the girls couldn't go an hour without casting some form of slander at their brother. Besmirching Sonny had become more addictive than Avon, cigarettes, and women's studies classes. It had become much more addictive than putting together picture puzzles. And Mattie was right.

"You can't go anywhere in this town without someone asking you about Sonny," said Rita. "I just tell everybody the God's truth. That's the only thing you can do. And then I ask them if they're at all surprised."

"At least CNN ain't carrying the full story," said Marlene. "They've just been showing the trailer every now and then, and mentioning that some nut up in Maine has taken a poodle hostage. It don't seem to matter that he's got those women, too. That's small potatoes these days, what with people going into McDonald's and killing everyone they see." Rita patted her hand about on the kitchen table, feeling around behind the plastic flower centerpiece that Mattie kept there.

"I can't find my cigarettes," she said.

"That's because they're out on the porch," said Mattie, "which is where smoking will take place from now on, at least while you're all staying in this house."

"Now, Mama," said Gracie. "You're overreacting again."

"I'm curious about something," said Mattie. "So just for the fun of it, fill me in. Why aren't you all in your own homes?" Marlene exchanged looks with Gracie, who peered anxiously at Rita.

"Well, I'll tell you," said Rita, as though she were talking to a ten-year-old. "We've been all through this before. You don't exactly have your thinking cap on tight when it comes to Sonny. And when them journalists find out the truth, which they will because even journalists can root up the occasional acorn, they're gonna come down on this house like locusts." She shook her head, tired of explaining the obvious.

"So?" asked Mattie. "I can handle a few locusts."

"Mama, listen to me for a minute, please." It was

Marlene's turn. Mattie directed her full attention to her middle daughter. Marlene was probably the prettiest of the girls, had been so when she was a baby, what with Lester's deep chestnut eyes and butterfly lashes, not to mention his ample lips. Mattie waited.

"Come on, Marlene," said Gracie, "say something or get off the pot."

"It's just that Mattagash, Maine, is kind of used to watching Sonny carry on. It's nothing real new to them, except that now it's on television." Rita seemed too eager to agree with Marlene for once. She was nodding so much, Mattie feared her neck might break and the head roll away. Or maybe it was the onslaught of a nicotine fit Mattie was watching unfold.

"Sonny always did stand out like a turd at a pee party," Rita said. Mattie shook her head. More pious talk from the Born Again. Rita must have gotten that from Deuteronomy.

"And you, Mama," Marlene continued, "well, you're what they call *vulnerable* right now. You could say and do anything. Everybody knows how you favor Sonny, and, well, if something tragic should happen, who knows what might swim through your mind." She was finished. Mattie watched her closely, watched her fidget in her chair. They never could take being stared down, the girls couldn't. *Swim through her mind.* What did Marlene think? A school of salmon was gonna swim upstream in Mattie's head and spawn there? She looked at Gracie, who looked again at Rita. Were these really the babies she'd born, anemic but healthy babies, babies who had missed out on those things, what the doctor called antigens? Were these three grown women her *kin?*

"We're just trying to help," Rita, one of them, said.

"This is one way," said Gracie, that schoolbook look on her face again, "for us four to finally bond, the way mothers and daughters should do." Now *they* waited, the daughters. Mattie thought about the consequences of throwing them out the front door, onto the porch with their cigarettes. They had been whining for almost thirty years that Sonny was the pet, Sonny was too spoiled, Sonny called the shots in Mattie's life. Well, she would sit it out another day, holed up in the house. Sonny had two women. She had three. And Mattie knew very well why the girls weren't taking turns watchdogging her. They were all afraid that if one spent too much time with Mattie, *bonded* too well without the other two being there to prevent it, the little mushroom of a house would go to that one daughter in Mattie's will.

"You'll smoke on the front porch," Mattie told them. "And that goes for all of you."

"Wesley says that Sonny's losing his charm when he has to take women at gunpoint," Marlene told her sisters, who both snickered. *Wesley.* This was Wesley Stubbs, from Watertown, who had swum upriver himself one day, to spawn with Marlene. Sonny used to say that if Wesley Stubbs had been born Indian, they'd have called him Brave Who Cheats Workmen's Comp. "He's a chiropractor's best friend," Sonny had told Mattie many times, and the two of them had laughed together, as the girls were now laughing.

They had *bonded*, she and Sonny, many times. "If it weren't for workmen's comp, Wesley would be putting the holes in doughnuts in one of them Dunkin' places," Sonny would say. And then he would have to quote his favorite line. "If Wesley Stubbs had been born Indian, Mama, they'd have called him Skidoo That Rides Like the Wind." It was pretty much general knowledge that Wesley spent the summers with his hands grasping a fishing pole, winters with his hands grasping the throttle of his yellow snowmobile. Mattie smiled, just thinking of Sonny and his crazy sense of humor. "If so-and-so had been born Indian" was the beginning of one of Sonny's many routines.

Rita went out on the front porch, letting the screen door bang behind her. Mattie watched through the window as she beat a cigarette out of her pack, lit up, and then exhaled. In seconds she was back at the screen door, peering through, her left hand cupping her right elbow as she held her cigarette aloft. Smoke rose up behind her head and wafted off in the general direction of downtown Mattagash, "the metropolitan district," as Sonny called it.

"Were you saying anything?" Rita wondered through the screen.

"You didn't miss a single syllable," Mattie reassured her. Marlene turned to Mattie.

"I ain't looked in my purse yet," said Marlene. "Are my cigarettes still in there?"

"They probably are," said Mattie. "I don't go looking in purses. I never did when you was all teenagers, and I ain't about to start now. I do, however, lay claim to what I find on my kitchen table." Marlene sighed a weary sigh.

"I don't smoke nearly as much as Rita," she said. "But you're sure none of us are allowed to smoke in the house." This came not as a question but as a statement. Mattie answered her, anyway.

"Ditto," said Mattie. Marlene took her purse and went out to join Rita.

"You got a spare match?" Mattie heard her ask. Now Mattie turned to look at Gracie.

"I'm trying to quit," said Gracie, foreguessing what was on Mattie's mind. "Smoking and exercise don't really mix." Mattie nodded. Well, maybe some good would come out of being holed up with Gracie.

In a few minutes, Rita and Marlene were back from smoking their cigarettes. Marlene measured coffee and water for the percolator and then plugged it in.

"If we get you a nice Mr. Coffee for your birthday," Marlene wanted to know, "will you use it, Mama? 'Cause there's no sense in getting you one if it ends up in the attic."

"I like my old percolator just fine," said Mattie.

"You gotta catch up to the world, Mama," Gracie now noted. "It's running ahead of you." Let it run, Mattie thought. And while it's running, she would sit on the front porch of her tiny house and have a cup of freshly perked coffee. That's what that word meant. *Perked.* Coffee that's been in a damn *percolator.*

"Not to change the subject," said Rita, who was famous

for doing just that, "but I run into Clarence Fennelson's mother at Craft's Filling Station this morning, and she told me it's been twenty-eight years since Clare died. June of 1966. Can you even believe that?" Mattie was now not only interested in what Rita had to say—she was caught with surprise, just as she was whenever Father Time revealed himself to her for the trickster that he was. Twenty-eight years since Clarence Fennelson was treading the highways and byways of Mattagash, Maine! Twenty-eight years that the town had carried on without him, had got up in the mornings and perked their coffee, had turned down their bedcovers at night. Mattie guessed it wouldn't have mattered a whit if Clarence had had an old-fashioned percolator or a Mr. Coffee. Except that the old-fashioned percolator might've kept him at home a couple minutes longer, and maybe he could have used that extra time to consider if he really wanted to take his own life. He had been such a nice boy, and such a neat dresser, his suntan pants always carrying a straight, orderly pleat down each leg, his white shirts always smoothly pressed. But then, Alma Fennelson had been his mother, and you could eat off Alma's kitchen floor. Everyone said so. Clarence Fennelson, who had once scored fifty points in a basketball game against Watertown and gotten his picture in the *Bangor Daily News* for doing so. When a small town loses one of its own, the death becomes a marker of sorts. "That was the summer before Clare Fennelson died," someone might say. Or "That was only a couple winters after Clarence Fennelson jumped off the bridge," someone else might say, and then time would do its snowball act, with the years rolling over each other, until the statistics of Clarence's life and death had faded into Mattagash history, no longer a yardstick to anybody but the folks who came to stare at his tombstone once in a while and ponder at such a short life span.

"I can still remember where I was the day he died," said Rita. "I was a junior in high school, and I was having my hair done for the Watertown prom, me and Lorraine and Theresa, at Chez Françoise Hairstyles, when Eleanor Ryan come running into the shop. She turned off all our dryers as fast as she could, one after the other, and that's when she told us." Rita had spent that time under the hair dryer for nothing, as Mattie remembered, because that star basketball player from Watertown High School had not bothered to pick her up and had later claimed he had never even *asked* to take her, that he was taking some Watertown girl instead. Poor Rita, and it broke Mattie's heart to see her, it really did. She had waited in her long white gloves and yellow gown, her French curls piled high on her head, like little brown bales of hay. That's probably why Rita would never forget where she was on the day Clarence Fennelson had died. With the clock ticking away the time and still no Watertown basketball star, she had asked Lester for the car and he had given it to her. Mattie still didn't know who gave her the bottle of vodka. The police *said* it was vodka, and they should know. They were the ones who found it in the car. And that's why they carried Rita from off that Watertown front lawn after the boy's mother phoned them, as if Rita was some kind of big unwanted dandelion in her bright yellow gown.

"I was helping to decorate the gym for graduation," Marlene said. "I must've been fifteen that summer. We heard the sirens coming full wail and we dropped all our pine boughs and run outside to see what was happening. That's when Emily Hart tripped on the pavement and broke her leg in two places, and that's the only reason they made birdbrained Debbie Plunkett the captain of the cheerleaders that next September. Emily's leg never did heal right."

"I was picking up some stuff at Blanche's Grocery," said Gracie. "I remember to this day what I was getting, too. It was a bottle of Pepsi, a pack of cigarettes, and a candy bar."

"Things ain't changed much," said Mattie. "Does that mean you were smoking even then?" Gracie nodded.

"Cripes," said Mattie, and shook her head. The stuff she learned from her girls when it was too late to do anything about it. Just as Clarence's mother had learned too late. "If we had only knowed Clare was feeling that low," Alma Fennelson had said for years, at every Tupperware party, at every fudge sale, at every PTA meeting, at every Christmas play, until no one had the heart to hear it anymore. "If we had only knowed," Alma would say, looking off at the past as though it were a place one might still get to, in order to change all the buttons on the time machine. "We might've done something to stop it."

"I was twelve," Gracie said. "Denny Plunkett stopped

in to Blanche's for something and he told us. He said that Clarence Fennelson had climbed up onto the Mattagash Bridge, made the sign of the cross, and then let himself fall, silent and still as a leaf. He went right out of sight and they still hadn't found him."

"Some still claim it was an accident," Mattie reminded them.

"*Some* are his relatives," said Rita. "The rest of us know the truth. You don't jump off a bridge by accident."

"It was awfully rainy that day, as I remember it," said Mattie.

"And slippery," said Marlene. "That was why Emily Hart broke her leg. Her legs were just like two little pencils, though, so it's no wonder."

"He might've just been trying to walk that rail," said Mattie, although she knew better. Tom Hart had come along and saw it all take place. He'd gotten out of his pickup and shouted when he saw Clarence standing on the bridge rail, in all that gray rain. "You better get down, son," Tom had shouted. But it was as if Clarence was in a daze, Tom said, and then he saw him make the sign of the cross. And that's when he fell.

"You don't jump off a bridge by mistake," Rita repeated.

The phone rang. Marlene beat Rita to it. It was Willard, Rita's green-haired child.

"Willie says to turn on the TV quick," Marlene shouted. "Sonny's giving another press conference!"

And that's what happened, no teaser, no time for the girls to pop up some popcorn or pick up a pizza. Sonny was back by popular demand, for now a crowd had swelled up in the background, ordinary folks who seemed excited just to be lined up on the road in front of the trailer. As the camera panned through the crowd, Mattie saw some of those folks waving happily.

"Hi, Mom!" one tall boy yelled, a baseball cap pulled down to his bushy eyebrows.

"What's happening?" Mattie asked. "Why are all those regular people hanging out at the trailer?" Marlene turned the volume higher. Rita and Gracie dropped down before the television set, pulled their legs up beneath them and waited, just as they did as children when professional wrestling came on. Of course, back then everyone thought the wrestling was real. Donna was back, and so was the thin-haired, thin-faced man, and the important-looking woman. But more new faces were now standing in front of the trailer as well, microphones in their hands, cameramen breathing down their backs. The Channel 4 camera focused in on a plump man in the sea of faces. He was pointing happily at a sign he had hoisted into the air, his chubby face a massive smile. The camera zoomed in. JOHN LENNON LIVES! the sign declared.

Donna was gripping her microphone in one hand, holding it up to her face as though it were a big black ice cream cone.

"Dan," she said to the camera in front of her, "there have been dramatic developments in the hostage incident here at Marigold Drive Trailer Park." Mattie could see the crowd growing even larger behind Donna's shoulder. Many of them seemed to be college students in a party mood. They were waving caps at the camera, making funny faces. If Mattie hadn't known better, she might have thought they were attending a football game. Others appeared to be there just for the sheer entertainment of the thing: *a man, two women, and a dog, all holed up in a house trailer.*

"What do you suppose the new developments are?" Marlene wondered. She was leaning back against the sofa, her knees drawn up.

"Shh!" said Mattie. "Donna's talking."

"Dan, we're told that Sonny Gifford, after intense phone negotiations with Chief Melon, has agreed to release one of the hostages," Donna said. She was slowly making her way to the area that seemed to be reserved for newspeople only, next to the yellow plastic ribbon that encircled the porch of the trailer. Police were motioning the spectators to move back, behind another yellow ribbon encircling the lawn itself, confining them to the road. People scattered in the background as Donna and the cameraman made their way toward the porch. Now the flock of television reporters with microphones in their hands seemed even larger and more important.

"I think that's a CNN camera!" Rita shouted, and pointed at the screen. "I'm going to Lola's!" She was on her feet in an instant, Gracie following. Mattie watched as they flew through the screen door and out to Gracie's car. An engine roared and pebbles flew, and then the sound of a disappearing car faded away to wind rushing in through the screen of the door.

"Are those two completely loco?" Marlene asked. The camera now did a quick pan of the scene on the road, where excitement seemed to be building further. Policemen were directing the spectators to stay behind the yellow plastic ribbon. But the crowd was having too good a time to care. Donna, who could not get to the trailer, put the microphone into the face of a young man, who had his arm around a freckle-faced girl.

"Why are you here today, sir?" Donna asked. Scarlet inched into the boy's face as he fought for the right words. Even on Mattie's small TV, she could see the color spreading.

"We just wanted to come by and tell Sonny thanks," the boy said, and the words were barely spoken before the crowd pressing in behind him to listen picked up on his comment and began to chant, "Sonny! Sonny! Sonny!"

"Are you an acquaintance of Mr. Gifford?" Donna now wanted to know. The eavesdropping crowd behind the boy quieted to hear what his reply would be.

"We don't know him," the girl offered, "but he's speaking up for poor people, and that's what counts." The group behind her liked this answer. They repeated their little song. "Sonny! Sonny! Sonny!" Another boy, wearing a University of Maine sweatshirt, pushed out in front and lowered his mouth to the microphone.

"As the great John Lennon once said, imagine if there was no hunger!" He held a fist into the air and the crowd went wild with enthusiasm.

Mattie looked at Marlene. "What's wrong with them people?" she asked. "Why ain't they home?"

Marlene shrugged. "Everybody needs a hero, I guess," she said, "and those poor, misguided souls think Sonny's theirs." Now the camera was back on Chief Melon, who was waving instructions to a line of policemen who had taken up strategic positions on the trailer side of the rope. Chief Melon raised what looked like a cheerleading megaphone and said something Mattie couldn't hear, and Channel 4 missed. She imagined Rita and Gracie getting the full story on Lola's satellite dish and resented them for it.

"I wish he'd let them both go," Marlene said. "Get this circus over with." Now Mattie watched as Sonny's silhouette appeared in the same window of the same door,

Sonny's balcony, his patio, his terrace, his courtyard. Mattie knew that, behind the window screen, he was again wearing his cheek-to-cheek smile. It had always been tough, even in times of great stress and difficulty, for Sonny to go anywhere without that smile. It was that very smile that used to get him into so much trouble with Lester. How many times had Mattie seen Lester strike the boy just because of that ear-to-ear grin? "Wipe that goddamn smile off your face," that's about the only sound advice Lester had ever given the boy. But Mattie also knew something else. She could sense it right through her skin as she watched the outline of her son in the window.

He's getting desperate, Mattie thought. She hasn't turned up from Atlantic City. She hasn't even called.

"Remember now," Sonny's voice was cautioning from behind the screen. "Just 'cause you can't see my hands don't mean there ain't a gun in them. So don't try anything foolish."

"I doubt it," said Marlene. "Sonny's too lazy to hold a gun on anyone. That'd be like lifting weights." Now the door of the trailer slowly opened an inch or two. Mattie could almost see a physical hush descend upon the crowd. Donna's face edged into the corner of the picture.

"Chief Melon has told Sonny Gifford to send out the hostage now, Dan," she said. "And he seems about to do that. At this point, we don't know if the released hostage will be Stephanie Bouchard or Vera Temple. Needless to say, Dan, the tension here is quite visible among the police officers as well as this crowd of fans who have turned out to catch a glimpse of Mr. Gifford. Someone seems to be coming out now, Dan!" Donna said excitedly, and then turned to watch the events on the porch.

"You can be sure he'll send out the homeliest one," said Marlene. Mattie's heart was beating so rapidly she couldn't reply. If he let one go, there'd be only one left. And when he let *that* one go, there would be jail time, yes, but it would be over. She would send him bulging packages of cookies and fudge, and a huge stack of those scary comic books he loved so much. Did they allow picture puzzles in prison? If so, she would dig out *The Desert with Night Moon*, that one puzzle she could never solve, the one with mostly black pieces in it. That would keep Sonny busy for his entire sentence. And what would he get? Surely, with no one harmed, with a judge able to gaze upon that broken heart Sonny was wearing on his sleeve, with good behavior and even more charm, he could be out in a couple years. Especially if that gun he claimed to be toting was a fake one after all. He could start all over. The door opened another six inches. Everyone waited. Reporters were silent, anticipating. And then, to everyone's astonishment, out trotted the poodle, a prance to its gait, its head held high, as though it were taking part in a beauty contest. It paused on the end of the porch and seemed to be scanning the crowd for a familiar face. One of the police officers scooped it up and, as Mattie watched, a bit of a struggle followed until the policeman threw up his arms and the poodle jumped to the ground.

"I think it bit him," said Marlene.

"You'll notice it didn't bite Sonny," Mattie noted for the record. He *did* have that invisible way with animals. Now Sonny seemed to be waving behind his screen. Reporters turned their attention back upon the door, which had again closed.

"This is a bit embarrassing," Sonny said from the window, "but it's getting quite dog dooey in here. It ain't like he's a cat, after all, and I can have some litter sent in." A chorus of questions rose up from the reporters. Why had he not released one of the two women? Sonny raised a sil-houetted hand to calm the storm of words coming at him.

"Well," Sonny said, "that's because my guests, these two very lovely ladies, girls from right here in Bangor, Maine—and let me say here and now that Bangor has some of the prettiest girls I personally have ever seen—these two young women are not exactly agreeable about which one should go."

"They *both* want to go?" a reporter shouted from the pack.

"On the contrary," said Sonny. "I don't want to brag or nothing, gentlemen, but they both want to *stay*. And just for the record, I'm going to expand my Great Americans list to include these two fine female specimens." He closed the door. His silhouette disappeared from the window. The crowd roared in jubilation. Mattie smiled. He had it, all right. Sonny Gifford could talk the Virgin Mary into dropping her pants.

"He released the *poodle?*" Marlene asked. Mattie found

herself smiling. She didn't want to since it was too serious a thing, but she couldn't help it. The laughter was involuntary, a nervous laughter that came from somewhere down in her stomach and was simply unstoppable. *While the world had waited with bated breath, Sonny turned the poodle loose!* The phone rang loudly and Marlene rose.

"Let it ring!" Mattie said sternly. She was no longer interested in what her Mattagash neighbors might have to say.

"What if it's Sonny?" asked Marlene.

"It ain't gonna be Sonny," said Mattie, "so let it ring."

Donna's face was back on the screen.

"This appears to be some kind of a joke on Mr. Gifford's part, Dan," she said. "Chief of Police Melon doesn't seem to be very pleased with how these negotiations have turned out." A man appeared behind Donna's back, unbeknownst to her, and waved his arms frantically at the camera. As Donna stepped out of the picture, the camera's eye fell upon the man's chest. He was wearing a T-shirt which announced: *I Visited Bangor and All I Got to Show for It Is Two Women and a Dog.*

"Make that *two women*," said Marlene. "He's gonna have to change his T-shirt now that the dog's gone. But they can print T-shirts in an hour these days."

"Sonny! Sonny! Sonny!" The pack was now howling.

"I feel sorry for them hostages," Marlene said. "This is like what happened to Patty Hearst. It's brainwashing, is what it is." Yes, it was brainwashing all right. But Sonny had been doing it to women ever since he grew his first mustache and his arms filled in with taut muscles, and his legs grew long enough to make him tall and give him that sexy swagger. And his voice developed that little pain in it when he talked about life and such things, a pain that so many women felt it was their duty to take away. His mother was one of those women.

Suddenly Mattie needed air, good old Mattagash air wafting up from the Mattagash River. She rose without a word to Marlene and went on out through the screen door. It slammed behind her. The porch was cool, caught up in the shadows left behind by the setting sun. On the porch, she could think. If only Elmer Fennelson were there for her to talk to, for her to say, *That boy's got to be careful, Elmer. He's carrying things too far this time. It's getting way out of control, growing bigger than something he can hold on to. I can smell what's going on, Elmer. I can smell it like it's something coming from the swamp, like them blue flags Sonny was always picking for me. That crowd is trying to make my boy a hero, and that's a job he ain't gonna turn down. That's a job Sonny Gifford's been applying for all his life.* This was the fear she was feeling in her heart, this knowledge of an upcoming sacrifice. There was a crowd turned out for Sonny all right, but another name for crowd was *mob*, and to Mattie they were one and the same: folks with nothing better to do, folks who should be home, folks sniffing for a little blood.

"Elmer Fennelson, where are you?" Mattie said to the curve of tarred road stretching past her house on its way to Elmer's. Nothing answered, except the whine of a distant truck that must have been climbing the portage. "I wish you were here, Elmer," Mattie said to the river that was winding itself away from Elmer's house, in the direction of the ocean. "I wish you were here because I think there's a fire being lit under Sonny's pants in a big way."

For a long time, Mattie sat on the porch. Down in the swamp, night peepers were making their racket, sounding almost like a pond of ducks. Stars were sprinkled overhead, a light dusting, overshadowed by the brightness of Venus. Now and then, a car passed on the road in a rattle of sound, then disappeared again, some Mattagasher headed to or from home. Mattie sank down into her rocker, but she didn't rock any, even though rocking had always soothed her, the way she remembered feeling in those early days when her own mother had actually rocked her. Those days before the kitchen knife and the fake stomach cancer and the jagged wrists and that blood-red valentine Mattie had made for nothing. But this wasn't a time for soothing. It was a time for sorting out the laundry. She stared at Venus, hanging like a crystal ball in the western sky. Funny how she had lived all her life thinking Venus was some magnificent star. Why hadn't anyone told her before? Why did she have to be so far into her life before her son-in-law Henry Plunkett would point up at that shiny ball and say, "That there's Venus"? Sitting in her rocker, Mattie felt as though maybe her life would've been different somehow, if she had known. She felt a little like she did the day she found out Lester had been sleeping with so many women all those years and everyone

knew but her. It was a feeling of being left out of a shiny
new secret.

"Venus," Mattie said softly, and now she could hear
the relentless nighthawks eating up their share of flying
ants and mosquitoes. A truck rumbled past and Mattie
heard radio music blasting from within its cab. "Sonny,"
she then said, as though maybe the two words were one
and the same. Maybe she hadn't known Sonny all those
years, either. After all, he was a boy without a name, the
way Venus had been without a name, all those sixty some
years it had dangled before Mattie's eyes, dangled like that
shiny pendant a hypnotist swings. But that was how Mattie
had lived her life, wasn't it? She had lived it like a woman
in a stupor. It was important that she outwit her husband,
Lester, outwit poor little birdbrained Martha Monihan.
And she had been so content on doing so that the years had
dissolved before her eyes. Her life had come and was nearly
gone, and what did she have to show for it?

"Venus," Mattie said again, and settled further down
into her sweater. But not even that soft Canadian wool—
this was a sweater Mattie had knit for herself, and let's
just see one of her girls knit something—not even her
handmade sweater could thwart the chill that was creeping into her bones. Trouble was in the air, trouble as real
as the nighthawks, as real as the two bats that were now
circling the night-light, looking for moths and bugs. Sonny
had taken his hostages on Monday and now here it was
Wednesday night. Mattie had felt the tension mounting

as she watched each news segment, tension growing as the crowd grew, silently, the way mold grows on bread. She could see Chief Melon's face go from relaxed and in control to edgy and nervous, his skin stretched on his face as though it were a wide elastic band. And the people who had turned up to cheer Sonny onward, well, that was trouble walking on two legs. A crowd of trouble. And now Sonny had done the unforgivable. He had made the chief of police and his entire department look like fools on television, in front of everyone. Mattie had felt, up to that point, that Chief Melon saw inside Sonny, too, almost the way she did. He had spent all that time on the phone with her boy and, surely, he had come to realize that Sonny Gifford's actions were forty percent broken heart and sixty percent county fair. Sonny couldn't turn his back on an audience, even if he *was* lovesick. But now things had changed. Mattie thought about Sonny's words earlier that day, when he told his listeners that he must boldly go where those *Star Trek* people went. It reminded her of another piece of the puzzle, something else Sonny had done as a child. He must have been about ten years old, as well as Mattie could remember, and he had had a bad dream, in the heart of a winter's night. Mattie could remember waking to his cries of terror and seeing the bed empty beside her, Lester not yet home. The latter wasn't unusual, but Sonny's cries were. In his room, she found him out of his bed, cuddled in a little heap on the floor, elbows and arms shielding his head as though something or someone was trying to hit him. Mattie reached out to touch him, calm him, eventually to hold him. But the minute he felt her hand upon his body, he cried out, "Beam me up, Scotty! *Please*, beam me up!" And Mattie took it almost as an insult. It had always seemed to her that Sonny was in search of a family, someplace he would feel safe. Some planet he could live on in peace. And this was in spite of all the love she had personally given him. But it wasn't enough. He needed Lester's love, too, and the love of his sisters. He needed to feel comfortable enough in his own home that when he drew pictures at school of his family, he could draw them all in one room, instead of placing himself apart from them. And there he was, wishing to be aboard the *Enterprise* rather than living in Mattagash, Maine. Daring to conquer new worlds, rather than abide in pain in the old one. He was looking for a father in the likes of Captain Kirk. Maybe a sister in that black woman who wore the short skirts. Yet, to this day, Mattie couldn't be sure where Sonny's pain had come from. Maybe in the way big, looming Lester had made him feel tiny as a mite. Maybe that was it. And no matter how big Mattie tried to make Sonny feel afterward, it never seemed to do any good. Maybe that was the answer, Mattie decided, sitting on her summer porch and gazing at Venus. Maybe that was Sonny's secret. He had lived as a handful of taffy between his mother and his father all his life. He had been pulled in so many directions, stretched here and there, that all he could do was plaster a mighty smile on his face and set about life hoping to become Mattagash, Maine's Biggest

Underachiever. And he had succeeded. But now he was underachieving on *television*, with a bevy of cops watching him do it, and trouble was floating in the air like a good old river breeze.

The girls were back, Rita and Gracie. They pulled up to the house in Rita's big black Buick, the radio playing loudly. Both car doors opened, slammed, feet trod upon the porch, and then they disappeared inside the house without having seen her sitting in the shadows. Her girls were home from the hunt, from the battle, from the assault on Sonny's life. Mattie released the breath she'd been holding, and it seemed as though even the peepers in the swamp heard her, for they grew still for a moment. A blinking light appeared in the sky above Venus and Mattie saw that it was an airplane. Or maybe it was the *Enterprise*. She watched as it slowly ate a path across the sky and then disappeared behind the farthest mountain range. The door opened again and Gracie ambled out, with that little bounce to her gait that she seemed to have acquired after Charlie left her for Sally Fennelson.

"It's a bit chilly out here, Mama," she said. "You want me to bring you a coat or something?"

Mattie shook her head. "Thank you, Gracie, all the same," she said, "but I got my handmade sweater keeping me warm." She smiled, and in the light wafting out from the living room window, she saw Gracie smile back. How long had it been since this kind of soft emotion floated between them? But every once in a while, and who knew for what reason, Mattie and her daughters, one at a time, seemed almost ready to bust down all the walls they had put up, those years of architecture. And then a little wind would come up and blow all those good designs away. And it did just then.

"You ain't sitting out here planning on sneaking a ride to Bangor, are you?" Gracie asked. "At least, we've been inside wondering about just such a thing. You think too much when you're sitting in your rocker, Mama, and I mean to tell you that you've thought up some doozies in your lifetime." So Gracie had come as a spy after all. Mattie smiled again at her youngest daughter, born in 1954, a mere month after Martha Monihan had stopped by the little mushroom house to announce to her best friend, Mattie Gifford, that Lester was in bed with Eliza Fennelson. Mattie still had an ornamental plate tucked away in her trunk of special things, a birthday gift from Martha, back when they were still in school. The artwork showed two little girls walking hand in hand across a meadow of blue-bells. The word *Sharing* was painted in red swooping letters above their heads. Below their feet, at the bottom of the plate, was the sentence *That's What Good Friends Are For*. Mattie had almost laughed that day she had finally tucked the pretty plate away in her trunk, where she wouldn't have to look at it. I didn't know you meant sharing husbands, too, Martha, she had thought as she wrapped the plate in tissue paper. And, if she told herself the truth, sitting there in her rocker, with Gracie hovering in the light drifting out of the living room window, she hadn't been in her best frame of mind to accept Gracie into a burdensome world. She had given birth to Gracie after losing her best friend to her husband. That had been Gracie's trousseau. Maybe Mattie even sent her a kind of jolt she never got over, right through the umbilical cord, a trait in life that would ensure that her own husband would be unfaithful. After all, why Gracie? Why not the other girls? Yet Henry Plunkett and Wesley Stubbs were as faithful to their wives as husbands could possibly get without being family pets. Only Gracie knew what it was like to wake up at night and feel how cold sheets can get on the empty side of a bed. But it was even wider than that, this scab that grew over their family life, this hideous scar. There was something about how Lester doted on his daughters—they were women, after all—that had always torn at Mattie's heart. This was true, wasn't it? Wasn't there anguish in seeing him tousle their hair, cuddle them onto his lap, tweak their noses, tickle them into silly confessions of childhood pranks? He had stopped touching his wife, stopped touching her in that loving and tender way that takes place in a kitchen, or in a living room, just weeks after they were married. He only touched her in the bedroom, until, with so many other bedrooms to keep warm, he even forgot about her there, too. But what was even worse, or as Mattie came to feel over the years, was that he never touched his boy, Sonny. "Because he's a boy, that's why," Lester would always answer. "We don't want him turning into a sissy right before our eyes." But then, the girls courted Lester, didn't they? Jumping him from behind doors, combing his hair into peculiar styles. All this while Sonny watched from that lonely distance that grew like a field between him and his family. One time, when they were in their early teens, the girls even put makeup on Lester, as a Halloween prank, and then goaded him into wearing a dress. Mattie remembered how she was struck with the fact that Lester was even beautiful as a woman, more beautiful, certainly, than she was. More beautiful than most Mattagash women, what with his full lips and naturally long eyelashes made even longer with mascara. That was the day she put their wedding picture away for good. She tucked it down into the trunk where the ornamental plate and other sad memories were lurking. There was no need to keep it out any longer. For one thing, the marriage had been bogus for years. And for another thing, it had become apparent to Mattie that, beautiful as he was, Lester had been both bride and groom on that day of their marriage. He had razzled and dazzled the troops, while she fought desperately to walk a steady gait in shoes that were killing her.

"Where's your mind right now?" Gracie asked, and Mattie remembered her daughter there, in the cool night air. "See? I told you it's dangerous for you to get into your rocker and rock yourself toward a deep thought." Mattie felt a sudden urge to say something important to Gracie, something a daughter could hang on to after a mother's death, words a daughter could bite into. She wanted to say, *Sweetie, I know how broken your heart must have been to find out about Charlie and Sally Fennelson. I know how even your breasts can ache on them lonely nights you sit up waiting, how all the veins running up and down your arms hurt. I know how loud the seconds can sound as you stand by a window and peer out into the night, a child sleeping somewhere in your house so that you can't cry out loud. I know what it feels like, so come here and let me hold you until some of that soreness goes away.* But Gracie had never admitted to her family that Charlie was the one to leave. Just as it had happened to Mattie, it had happened to Gracie: all the town knew but the two of them. Mattie hadn't known about Charlie either, or she would've told her daughter. Mattagash had managed to pull the wool twice over Mattie's eyes. When Gracie told Charlie to get out because he was never home anyway, she probably knew in her bones something was going on somewhere. But it gave her a parcel of pride that it happened the way it did, and Mattie felt good about that. A week after Gracie officially told Charlie to leave, Sally Fennelson threw her husband, Duane, out of their house trailer and long, lanky Charlie Craft moved into Duane's shoes, into his life. "She can have him," Gracie had announced about Charlie, "now that I got rid of him." Mattie herself didn't know the truth until Rita and Marlene just up and told her one day, let her hear all about the soap opera. Charlie had been seeing Sally for a year. Well, peace of mind comes in the strangest boxes. But Gracie's fake pride prevented Mattie from some of that *bonding* Gracie was forever talking about. Besides, how could Mattie tell her girls what a rogue their beloved father had been? They really believed he had been playing poker all those nights, as he used to tell them. Maybe word of his actions had reached the girls finally, as adults, but they grew up thinking he had strung the stars. And Mattie let them. But then, Jupiter and Venus had been two of those stars, or so they thought.

"I was just thinking of your father," Mattie answered, finally. It was the truth. "I was just thinking of Lester. It'll be almost five years since he died. And I was thinking, in a way, of Clarence Fennelson. Twenty-eight years. Imagine that. I must mention this to Elmer if he ever turns up again. Clarence was his favorite nephew."

"Where *is* Elmer?" Gracie asked. "You two are like ticks on a dog and yet I haven't seen him once since I been over here."

Mattie shrugged. "Yesterday I called Pauline and told her to peep through the windows during her Avon rounds. But his pickup truck is gone, and so is Skunk. So Elmer's kicking up his heels somewhere. Pauline said everything looked fine through the windows." A speeding car passed in a screeching of wheels as it rounded the bend in the road, music pounding from its interior, and then it was gone.

"Crazy young fools," said Mattie.

"I gotta tell you that I'm glad in a way Elmer isn't here," said Gracie. "I know darn well he'd drive you to Bangor, and I can see the two of you now on television, with Skunk sitting up between you in Elmer's rusty old pickup." Mattie said nothing. The nighthawks were still busy. *Pee-ik.*

Pee-ah. The bats circled the pole light frantically, swooping and diving. The summer peepers kept up their strain, filling the swamp with their own music. Behind the house came the sound of the Mattagash River, gallons of water tumbling over one another in order to get to the ocean. Mattie waited. Gracie waited. At first, Mattie thought her daughter might say something, might try to tear a brick out of that wall of bricks between them. Did she even care anymore? The truth was that, with Elmer vanished into the Mattagash Triangle, Mattie needed a friend, someone to talk to, someone who would listen patiently and then give up some honorable advice. A car's headlights swung around the turn in the road. Mattie heard the engine first, and now she waited as another neighbor roared past the house, this time in a long white car. There was only one long white car in Mattagash, where cars were as recognizable as people. As it passed the house and went on its way, following its beams of light, two heads rode silhouetted inside.

"Oh, Jesus," said Gracie softly. "That was Charlie's car. That was Charlie and Sally Fennelson." Her voice sounded old suddenly, older than Mattie's, an old, old woman talking now, there in the evening shadows, singing out with the nighthawks. Mattie knew the sound of that voice. She knew. It wasn't that Gracie hadn't seen them together before, or at least *expected* to see them. It's just that it could catch you off guard now and then, stick a knife into your fortitude if you weren't expecting it. Mattie reached out and gripped Gracie's arm.

"That's just two people riding in a car," said Mattie. "That's just two people using up the highways and byways of Mattagash, Maine. Don't you give them any more credit than that, honey. Don't you let them be something bigger than they are. They're just two heads in a car." In reply, she heard what sounded like a small gasp, there in the unlit shadows, and then Gracie's voice, opening up for the first time since all this happened with Charlie. Gracie finally talking.

"I wish I could live my life over," she whispered. "I wish I could live it over so I could leave out all the bad stuff." Mattie said nothing, and when she realized that Gracie was actually waiting, *waiting*, for a comment from her mother, she cleared her throat. She needed now to say the right thing. That Gracie was her daughter should have been reason enough. But what was suddenly more important to Mattie was that Gracie was *another woman*, another woman scorned by a heartbreaking man.

"I'd leave out all the bad stuff," Gracie said again, "if I could just live my life over." Mattie thought about this statement.

"Trouble with that, sweetie," she said, "is that it can't be done. Living life is like knitting a sweater. You drop a few stitches here and there. The only trouble is, when you go back to redo them lost stitches, when you go back to repair the damage, you gotta unravel a whole bunch of good stuff to get there. And you don't want to do that, Gracie. You never mind about Charlie Craft. You never mind about them dropped stitches. You just go ahead and remember all the good stuff that life has shoveled up." Mattie stopped for a minute to think about this. Funny, but it had come out of her mouth as the gospel truth, and it sounded right, sounded like good advice to a woman with tainted memories of her marriage. Yet Mattie herself had done just the opposite all her life. Mattie had undone a million sweaters in going back to examine lost stitches. She would tell Gracie this, she decided. She would say, *Look at me. I'm the perfect example of what not to do.* She wanted to say much more, pass on her experience to the next generation, her knowledge and lore and home remedies for a broken heart. But before she could speak again to her youngest daughter, before she could finally hope to pry open that bulging can of earthworms, the front door opened instead and Rita bustled out onto the porch, noise following her like a dark cloud of grackles.

"What's going on out here?" Rita asked. "Are you two coming in to watch the late news? Any mosquitoes out yet? Willard told me that if you wear dark clothes and aftershave at dusk in the summertime, you're just asking for mosquitoes to flock to you in droves. Who would've ever thought?"

Gracie took this opportunity to leave. She opened the door and disappeared back inside the tiny house, the way Charlie and Sally Fennelson had just disappeared in the sound of their own engine, two broken marriages trailing after them like tin cans. Now the nighthawks and peepers had only a brief chance to be heard before Rita started up again.

"Wow," she said, and pointed at Venus. "Look at that big bright star over there in the sky."

13

The next morning Mattie stayed in bed until the girls finally crawled out from under their own blankets. She could hear them in the bathroom, arguing over the toothpaste, towels, combs. She could hear them in the kitchen, quarreling over the coffee, the cups, the toaster. And, as she drifted in and out of sleep, her mind running between the voices in the kitchen and the dream images in her head, it seemed as if time had caught its hook into the person she'd been almost thirty years ago, when her daughters were still in their teens and Sonny just starting school. Time had hooked the old her and was reeling her back. The funny thing was, Mattie didn't want to go. Oh, she knew for certain there were all kinds of people who craved their youth, who would run like gazelles toward that fishhook of time, peeling off the years like old imagined skins. But not her. Not Mattie. Time meant heartaches and loneliness and lessons learned too hard and too late. No, not Mattie. So she had struggled to come out of her reverie, one in which she imagined the school bus was in the yard, honking its horn as it used to do, for the girls were always late. And this was when she remembered Sonny. What would he be then? Six, seven years old? He might be young enough to save, if she let time reel her back to the shores of the past. Sonny might be salvageable, like a shiny coin that's driven into a river bottom, something good enough to dive for. She could take him away and let him grow up as another boy, in another town, in another life. As the squabbling voices of her daughters leaked into her dreams, Mattie could see Sonny's blond head bobbing through the hay field, a bunch of smelly blue irises held aloft as a prize just for her.

"Sonny," Mattie said, "I'm over here, sweetie." But Sonny just kept on walking, his supple frame heading toward the creek, a ghost boy walking in a ghost dream. Mattie could see the green of his jacket, that jacket she had bought him at Buzzel's in Caribou, a jacket she'd not given an inch of thought to in almost thirty years, but there it was, as new as the day she took it off its hanger. Sonny, still young enough to shape, to mold. Sonny in his bright green jacket. Mattie would make him study this time around. This time around, there would be no wild, poetic stories, no running off from school, no masterpieces painted on frosty windows. And when he drew crazy pictures of lighthouses and sharks and silos, she would rip each of them up. She would make him draw canoes in the Mattagash River, like the other boys. She would make him draw pulp trucks and chain saws and skidders, like the other boys. But just as she was reaching out a hand, hoping to get close enough to grab the collar of that green jacket, just then the murmur of voices brought her full awake. The girls had moved from the kitchen because now whispers were coming from outside Mattie's bedroom door. Her daughters were rallying themselves toward a plan. She could hear them. *Let her sleep. But it's not like her. Do you think she's okay? Open the door and take a quick look. She needs the rest. It'll keep her mind off Sonny. It'll keep her from getting into any trouble.* Mattie heard the door open gently, a sweet little squeak disturbing the silence. She kept her eyes closed, her right arm flung upon her chest. The sweet squeak again, then the door closing. Mattie opened her eyes and waited, waited for the rustle of their coats, the thump of their big purses against the hallway walls, the front door opening and closing, cars coming alive in the driveway, pebbles grating against tires, and then the sounds of car engines fading away in the distance.

For a long time she did nothing but stare at the ceiling. Then she studied the wallpaper she had gotten in Watertown, a pale yellow background with tiny clusters of purple flowers here and there forming a nice pattern. She had bought a lavender bedspread to match it, and lavender curtains. A fluffy yellow rug lay on the floor at the foot of the bed. She couldn't keep a fluffy rug with Lester living in the house. He never bothered to take his work boots off, not even when he came into the bedroom. Then, as soon as Gracie was finally married and gone, in 1974, Lester had moved into the girls' room. He had not mentioned this decision to his wife, as if it were nothing more than changing coats. Mattie waited a full week, and when it was apparent that Lester wasn't moving back, she got Rita to drive her to Watertown and she bought herself the fluffy yellow rug. She bought the pale yellow wallpaper with the purple clusters and the lavender spread and the lavender curtains. And then, for fifteen years Mattie had lain beneath her lavender shroud and watched the moon inch across the orbit of her bedroom window. She had watched the snow pile up on the horizon of her windowsill. Rain. The occasional hail. Autumn leaves fluttering. For years she lay there and listened to her husband's breath coming and going like a runaway train, on another track from hers. She lay there and wondered what Lester was thinking of just then, what he was thinking of the day he asked her to marry him. That had become the great mystery in Mattie's life. Not why he wanted other women. There was no puzzle in that. But why he wanted *her*. In 1978 Sonny moved out of the house, moved in with some woman from Watertown who couldn't wait to jump up at the crack of dawn and cook him pancakes and squeeze him some orange juice into a glass, all while wearing a see-through negligee. Never having had fresh orange juice before, Sonny was convinced that this was a life experience he couldn't turn down. "She even puts the sugar into my coffee, Mama," he had told Mattie. And so he had shed the narrow bedroom, with the Rico Petrocelli baseball, and the lewd pack of playing cards, and the posters of beautiful women. Up until that day, Mattie had been able to bear the loneliness, knowing that Sonny was just next door, knowing that, in the heart of the night, Sonny'd be home from some fascinating date and he'd come in and sit on the edge of her bed and make her laugh with his crazy stories. Then he'd go off to bed and she'd feel less alone, there in her lavender grave, able to hear his occasional cough, his bed squeak as he rolled over with a dream, could imagine him all tucked in safe for the night. So four of those fifteen years weren't so bad. But the last eleven were. When you don't know enough about life to know what you might have missed out on, your imagination plays wicked tricks on you. For a few years, Mattie could see herself married to a millionaire somewhere if she hadn't married Lester, burning up money like it was a pile of dead leaves. At the last of it, she came to know the truth: she would be happy for someone who would reach out once in a while and pat her hand. Sometimes, you need to be touched to know you're still alive. Those were the nights that Mattie rose in the darkness, or in moonlight, and padded her way down the hall to Sonny's room. And, lying on Sonny's bed, surrounded by all those skimpily clad women on Sonny's posters, she felt less alone. After all, Sonny's friends were her friends.

Now, with all three girls safely gone, probably to feast at Lola Monihan's satellite dish, in case CNN had any *new developments*, Mattie made the decision to get up out of bed. Only when she had the flu so bad she couldn't move, that sick time she mentioned to Henry a couple days ago, could she remember ever lying in bed as such. But it had occurred to her that maybe life's truth was something she could escape, if she stayed in bed long enough. The same reason Gracie was sleeping later and later into the day, women's studies or not. But it wasn't. Left behind in the air now seeping under her door was the smell of leftover breakfast, of coffee and burnt toast. And it was enough to get Mattie up.

Pauline Plunkett had obviously been by. Sitting on the kitchen table was a brown bag with *Mattie* written in black letters across the top. Inside, Mattie found a large bottle of Skin So Soft and that morning's copy of the *Bangor Daily News.* Bless Pauline's heart. She was always thinking of others, even on those early morning runs to Watertown to pick up Avon shipments. The girls must not have looked inside the bag. If they had, the pages of that newspaper would've been scattered like autumn leaves all over the house. Poor Simon Craft. This would make two days that he would be denied the joy of putting Mattie's *Bangor Daily News* into her hands, Sonny's name plastered across the front page. Yesterday, Mattie had watched from behind her curtain as Simon fidgeted in his mail car, pretending to be sorting and arranging letters, before he'd finally given up. She had no doubt that he'd discussed the hostage incident fully, at every single stop along his route, and was most anxious to pass some of his gleanings on to her. Sonny had once remarked that Simon Craft was Mattagash's first satellite dish. "The mobile kind," Sonny said.

Mattie took her freshly perked coffee, her bacon and

toast, and arranged herself in the living room, her plate before her on the coffee table. The *Bangor Daily News* carried almost bouncy headlines. THE GIFFORD TRIANGLE: WOMEN STAY, POODLE GOES. Beneath the announcement were photos, including one of the hostage poodle as it stood trembling on the trailer's front porch, looking like it might prefer to be back inside with its captor. Other photos were of the crowd, including the man who was wearing the specially designed T-shirt. In another shot, the JOHN LENNON LIVES! sign loomed over a mass of heads. Mattie studied the photos carefully. All the faces in the crowd were cheering Sonny onward, no doubt of that. But here and there Mattie could pick out the grainy face of a policeman, grim and tense. The article went on to talk about Sonny Gifford's "soft voice and folksy mannerisms," his "Great Americans list, which includes Jackie Kennedy Onassis and Sheila Bumphrey Gifford, his estranged wife." The article then mentioned the arrival of other journalists, from Boston and New York, and spoke of how the story of Sonny Gifford seemed to be growing. "Americans look for heroes in the strangest of places," the article stated, "and Sonny Gifford seems to speak for a generation of unemployed, unempowered, and disillusioned young men who are seeking answers by taking control of a situation in which they feel helpless. Sonny Gifford may very well be Maine's first Angry Young Man."

What the hell does *that* mean? Mattie wondered. And then there was Sonny, standing beside what looked like a barbecue, in what must have been someone's backyard. It was an unusually good photo, although Sonny never took a bad picture in his life, not even with his eyes closed. When his eyes were closed, you could see those butterfly eyelashes just lying there on his face. Beneath the picture were the words "Contributed Photo," and Mattie supposed that a Marigold Drive neighbor had dug it up. Sonny had his usual grin spread across his face, that devil-may-care smile. The rest of the article stated only what Mattie already knew: a recap of how Sonny saw John Lennon's face telling him to speak out for poor people, the bank, the women, the poodle, the trailer, and Sonny's demand for public negotiations, rather than private. Waco, Texas, was mentioned and that crazy David Koresh, which displeased Mattie. Sonny might've been a live wire all his life, but he was as sane as the next person. And it seemed that the Bangor Police Department, keeping Waco in mind, wanted to achieve just the opposite results. "As soon as Mr. Gifford states his demands," said Chief of Police Patrick Melon, "we feel confident that they'll be met. For now, he's asking to speak with his estranged wife, Sheila Bumphrey Gifford, who is rumored to have gone to Atlantic City for the weekend. We urge anyone who has any information on Mrs. Gifford's whereabouts to come forward at this time. We want to assure the families of the hostages that we're doing everything that can possibly be done to avoid any kind of mishap." Mattie put the paper aside.

"What about the family of the hostage-*taker*?" Mattie wondered aloud. "I could use a little assurance, too." A board creaked on the front porch and Mattie felt her heart lurch. Maybe it was all over and Sonny had come home. This thought, accompanied by a splash of logic, soon faded, and Mattie then hoped it was Elmer. Elmer would drive her to Bangor. Just that morning she had changed her mind again, had decided that she would ignore Sonny's advice about staying put and letting her teeth soak. The boy was slowly turning into a movie star, and with that future in store, Mattie feared for his safety.

Nobody likes for the hero to walk away, Mattie thought again as she waited for a face to appear in the window of the front door. One did. It was Roberta, Mattie's only granddaughter, soon to be the mother of Mattie's first great-grandchild. Lumbering along behind her was Willard Plunkett, Rita and Henry's six-foot-three oldest child, the boy with kneecaps the size of softballs. Robbie waltzed right in, but Willard had to bend in the doorway of Mattie's house so as not to hit his green hair on the doorjamb.

"Why, Robbie," said Mattie, rising to give her granddaughter a hug. "What brings you out on such a nice morning?" Robbie hugged her back.

"We just come to see how you're handling everything," said Robbie, "what with Uncle Sonny and all." Willard finally made it inside the door.

"Hey," he said to Mattie, his right shoulder jerking and his left eye blinking uncontrollably. "How's it going?" He seemed to be looking for a place to spit.

"If it ain't Willie," said Mattie. She stretched upward

in order to give Willard a loose hug. Her arms could reach just above his thin waist, so she squeezed that part of his long body. Willard stiffened in this embrace. Like most Mattagash men, he wasn't big on displays of physical emotion. Bending down toward her, Willard appeared almost cartoonlike, Big Bird, maybe, from *Sesame Street.*

"Hey," Willard said again. Aside from the nervous blinking, and the twitching of his shoulder, Mattie sensed something else amiss with her grandson. The rims of his eyes seemed abnormally red, and for a person with green hair, well, the eyes stood out more than was their bodily duty.

"We just came to see how you are," said Robbie, "and we were wondering if you need anything in Watertown." Mattie looked at her grandchildren hard and long, Robbie with her sweet little face, a face already talking about sadness and rushed lives. Willard, looking like a leftover from a bad yard sale. Blood of her blood, bone of her bone. She gave Willard the longest look, having not seen him in a few months, not since he'd dyed his hair and begun experimenting with marijuana, if what Rita said was true.

"Hey," Willard said, shifting his long legs inside their big long shoes. Shoes designed for a circus clown. And twitching his shoulder as his crossed eyes worked overtime. Maybe the boy would grow into something worth looking at a few years down the road. Maybe all his features would straighten themselves out. But right now he was all limbs and shoes and nervousness. He reminded Mattie of something you'd construct from a can of Tinkertoys. Her heart did a little flip-flop. Poor boy, poor Willard, what with Rita poking him daily with a pitchfork of criticism. Mattie looked back to Roberta, to her tie-dye dress and her short hair, cropped like a boy's, and her Black & Decker big-soled shoes. Clunkers. Army boots for little girls. Everyone wanted to act tough these days, even Robbie, with the tiny face of an angel, lips painted almost like a doll's, skin as white as a porcelain dish. Her only granddaughter.

"Whose car are you driving?" Mattie asked.

"Mama's Buick," Willard answered. Mattie looked out into the yard. Sure enough, there was Rita's big black Buick. The Road Hog, Henry called it.

"Willard ain't got his license yet," said Robbie, "so Aunt Rita is letting *me* drive the Buick."

"Where's the For Sale sign?" Mattie asked. She knew Henry had made one for the back window of the Buick. *Good Condition. Tires Like New. Will Accept Best Offer.* She had heard Rita telling Gracie about it. Mattie assumed that Henry was finally flaunting signs of good salesmanship. How could tires possibly be like new with Rita at the wheel?

"Mama don't put the For Sale sign in the window unless Daddy's around," said Willard. "She's afraid someone will see it and want to buy her car."

"Any gas in the Buick?" Mattie wondered. Roberta gave a quick little nod, her angel lips pursing themselves into a smile.

"I know what you're up to, Granny," she said. "I already been grilled about whether or not you've asked me to take you to Bangor. You know Gracie will kill me if I do." Mattie looked down into her grandchild's eyes, down to where the good stuff about a person's life is kept, the meat of their soul. That's what makes them stand up to the winds of adversity or fall down. There was all kinds of good stuff about Robbie there in those eyes, the things Mattie knew about her from when she was just a little girl. She loved animals and flowers and was kind to all living things. She loved her grandmother, too, and used to sleep on Mattie's back porch while Mattie weeded the garden, just so that she could be close by. She was a good child, a good pregnant teenager. Lucky Lester hadn't lived to learn the news about Robbie. He liked to take women to bed himself, but he wouldn't look kindly at Peter Laforest doing it to his granddaughter. Mattie turned her attention upon Willard.

"I'll pay you well," she said. "We can go to the Bangor mall after we talk to Sonny, and shop for us a nice little present, all three of us." She winked at Willard. What would it take? Some loud record? A movie video? More colored hair dye? She'd dip—no, she'd dive headfirst into her rainy day money. Robbie put a hand on Mattie's shoulder.

"Granny," she said, "Mama would kill us. And then Aunt Rita would kill whoever is left." She shook her head sadly. Willard shifted about on the great boats of his feet. His shoulder twitched fiercely. Sunshine filtered in around his head, through the top glass in the door. In its sheen, Willard's hair was suddenly beautiful, like the pot of shamrocks Mattie kept in her bedroom window, green and billowy. It was as if Willard were carrying a small hill upon his head, a virgin meadow, a peaceful place where one could go and lie down and rest.

"I'm sorry, Granny," Robbie was saying.

Mattie patted her tiny hand. "Will you at least think about it?" she wondered, and Robbie promised that she would.

"Why don't you come to town with us?" she asked. "I need to pick up a prescription and Willard is looking to rent a movie. We'll be back in no time."

Mattie shook her head. "I got to stay in case there's any new developments," she said, remembering Gracie's words, remembering the new language she was now learning, thanks to Sonny's latest world dealings.

"Stop in again, Willard," Mattie said to the long, retreating form of her grandson.

"Hey," Willard said, and waved back at her. Mattie realized now that *hey* didn't just mean *hello, yes, thanks, maybe, okay*, and so on. It also meant *good-bye*.

"I've been to see the doctor," Robbie now whispered to Mattie. "Everything looks just fine." Mattie smiled. She squeezed Robbie's hand. Everything looked just fine for a pregnant eighteen-year-old, in a crazy-colored dress, wearing shoes fit for a storm trooper, and chauffeuring a twitching, blinking cousin with green hair. This was the new world, but after having lived for almost seventy years in the old world, Mattie was beginning to like this new one better. Things were strange there, but the kids seemed to make a little bit of sense. Robbie and Willard were doing strides better than their own parents. And one thing was certain. Mattie wished she'd have had Robbie's clunkers to wear on the day she actually married Lester Gifford, instead of those tall, pointy-toed things. She wished they'd been shoes she could run in. She wished she'd had a driver's license. Who knows what mountains she might have scaled with those two things on her side. Mattie watched as the car pulled away, Robbie's tiny body hanging on to the big steering wheel, Willard's green head rubbing the top of the car's roof, like the head of some exotic parrot. The new generation.

Mattie went immediately to the telephone. There on the counter was the number she had asked for just that morning, from information, the number of the Bangor Police Department. She had been afraid to punch in the numbers after the operator gave them to her, afraid that once she told the truth, that Sonny wasn't adopted, that his mother was alive but not well because she feared the worst for her son, that all hell would break loose. At least that's what born-again Rita had been prophesying for the past three days. "All hell's gonna break loose when them reporters find out the truth," Rita had said. "When they find out Sonny's got relatives up here, we may as well head for the hills."

The phone rang twice, way down in Bangor, at the police department, before Mattie heard a woman's voice answer with a curt, crisp "Police department, can I help you?"

"I want to talk to the chief of police," Mattie told her.

"And what is this regarding, ma'am?" the voice asked.

"Sonny Gifford," said Mattie. "It's regarding Sonny Gifford, who's holed up in that house trailer." The voice on the other end of the line sighed.

"And what message would you like to leave for Chief Melon?" the voice wanted to know, a bored voice, a voice tired of the conversation already. And Mattie hadn't even begun.

"It's personal," she said.

"Ma'am." The voice was annoyed now. "You'll need to tell me what this is in regard to. Chief Melon can't take every call that comes in. He's a very busy man right now." The voice waited, impatiently. Mattie could hear some kind of rhythmic tapping on the other end. A pen against a metal desk, maybe.

"It's personal," she said again. Now *she* waited. Sunshine was beating its way through the kitchen window and Mattie felt instantly warm. Too warm. Tiny beads of sweat broke out above her upper lip.

"Well, you'll need to tell *me* first," said the voice. "And if I decide that it's important, I'll see that Chief Melon gets your message."

"But I'm his mother," said Mattie. "I'm Sonny Gifford's mother. Ain't that reason enough to talk to the chief of police?" The voice was now more annoyed.

"Ma'am," the voice said, a city voice to Mattie, a voice of some authority. "John Lennon himself called here about an hour ago. He wanted to talk to Chief Melon, too. And ten minutes after that Hillary Clinton called and said she wanted to make Sonny her running mate in 1998. And just after Mrs. Clinton called, Shirley MacLaine took time out of her busy schedule to phone and say that Sonny is really just a mouthpiece for a four-thousand-year-old Tibetan priest. And yesterday Boris Yeltsin called, offering Sonny political haven in Russia. And in between all those *personal* phone calls were dozens of calls from just plain ordinary folks who wanted to wish Mr. Gifford the best. Now, do you think I can bother Chief Melon with each and every one of those phone calls?" The voice waited. Mattie's mind was reeling. At first, she had taken what the voice said to be the gospel truth. Boris Yeltsin? Hillary Clinton? Shirley MacLaine? After all, with CNN carrying the story, it was more than likely that all kinds of important people now knew about Sonny. But then she remembered the John Lennon call. John Lennon was dead, or so Sonny himself had announced during his first phone conversation with Chief Melon. Now Mattie's mind was able to process what had been said. The woman with the stern voice was getting all kinds of crank calls and she was fed up.

"And as soon as you hang up," the voice continued, "I'm sure that Steven Spielberg will call for the movie rights, and then Elizabeth Taylor will call for a dinner date. She likes the wild, scruffy type these days. And then, more than likely, the Martians will call." The voice waited.

"But I'm his mother," Mattie said softly. She almost doubted herself in this matter. She could hear the voice telling the next caller, "And just after Shirley and John and Boris and Hillary called, his mother called, which is unusual for a woman who is dead and buried in Mattagash, Maine."

"You're his *mother?*" The voice was entertained by this.

"Yes," said Mattie. "I'm his mother, from Mattagash, Maine, and I want to talk to Chief Melon."

The voice sighed again. "Leave me your number, ma'am, and I'll see that Chief Melon gets your message." As soon as Mattie delivered the last digit, the voice disconnected her without so much as a *thank you* or a *good-bye*. Not even a *hey*.

14

And then, it all seemed to happen at once, as though the years of Mattie's life had piled up on each other, all sixty-six of them, waiting like logs in a slough for the one major event that would mark her existence on the planet. And when that finally happened, those years came cascading down around her. The years of her life tumbled out onto the floor like marbles that she would never be able to gather up again in one bowl. The years of her life had been a made puzzle that one day gets unmade, the pieces all scattered. It had begun with her not planting a garden for the first time in years, with Sonny turning up on Channel 4, with her best friend, Elmer Fennelson, disappearing like smoke, with her three big girls all back inside the little house trying to live their teenaged lives over again, with Robbie turning up pregnant, with Mattie now sleeping late, with time trolling a second chance before her eyes, another chance to save Sonny. And then the rude, impersonal voice on the phone, a voice that suggested to Mattie that Sonny now belonged to other people, not to her. It all came undone, unmade, in a matter of days. Or was it years? Seconds? Does anyone know the spot in time when something happens that will snowball into a future event? If she had beaten Sonny for his windowpane art, if she had made him wash his own laundry, take down his dirty pictures, could she have prevented the next few hours? Could she have changed his life for the better?

Mattie had hung up the phone and was now in her bedroom, with Lester's old suitcase opened onto the lavender bed, waiting for a few items that she would carry to Bangor. She would get there some way, she knew that.

"All God's children got traveling shoes," she said aloud as she placed two folded pairs of underwear into the empty suitcase. Funny, but she still couldn't call them *panties*. The girls laughed aloud whenever she said *bloomers*, but until the day Mattie died, she would consider them such. And a *bra* was a *brassiere*. And she would never use a Mr. Coffee, or a microwave oven. She would fry her eggs in bacon grease and be damned, thank you very much. But those thoughts were all lost in the wave of events that happened next.

First, Rita came running into the house. She'd hitch-hiked a ride with Rachel Ann Parsons, who was responsible for Rita finding Jesus in the first place. Rita ran in all aflutter, just the way she did three days earlier, on Monday afternoon, when she came bearing the bad news of Sonny. Rita the messenger. But now she had different news.

"Have you seen Willard?" Rita panted. "Where's Robbie?

Where's my Buick?" At first Mattie thought there had been more of those blasted *new developments* on Sonny. But no, this was something nearer and dearer to Rita's heart. Her beloved Buick. Her big black Road Hog.

"They're gone to Watertown," said Mattie. "Now calm down and tell me what's going on." But Rita was at the telephone now, frantically licking her thumb and dabbing it at the flimsy pages of the phone book.

"They'll be going to Watertown Video," said Rita. "I can catch them there." She threw the phone book onto the counter and began dialing. Through the kitchen window Mattie could see Rachel Ann Parsons, waiting in her little blue car, her white arm resting against the glass of the driver's window.

"What's going on, Rita?" Mattie said again.

"Busy," said Rita, and hung up the phone.

"Don't make me keep asking," Mattie warned. Rita turned to Mattie then and grasped her shoulders with both hands. Instant tears turned Rita's eyes all watery.

"Oh, Mama," she said, "it's just the most wonderful thing. God spoke to me. He talked to me, Mama." At first, Mattie saw this as a good sign, that maybe God was offering some sound advice about Sonny. Why He chose Rita was another example of those "mysterious ways" in which He was forever operating. Mattie could only hope that this was genuine and not another of Rita's dramatic outbursts.

"What did He say, child?" Mattie asked. *Drive your mother to Bangor*, that's what Mattie was hoping for.

"He told me to sell the Buick!" Rita said. At first, Mattie simply stared at her daughter, at the tears of heavenly glory that were now spilling out of Rita's eyes, at the profound smile on her face. Mattie supposed that this was what was meant by "a look of bliss."

"He told you what?" she asked.

"He told me to sell the Buick!" Rita shouted. "I was doing the laundry, in the middle of sorting my coloreds from my whites, when what do I hear but this big booming voice. 'Rita, honey,' the voice said. 'Obey thy husband and sell the Buick.' Rachel Ann told me that God only talks to the real pious. Oh, my heart is still beating so fast, Mama, I can hardly talk!" She let go of Mattie then and was on her way back to the door.

"Could it have been Henry?" Mattie asked. "Could you have heard Henry Plunkett? After all, *he's* the one wanting you to sell the Buick." But Rita was already halfway out the door.

"I gotta put that sign back in the window!" Rita shouted. "Every second it ain't there dishonors His name." And then Rachel Ann's little blue car pulled out of Mattie's yard and pointed its nose at Watertown. Well, there went any chances of Mattie talking Robbie and Willard into driving her to Bangor in Rita's Road Hog. And she had thought that she might be able to do just that. Robbie seemed almost wavering when Mattie had asked earlier. And Willard, well, who could tell if Willard was wavering or not, what with all that twitching he did. But now it seemed those chances were squelched, now that God had gone into the used-car business. Mattie was sorry to hear this. How could He keep an eye on Sonny if He was concentrating on *Good condition, Tires like new, Will accept best offer?*

Mattie had just gone back to her packing, thinking that maybe, if she asked again, if she promised something big, the house itself maybe, Marlene would crack and drive her down to Marigold Drive Trailer Park. Or maybe Elmer Fennelson would finally appear from his disappearing act. Elmer would take her for sure, and she would be ready, Lester's old suitcase packed with a clean brassiere and two clean pairs of bloomers, two dresses, socks, her toothbrush, her big jar of cold cream. She wouldn't need much. Or if Pauline ever did get off the road with her sacks and boxes of Avon so that she could answer her telephone, maybe Pauline would take her, tired as she was. *Someone* would take her. Mattie had even thought of calling a taxicab, but where would the nearest taxi service be? Caribou, maybe? It would take him almost two hours to get to Mattagash, and then they would have to turn around and drive another five hours south to get to Sonny. What would that cost? Would the four hundred dollars she had in the bank be enough for that? She thought not.

"Not with what things cost these days," Mattie said. Then she would be broke, no money for a motel room, for food. And her social security check wasn't due for another two weeks. She stood in the middle of the living room and waited, listened to the sounds of the little house, ticking like a bomb, the quiet of things when one stands alone in one's own home and thinks. Water in the pipes. A creak in the walls. The grating of the electric furnace. An outside wind. And then silence. And when that silence comes, there's nothing left to do, no distractions to keep you from facing up to the facts of your situation. There's just the quiet of the truth, floating all around you like a bad perfume, like the smell of those swamp irises.

"I ain't ever gonna get to Bangor, am I?" Mattie asked aloud. Nothing in the house answered. Somewhere in the distance a car door slammed, probably at Pauline's house, and the sound of it reached her through the screen of her back door. She could ask Jesus. It wasn't as if the heavenly ice hadn't already been broken. After all, his father was on speaking terms with Mattie's oldest daughter, Rita. She could slide *Easter Rising* out from under the sofa and ask the kind face in the picture, the one with the sad blue eye and blondish hairs growing like peach fuzz on the boyish chin. "I ain't ever going to Bangor, am I, Jesus?" she could ask. But she already knew the answer. No need to put one more burden upon the boy's thin shoulders. She heard the grackles in the backyard and imagined their bluish heads, bobbing. She could almost see the towels she'd hung out on the line yesterday, after that light rain, so much did she want to leave her earthly body and go where the truth wouldn't find her. But she couldn't. And then the quiet broke, like a dam, and life rushed down onto her head, wave after wave of helplessness. *She would never get to Bangor, Maine. She would never get to Sonny.* And that's when she heard another car in her yard, her peaceful little yard that had been such a nice place before all this trouble. She thought of her tiny square of lawn, where the St. Francis of Assisi birdbath served as a friendly swimming pool for the neighborhood birds. She thought of those sweet bygone days when she and Elmer Fennelson would sit upon her narrow front porch and discuss their lives as though they were books they had once read and then put away on the shelf.

She hoped that it might be Rita again, that God had changed His mind and demanded that Rita drive her mother down to Bangor. "Keep the Road Hog, honey," Mattie could almost hear God advising in a booming voice that only God or Charlton Heston could have. "Put the pedal to the metal, sweetheart." But it wasn't Rita. It was Pauline. Mattie opened the door to let her in. She seemed more tired than ever, her big body having a hard time keeping up with her feet.

"I know that bubble bath ain't here yet," said Mattie. "I just ordered it Monday. And I found my bottle of Skin So Soft this morning. So does this mean you're actually gonna sit down and have a normal visit with me?"

Pauline shook her head. "You got your TV on?" she asked.

"Why?" said Mattie. The truth was, she *didn't* have the television on. She was tired of looking at it and not being able to do anything to help Sonny. She was now intent on seeing Sonny in person, and not on Channel 4. So she had turned the television off and set about packing her suitcase.

"I just stopped off at Lola's to pick up Little Frank,"

Pauline said. "Sonny's ex-wife has turned up in Bangor. She even brought the dog." Mattie said nothing. She just looked at Pauline's face, a nice, round face, tired, filled with a lifetime of honest work, filled with kindness. Would God forgive Mattie for the many times over the years she had wished Pauline was her own daughter? Would God forgive her for coveting Pauline when she had three daughters of her own? Another car roared into the driveway and Mattie suddenly felt weak, her legs turning into rubbery things. Pauline reached out for her, pulled her toward the recliner.

"Sit down, darling," said Pauline. "It's gonna all be over soon and Sonny'll be just fine." She kneaded Mattie's shoulders as she said this, and, because of that, because of that tender touch of one human being to another, Mattie believed her. And then Gracie and Marlene flew into the house, excited bats, their purses sailing like Frisbees toward the sofa. Couldn't they just walk over and put them down? Did they have to hurl things?

In no time Marlene had Channel 4 cranked up, and Gracie was telling Pauline all about the newest of the new developments. Mattie looked up at the clock. One thirty. Martha Monihan would be very unhappy that Channel 4 had disrupted her soap opera for Sonny Gifford, Mattie's only boy. Who would have ever dreamed? All those years that Mattie and Martha had watched folks on television get born and have affairs and sometimes die, who would have ever dreamed that one day their favorite soap would be interrupted because of something Sonny Gifford did?

"It'll soon be over, Mama," Marlene was saying. "He'll come out now and let them two women go." Mattie tried to reason with herself. They were all saying it would be okay, even Pauline, so why couldn't she believe it? What made her motherly heart so sore? The television screen had now come to life, and it carried a picture of the same trailer, white, with the fine red pinstripe cutting through its middle. The lawn was awash with people. A sign held aloft, over the heads of just regular folks with nothing better to do in their own homes, listed an address for the Sonny Gifford Fan Club. Reporters and policemen were everywhere. Donna's hair was flying in the wind. Mattie tried hard to concentrate.

"Pauline," she said, and Pauline bent down to listen. "I'm afraid."

Pauline rubbed Mattie's shoulders. "You want a cup of tea?" she asked. "A glass of soda pop?" Mattie shook her head. Gracie and Marlene were hovering in front of the television like excited hens. And then Donna was back, with her microphone welded to her hand, her eyes awash with the biggest story of her lifetime.

"Dan, it looks as though things will soon be resolved here at Marigold Drive Trailer Park," she said. "As you know, Sheila Gifford, Sonny Gifford's estranged wife, has contacted Chief Melon and is willing to come forward and speak to her ex-husband. Apparently, Dan, there was a dispute between the couple over the ownership of their dog, Humphrey. This is the dog Sonny Gifford mentioned to the press two days ago. It seems that both parties wanted the dog, so Sheila Gifford took the dog with her to Atlantic City to prevent Mr. Gifford from having him."

"They're fighting over a *dog?*" asked Pauline. But Mattie knew that Sonny's dogs were his babies.

"There was a couple on *Geraldo* last month," said Marlene, "who spent over a hundred thousand dollars each on lawyers because they both wanted custody of their miniature collie."

Pauline sighed. "What I could do with money like that," she said.

"Is Sheila Gifford there at the trailer park, Donna?" Dan's voice asked. Mattie was growing tired of these two people, two strangers discussing her son, examining his life under a microscope.

"Yes, Dan, she is," Donna answered.

"Look!" said Marlene, and pointed at the screen. The camera had fallen upon a woman standing next to Chief Melon, who seemed to be giving her instructions. Mattie saw his hands moving like batons as he spoke, his head bobbing at the trailer. "That must be her!"

"What's so special about *her?*" Mattie heard Gracie say. The woman on the television screen had long, stringy hair, brownish-blond, tired hair that looked as though it could use a good washing. Of course, Sheila had probably driven all night from Atlantic City. The camera zoomed in tight on her face.

"Sheila Gifford," Mattie could hear Donna's voice announcing somewhere in the land of television. Sheila's eyes were almost too big for her narrow face. A heavy, dark line ran beneath both of her bottom lashes, and Mattie knew from having daughters that Sheila's mascara had outlived its usefulness and had fallen off, creating black rings beneath her eyes. She looked as though she could use a good shower. She turned her head and spoke to a woman standing behind her, a friend, relative maybe, and Mattie could see the narrow bridge of her nose, long and thin, as if it didn't belong on her pale face, a face made for a shorter nose.

"Lord," said Gracie again, "*this* is the face that launched a thousand ships? What does Sonny see in *her?*" Mattie had no idea what Gracie was talking about, what with college loading her head full of all kinds of nonsense these days. Things you couldn't use in times of emergency. As a result, Gracie was a truckload of information with no brakes. Just a couple weeks earlier she had called Mattie up and said, "Mama, did you know that the Mayans were chewing gum over a thousand years ago?" Well, no, Mattie hadn't known that. Another time, Gracie had been sitting at the kitchen table, having coffee, when she looked right at Mattie and said, "The ancient Egyptians kneaded their bread with their feet." Mattie had tried not to think about this, about dough being squished up between brown Egyptian toes. It seemed almost as if Gracie needed to fill her head up with this stuff to keep thoughts of Charlie from seeping in. So what harm could it do? So much for *launching ships*, but as far as what did Sonny see in this woman? This was something Mattie understood but couldn't answer. What did Charlie Craft see in Sally Fennelson, that he left Gracie behind to take up with her? What did good, soft-spoken Henry see in Rita? What did Lester Gifford see in Mattie that he came into her garden that day, still wearing his army uniform, still nursing his war wound by limping on that bad knee? What did anyone see in the people they either love or need?

"Maybe he *does* have to take women at gunpoint now," said Marlene, "like Wesley said." But Mattie knew the truth about it. She knew Sonny had found something uncommon in this common woman, something soft and caressing. Maybe it was how she ran her fingers through that stringy hair, how she walked, the way her mouth moved when she talked. Maybe it was the velvety way she held her children, as though they were fragile petals. Maybe it was how she held *him*. Whatever it was, there was some kind of magic working there for Sonny, and it had lifted this Sheila woman up and above all other earthly women he had known.

"Hush!" said Pauline, and Mattie was relieved to have her there, to feel those big hands upon her shoulders. Donna's face was back.

"It seems that what Mr. Gifford wants at this time, Dan, is his dog. A few minutes ago, in a telephone conversation with Chief Melon, he indicated that if he gets the dog, he will let the hostages go." Before Mattie could hear more, the door burst open and Rita blew back in. Mattie hadn't even heard the sound of a car, so caught up was she in

Channel 4. Rachel Ann's face was peering like a pale balloon from behind Rita's shoulder. Rita obviously hadn't found the Buick. God had told her to sell it, but He apparently couldn't tell her *where it was*.

"Has he come out yet?" Rita asked. "We heard the news while we were gassing up at Blanche's Grocery." Her hair seemed electrified. She'd had quite a day. Her purse sailed across the room and landed next to Gracie's on the sofa. Pauline held up a hand that said *be quiet*.

"Is the dog there, Donna?" Dan asked. The camera swept the crowd and then stopped again at Sheila Bumphrey Gifford. Police were working hard to keep the onlookers back. Signs were everywhere. University students, with big *U of M*s on their T-shirts and sweatshirts and sweatpants, were waving vigorously at the camera.

"Yes, it is, Dan," said Donna, "but we haven't seen it yet. From what we're told, Chief Melon is talking with Sonny Gifford at this time. It looks as though this unfortunate matter will be resolved soon." And then, with a promise to interrupt the regularly scheduled program when negotiations were completed, Channel 4 went back to Martha Monihan's favorite soap opera.

"Do you want me to stay?" Pauline asked Mattie. The three girls were in the background, discussing whether they should go to Lola's in case CNN was still covering the hostage incident, or stay with their mother, who was still, as Marlene once said, *vulnerable*.

"No," said Mattie. She stood up and turned the sound

of the soap opera down. The girls would be sure to crank the volume back up when things started happening again at Marigold Drive Trailer Park. Mattie had no doubt about this. She had unwittingly raised three good watchdogs. Nothing would be missed, and a good time would be had by all. "You go on home and see about your kids," she told Pauline.

"I'll call you later," Pauline said, and Mattie held the front door for her.

"Is Elmer home?" Mattie whispered as Pauline edged past. "Is his pickup back?" There might still be time. What if it took a few hours before Sonny agreed to send the hostages out? Pauline turned and looked closely at Mattie's face.

"He ain't back," Pauline said. She paused, as if uncertain about what she could or should say. "I know where your mind is right now," she finally told Mattie. "And I'd drive you myself if I could. But my car probably wouldn't make it past Caribou. I'm lucky it ain't gone out on me already. And then, I can't leave Frank with the kids, sick as he is."

Mattie shushed her. "I know all about it," she said. "You just go on home."

Before Pauline drove off, she threw Mattie an invisible kiss, and then a thumbs-up. Mattie waved her out of the driveway before she closed the door. Marlene and Rita were in the kitchen making sandwiches. Rachel Ann Parsons asked directions to the tiny bathroom, so that she could relieve herself and then go on home, go back about her usual business of saving lost souls. Gracie had started her exercises now, her legs bicycling around and around in the air, going nowhere.

"Marlene?" Gracie shouted out to the kitchen. "Bring me a glass of water."

"What's the matter with *you?*" Marlene wanted to know from the kitchen. "Your feet gone to lunch or something?"

Rachel Ann came out of the little bathroom, the sound of flushing water rising up behind her. She paused at the kitchen door and listened for a bit to Rita and Marlene, who were arguing over the intricate makings of a sandwich.

"You put the bacon on the *top*," Marlene was instructing Rita. "The lettuce goes on the bottom, and the tomato goes in between."

"Well, *you* can put the bacon where you want to," Rita said. "But I personally believe in the *tomato* going on top." Rachel Ann moved away from the kitchen door, saying nothing. She found her own purse from among the collection of purses on the sofa, and threw the strap over her shoulder. She stopped before Mattie and stood for a minute, waiting, searching, it seemed, for the right words.

"Do you want me to pray with you?" Rachel Ann asked. She seemed about to collapse from exhaustion. After all, it was a big, big world, and there were so many wretched souls to salvage. Just the follow-up on saving Rita had obviously worn her down. "I'm more than willing to pray with you," Rachel Ann offered again.

"Thank you, Rachel Ann," said Mattie. "I appreciate your offer, but I been praying alone now for over sixty years, and well, I've grown kind of accustomed to it." Still Rachel Ann lingered, looking back again at the kitchen, listening to the music of Rita's shrill voice.

"God first spoke to me in 1972," Rachel Ann said now, as though she were answering a question on some test. She looked at Mattie, her small eyes expressionless. "And now He's talking to Rita, too."

"Ten!" Gracie announced from her spot in front of the television set. She was doing sit-ups now, her legs having stopped their useless cycling.

Rachel Ann went on out to her little blue car. Mattie stood in the door and watched as it pulled out of the driveway and pointed itself toward the life Rachel Ann had chosen to live for herself, her own Mattagash version of time spent on the planet. Then Mattie closed the door to her mushroom of a house.

"I wish God would tell you how to make a BLT," she heard Marlene tell Rita.

15

They waited. Within a half hour the house had filled with grandchildren. News travels fast, especially in Mattagash, Maine. Robbie was back, in her crazy tie-dye dress, her face eaten up with concern for Uncle Sonny. Willard had found a spot on the corner of Mattie's sofa and was reading some magazine while he twitched and blinked. With his greenish head bobbing, with his long stick arms bent at the elbows, he reminded Mattie of a praying mantis. Steven and Lyle, Marlene's two boys, were sitting cross-legged in front of the set with Gracie, who looked younger than ever, a neon sweatband encircling her forehead, her fetlock stockings about her ankles in neon colors. Mattie feared that Gracie was growing so young, so fast, with each passing day that Charlie stayed gone, that she might just up and disappear. She might die of young age, instead of old age. Rita's younger son, Josh, had fallen asleep in the recliner. Marlene was taking a shower and Rita had water boiling in a pan on the stove, hoping to make a big enough pot of spaghetti to feed this unusual family reunion.

"Henry's coming over later," Rita told Mattie, and she nodded. It'd be good to have Henry around. He was solid, the way Elmer Fennelson could be solid. "Wesley's fishing," Rita added, "or we'd all be here, the whole family, all except Sonny, of course. I wonder if this is what Gracie means by *bonding*." She broke a handful of spaghetti in two and plunged it into the boiling water.

"If Wesley Stubbs had been born Indian," said Mattie, "they'd have named him Skidoo That Rides Like the Wind." She looked at Rita, and Rita smiled. "They'd have named him Brave Who Cheats Workman's Comp."

"It sounds like Sonny *is* here," Rita said.

Mattie fixed herself a glass of vinegar and water for her varicose veins, not knowing what else to do. Waiting for news of Sonny, she felt as if she were at some kind of funeral wake. But not a wake like in the old days. In the old days, when someone died, folks skilled in funeral things would come to a person's house and dress the dead body, get it ready while family and friends set up a vigil downstairs. There was a softness in this kind of waiting, with the clock ticking on the wall, with someone boiling tea, someone stoking the fire. Mattie had seen her father leave the world this way. She had brought a funnel cake to Eliza Fennelson's home, while Eliza lay upstairs in her own bed, struck down by cancer instead of Cupid's arrow, but free of sin. And Constance Mullins. Horace Craft. A whole bundle of

Mattagashers. And then people started dying in hospitals, where rules existed, rules that said, "You can touch your loved one between the hours of such and such. Outside of that time, toodle-oo." These days, when people died, they were whisked away by professionals, whisked away in a hush-hush manner, as though dying was an embarrassment, as though dying had disgraced the whole family. And when the body appeared again, in its casket, in some joyless room built just for *holding dead bodies* and not for raising up big families like a real home is, when the body surfaced again it would be all prettied up. Mattagash women who'd never worn rouge in their lifetimes went to paradise with cheeks round and red as a clown's. Mattagash lumberjacks who'd never had clean fingernails in the flesh would be manicured to the hilt. This was how Mattie felt, waiting for news of Sonny. It was a sterile feeling, as though the house had been disinfected. Professionals now had her son's living body, and they would let his mother view it again when they were good and ready. Mattie let out a weary sigh. There was nothing quiet in this present waiting. How could she hear her old clock ticking from its spot on the shelf when a living room full of noise was competing with it? Steven and Lyle were now fighting over some handheld video game. Gracie was watching Channel 4, the volume ricocheting off the walls. Robbie was washing dishes. Willard was flipping the pages of his magazine with a steady, annoying *flick, flick, flick.* Rita was shouting instructions to the boys. And Marlene had yet to get out of the shower and add her own two cents. Maybe in her bedroom, Mattie could find a lavender patch of quiet from the newly gathered family.

"Call me," she said to Gracie, "the minute something happens. I'm going to take a nap." Gracie nodded, a thick ponytail bouncing like a teenager's off the left side of her head.

It was on the way to her bedroom that Mattie spied the little piece of puzzle, the blue eye of Jesus, lying beside the leg of a kitchen chair. She picked it up before anyone could see it there, and stared down into the sad pupil, into the very soul of a young man who had all of humanity resting upon his narrow shoulders. As she slipped the piece into her apron pocket, she felt from far down within her a surge of anguish rise up, a mother's anguish for a lost boy. But Sonny was more than her boy. He was the side of her that she herself had never developed. He was her sense of humor, a thing she had owned once as a girl and then lost somewhere, maybe at the bottom of that trunk where she still kept her wedding picture and Martha Monihan's friendship plate. Only with Sonny had she truly felt the power of pure laughter. Theresa Something-Polish had said that very thing, on the phone to Mattie, from her new home and life down in Connecticut. "I heard that Sonny won a hundred dollars in the lottery," said Theresa, "and that he quit his job as a result." Mattie smiled, remembering. It was true. Sonny quit his job with Watertown Electrical Repair, which he had held for almost three months. "I did it for all them folks too stupid to quit when they win millions," Sonny had explained. And the event had gone into the big book of laughs Mattagash had been keeping on Sonny Gifford. "Nobody in my whole life since I left Mattagash, Maine, has ever been able to make me laugh the way Sonny did," Theresa told Mattie. Mattie knew what she meant. That's how she herself felt around Sonny, that she was his favorite girlfriend, the one he would never walk away from. She felt *courted*, didn't she, the way Lester had never courted her. All Lester had done was wear his army uniform and look handsome until one warm August day when Mattie heard herself saying, "I do," and then it was all over.

From her window, Mattie stared at the river while the yellow walls of her bedroom rose like pale wheat all around her. This was where she had stood, all those lonely nights, pondering the whereabouts of her husband. Now the window seemed like a picture frame, designed to encircle a picture puzzle. *Woman Waiting at Window*, the puzzle might be called. It had bordered a good part of her life, this window, this frame, and now here she was again. It reminded her of the day she had stood at the window of her childhood bedroom and tossed her mother's valentine out to the wild winds. *A mother's heart is always true, even if her heart is blue.* And now, nothing could change Mattie's own blue heart, for she knew things were not going well in Bangor. Never mind that Pauline said it would all work out. Never mind what Donna, the reporter, said. Or what Chief Melon was hoping for. Never mind all of that. Mattie *knew*. Just like that mother whose son had been aboard the space shuttle when it exploded and came falling back to earth. She told everyone who listened that she knew her boy was still alive when he went into the ocean. And that he lived for some time after that. Never mind what NASA said. This mother *knew*. And so did Mattie, even before Gracie screamed out from the living room, from her vigil in front of the television set, to come quick, Mattie knew.

"That poor boy!" Mattie thought she cried out, in answer to Gracie. Then she realized that she hadn't said a word.

"Them poor dead boys," Mattie now said aloud. And she reached into her pocket and touched a finger to the blue piece of eye puzzle.

"Turn it up, quick!" she heard Rita shouting from the kitchen, and then the scuffle of feet, the tinny voice of a newscaster. Didn't those newspeople have better things to do? Didn't they have their own children to fret over?

"Sonny's coming out!" Gracie shouted.

"Stevie, quick!" Marlene's voice. She must have finished her shower. Mattie knew without seeing her daughter how she'd look, a towel wrapped about her wet hair, wearing Mattie's old tan bathrobe, which tried to mind its own business on a nail behind the bathroom door. "Make sure the VCR is taping!" Marlene instructed. "Your uncle Sonny is about to make his splash!"

And so Mattie came out of her bedroom and stood before the great set, surrounded by all of her family, grandchildren and children. They were all there but Sonny. She stood before a box of magical dots and wires and transmissions, things she didn't understand, things no one she knew understood. You just turn a button and it speaks to you. Mattie stood before the television and hoped the dread that had settled into her heart was not a real dread but a mother's fear. She stared at the reporters, those midwives to her son, those people who now saw him more often than she did. They had all materialized. Like ghosts, their bodies had used those magical dots to take on shapes. They had all come.

"There has been a remarkable turn in the Gifford hostage case, Dan," said Donna. Her small face seemed almost sad, drained of energy. Rita cranked the sound up yet again and now Donna's words seemed to be rocking the house, pitching it to and fro with excitement. "As I stated earlier, Sheila Gifford, the estranged wife of Sonny Gifford, who has barricaded himself inside this trailer with two hostages, has now come forward." The camera was back to its usual panning, capturing all the principal players. Chief Melon had returned for an encore, busy with instructions and concern. Sheila Bumphrey Gifford stood straight, looking like a zombie. The house trailer loomed sharper than ever, the pinstripe running like blood across its middle. Even the crowd seemed more lively. Maybe it was a stunt crowd, flown in just for the occasion.

"Apparently, Dan, Sonny Gifford wished his wife well a few moments ago in a telephone conversation," Donna was saying. "All he wants now, he says, is his dog, Humphrey. But once the hostages are released, the question will be whether or not Mr. Gifford will surrender himself to Bangor police. We understand that Sheila Gifford has offered to take the dog into her trailer, in the hopes of talking her estranged husband into giving himself up. But Sonny Gifford has declined this offer." Mattie wasn't surprised. Sheila had run off with another man, after all. Sonny had his pride, especially while he was on television.

"And attention," said Marlene. "All he wants is attention."

"What does he *see* in that woman?" Gracie asked, her ponytail wiggling.

"It'll be over soon," Robbie whispered to Mattie. "Uncle Sonny's gonna be just fine." She put her small hands on Mattie's shoulders and began kneading, the way Pauline had done earlier. Did the Egyptians knead shoulders with their toes?

The television picture jerked about as the camera rushed into a new position, Donna keeping just ahead with her microphone.

"We're told that Sonny Gifford is getting ready to release the hostages now, Dan!" Donna said excitedly. Mattie could see the chief of police talking on a handheld telephone. He must be talking to Sonny. She wished she could butt in, interrupt the call, hear Sonny's voice for her-self. *Take it easy now, boy*, she'd tell him. *Take it easy and keep your head. You can still walk away from this movie with some dignity. You can still avoid this big fire blazing away under your pants. Hillary Clinton has called. Shirley MacLaine. Boris Yeltsin. By the looks of things, after a few months in jail, you might even get your own talk show.* Her heart started to thump and Mattie wondered if Robbie could feel it, right through the bones of her grandmother's body.

Rita and Marlene kept up their running commentary, on everything from Sheila Gifford's hairdo to how the lawn in front of the trailer needed mowing. Their voices filled the house with noise. Shutting them out as best she could, Mattie kept her eyes welded to the action on her television set. She noticed policemen at the edges of the screen, poised, holding rifles with scopes.

"Oh my God," Mattie heard her mouth say. And then the camera pulled back enough that the door of the trailer zoomed into view and Mattie saw it open, saw two women step out onto the porch, Sonny's face appearing in the door behind them.

"The hostages," Marlene whispered. One had long brown hair, just as in Mattie's dream, pretty brown hair. The other one, with short blondish curls, said something to Sonny, over her shoulder, and Mattie could see him nod. They appeared to be working well as a team, these hostages and their captor. The two women stood on the porch, their hands at their sides. Mattie could see only one of Sonny's hands, the left one, which he had clasped around the upper arm of the long-haired woman, holding her firmly before him. Did he have the plastic water pistol in his other hand? Mattie had known right from the very beginning that Sonny wouldn't hold a real gun on human beings. And not because holding a gun was too much work, as Marlene had said earlier, but because Sonny had another way with people. He didn't need a gun. He held most folks to him just by being Sonny, just as this huge wild crowd was now held to him. Sonny should've gone to Hollywood, that's one thing for sure.

The hostages stood stiffly, staring out at the crowd as though they were a couple of manikins. Or two of those blowup dolls Sonny was always threatening to order one day. Mattie still couldn't see Sonny's right hand, which was concealed behind the long-haired woman's back. He had stepped out of the trailer now, the hostages inching forward on the tiny porch to give him room, reporters still vying for the closest spot to the plastic yellow ribbon. And then Sonny was telling the camera hello, bidding America good day. Questions began to fly instantly, like a swarm of summertime blackflies, good old Maine blackflies, with reporters shouting out to Sonny as they pushed and scrambled about on the lawn. "Is Sheila Gifford willing to give up the dog?" "Will you give yourself up?" "What will happen once you release the hostages?" This last question came from Donna and was the one that Sonny accepted, smiling down at Donna's little dog face, selecting her from out of the crowd. She had been, after all, his *first* reporter on the scene, and Sonny would remember her the way one remembers that first true love. Sonny had a loyal streak running through him the way white runs on a skunk. Mattie wouldn't be surprised if, this very next Valentine's Day, Donna found an anonymous valentine in her mailbox.

"I can't believe this," said Marlene. "They're letting him have another conference?"

"That's because he's still calling the shots," Rita prophesied. "But wait until he turns them women loose. I daresay this is Sonny Gifford's last press conference." Gracie threw a pillow from off the sofa at Rita and it bounced off the top of Rita's head. But she didn't seem to notice this. Rita was accustomed to having pillows thrown at her head during made-for-TV movies and family functions of all kinds.

"Park your lips, Rita," said Gracie. Sonny had used one of his famous long pauses while he pondered the answer to Donna's question, the camera lingering on his face while it waited.

"I intend to spend some quality time with my dog," Sonny finally told her. "Whoever said a man's best friend is his dog must've been married at least once in his lifetime." This said, Sonny produced his explosive grin. The crowd roared with approval. It was good to see Sonny's face again, without the window screen hampering his fine features. Funny how a camera adored Sonny Gifford, lit up all his best intentions. Mattie had never seen a picture of herself, in all her sixty-six years, that she felt comfortable with. Sonny had inherited his friendship with the camera from Lester's side.

"In that case," said Marlene, "I hope they allow dogs in prison, 'cause that's where that brother of mine is headed." Then another question flew into the air that Sonny seemed to like. He pointed at someone in the crowd and then cupped his ear, asking for a repeat.

"Donnie Henderson says you're the inventor of the Le Mans Birth Method, Sonny," the reporter's voice cried out.

Mattie couldn't see where the question came from. A male voice. Maybe that thin-faced, thin-haired man. "Could you tell us what the Le Mans Method is?" Sonny shook his head, a look of great fondness on his face, as if he might be remembering Donnie. He and Donald R. Henderson had been such good friends, burning up their childhood years in pursuit of baseball and mischief, which developed, later, into *girls* and mischief.

"Oh please, God," Rita wailed. "Don't let him tell that story and embarrass the daylights out of me on television!" Sonny stood on the porch now, his left hand still holding the long-haired woman's arm, the reporters waiting, the fans waiting, all of America *waiting*.

"Now, that there," said Sonny, "is a scientific secret and Mr. Donnie Henderson should know better than to think I'd reveal it here on TV."

"Thank you, Jesus," said Rita. Mattie was having a hard time telling reporters from the well-wishers who had been mobbing the trailer park, folks cheering Sonny onward. They seemed now to be one and the same. No one was asking important questions. Mattie longed for that tight-faced—what Sonny called tight-assed—woman who had kept things on a serious keel. But she was nowhere to be seen. And then a new actor materialized, a debut moment as the dog, Humphrey, made his appearance on the end of a leash held by a policeman. Mattie could feel the crowd's delirium all the way from Bangor, could see them rising to the occasion. *Humphrey is here. Humphrey is here.*

"There's the dog!" shouted Marlene.

"A German shepherd," said Steven. Mattie nodded. Sonny had always loved German shepherds, had owned three or four of them in his lifetime. The German shepherd seemed caught up in the ruckus. He pulled back on his leash, straining to run, but the policeman held him as best he could, calming him down with a friendly pat.

What happened next seemed to Mattie to occur in slow motion, as if maybe the television had delayed the action so that no one would miss anything, no viewer out in Washington State, where Sonny's cousin William lived, or down in deserty New Mexico, where his aunt Frieda, Lester's sister, had hidden for most of her life after marrying that air force man and abandoning Mattagash, or down in Connecticut, where Theresa Something-Polish was still carrying her torch for Sonny. It only took a few seconds, but time kindly slowed itself down so that Mattie and others could watch it all unfold. Seconds.

"I'd like to take this opportunity to thank the Bangor Police Department for their patience," Sonny announced.

"Who does he think this is?" Rita asked. "A politician?" But before Sonny could say anything else, before he could dole out more of what the papers called his "soft voice and folksy mannerisms," his dog suddenly heard his master's voice for the first time in days. At least that's what it looked like, for Humphrey went crazy, jumping into the air, twisting his body, fighting to get free of the leash.

"He thinks they're hurting Sonny!" Mattie cried out.

Sonny's other dogs were the same way. He used to show their devotion off to his friends. "Just pretend you're hitting me," Sonny would urge Donnie Henderson. And the dogs would bare their teeth at the sight of Donnie's raised hand, would go crazy to protect their beloved owner. "He thinks them hostages are hurting Sonny!" Mattie cried again. And then Humphrey pulled away from the policeman who was trying frantically to hold him, pulled away and bounded toward Sonny and the two women. The crowd broke into screams. A loud eruption of chaos. Frenzy on the loose. Mattie realized that Sonny must have seen the dog coming, for he pushed his hostages aside so that Humphrey would see he was unharmed. But it was too much action for too few seconds. Too many pictures for brains under stress to process. As Sonny flung the women away so that he could grab Humphrey up into his arms, one of the policemen panicked. Mattie didn't see which one, for there was too much commotion. She didn't even hear the gun firing, for the crowd was thunderous.

Instead, she stood paralyzed before the television's face, stood peering at the ruination of her son. The bullet hole between his eyes looked like the mark of Cain, except that Sonny wouldn't hurt nobody, much less kill his brother. He didn't even have a brother. He just had those awful sisters. Mattie watched as the two women hostages knelt beside Sonny's body. They reminded her of women she'd seen before, women in the lumber camps who'd lost a husband beneath a fallen pine. Women she'd seen on TV during the Vietnam War, who wept over the mangled bodies of their children. Women who'd lost their brothers, sons, even themselves somewhere on the bumpy road through life. The two women wailed. Mattie saw them throw their throats back, like coyotes. They wailed for her lost son, her dead boy. In other days, other times, they'd have been allowed to dress the dead body, carry it home, mourn for it in private, the way everybody in Mattagash used to do before they built that funeral home in St. Leonard. But not these women. People who knew them, anxious relatives and friends, rushed in and pulled them both away.

"He didn't have a gun," Robbie was saying now. "He didn't have a single thing in his hands." With the rest of the family staring in shock at the television screen, Mattie moved away from the set. She could stand it no longer. Strangers were there with her child and she was in Mattagash, wringing her hands as though they were mops. She heard Rita sobbing and wondered why. And then Marlene followed suit, Marlene, the middle daughter who seemed to have no identity, who always had to do everything Rita did, even when they were children. Marlene and Rita, shrieking now like hyenas. Willard had dropped his magazine and was standing in front of the set, staring down at the commotion taking place in Bangor. In the breeze coming from Mattie's little portable fan, which sat on top of the television, Willard's green hairs were waving like blades of grass, and, crazily, Mattie thought of her cemetery plot in the Catholic graveyard, down by that clutch of pine trees near the old meadow, a slice of land lying next to Lester's slice. "Looks like you both got a piece of the American pie," Sonny had said the day he drove Mattie out there so she could plant a red geranium on Lester's grave. Sonny had been unable to finish reading the words on his father's tombstone. *Beloved Husband, Beloved Father. His earthly toils are over. His heavenly rest begun.* Instead, he walked along the meadow's edge, kicking his boot at invisible rocks, until Mattie finished. "Because I got nothing to say to him," he told Mattie later, when she asked why. Now, with Sonny himself lying dead in Bangor, Maine, Mattie pushed Robbie's arms away, for they were encircling her, taking her breath.

"It's okay, honey," Mattie's voice said, an impersonal voice, a voice like the one on the telephone earlier. *You're his mother, you say?* "I just need to be alone for a bit." She squeezed Robbie's hand and then let it go. Gracie was now reaching up for Robbie, stretching out her arms. Her ponytail had gone slack.

"Oh Lord, oh Lord, oh Lord," Gracie was saying.

In the kitchen Mattie leaned against the sink and tried to breathe. What should be done now? What steps should be taken? Where was Henry? Henry would know. He couldn't sell whores in a lumber camp, but he'd know what to do in a mess like this. A knock suddenly rattled the screen on the back door. Mattie tried to gather her thoughts. Was it one of those ghost knocks? A spirit beating on the window to let you know someone has passed over?

She'd known about such things since she was a little girl. Hadn't the wind beat its fists at her own window the night her mother died? Another knock, this one sounding more human than the last. Mattie stood, straightened her hair as best she could, and then felt silly. *Fixing her hair, and Sonny just dead!* The girls were still all pasted about the television set. There wouldn't be any more *teasers*, that was one thing for certain. Her hand shaking, Mattie opened the back door and saw Elmer Fennelson standing there, hat in his hands. Of course, it would be Elmer. Elmer always came to the back door like some railroad bum, some runaway slave. Poor Elmer. Not wishing to make any more racket in the world, any more fuss, than was necessary. *Hanging back.*

"Where've you been?" Mattie asked. She could feel tears filling her eyes, turning the world all watery. Elmer seemed to be trembling. Had he already heard of Sonny and come to comfort her? No, he couldn't have. Sonny had just now died. Even if Elmer had jumped into his old pickup, Skunk on his heels, it would've taken him more than five minutes to get to Mattie's house.

"I been camping out, over on the hardwood ridge behind my house," Elmer said quietly. "Me and Skunk, we been camping out without telling a soul." He waited. Mattie held the door ajar with one hand, not knowing what else to do, what to say. She could hear the racket of her daughters and grandchildren behind her.

"Camping?" Mattie asked vaguely.

"Camping and doing a parcel of thinking," Elmer said.

He shifted his long, thin frame from one foot to another, twirled his cap. "But I see you got company."

"Thinking?" Mattie asked.

"Well, what I come to ask you is this," Elmer said finally. He cleared his throat. Mattie tried to understand what was happening, what her good friend Elmer was working toward, but all she could think of was Sonny. It occurred to her that she might faint, like that day in church when she married Lester Gifford. Elmer had been there to catch her that day, too.

"I know we're both older than two old hound dogs," Elmer said. He looked off toward where Mattie's garden usually lay. "But I was wondering if you might consider the idea of you and me getting married." Mattie couldn't respond. She tried to remember why these kinds of big things in life usually don't happen at once: a child's death going hand in hand with a proposal of marriage. That wasn't the way it was usually done, was it?

"Married?" Mattie asked.

"We could live in the house of your choice," said Elmer, "although I've grown real partial to mine." Mattie stepped out onto the back porch and let the screen door close behind her.

"Elmer," she said. "They shot my boy. They just shot Sonny down on television, like he was some kind of outlaw. They just put a bullet into his head. My boy is dead, Elmer." Then she went back into her house and closed the door.

With her daughters still stunned before the television,

jolted by death, dazed and astonished, saying nothing for the first time in years, Mattie pulled a chair away from the kitchen table and sank down into it. Funny, but the pattern on the tablecloth, with the tiny rose flowers and wispy green leaves, seemed large suddenly, important in some way. Everything seemed to be a clue to the hereafter, now that one of her own had gone there, was *on his way there*, since Mattie had no idea how long it took a soul to depart its earthly woes. She wondered if Sonny would be stopping by Mattagash, Maine, on his way out, maybe to see if Mattie's teeth were really soaking, pick up his Rico Petrocelli baseball and his *Best of Ricky Nelson* CD. Now, Mattie remembered, *remembered wildly*, for it seemed that her mind was reeling with this new information, this new intimacy with death, that Ricky Nelson was also dead. Killed in a plane crash. She hoped that he knew how much Sonny admired him and, maybe, would be there to help her boy in some small way, with any kindness. For Sonny needed *kindness*, that was all. Kindness and attention, and it seemed to Mattie that folks on the other side would be kind to one another, and especially to a newcomer. She should probably wait in Sonny's room, she was thinking, since that's where he kept his CDs, and his cherished baseball and those awful playing cards of naked girls. Mattie hoped, in case Sonny *did* stop by, that he wouldn't take the cards with him. Then she remembered that ghosts don't pack their personal belongings before they go. Ghosts don't get that kind of head start, the way businessmen and stewardesses and such folks do. Sometimes, Mattie had read, this is what keeps ghosts locked to the earth, that sweet burning need for something they loved and gave up too soon. Considering all that, Mattie decided that maybe Sonny Gifford would still be hovering in Bangor, hoping to get one last look at that Sheila woman he had loved and married and lost, maybe hoping to touch her stringy hair one more time, smell the dried sweat of her skin, hear her breath coming at him while she slept. Sonny would be in Bangor, chasing the woman he loved, no doubt about it.

"Sonny's dead," Mattie said to no one. She thought about the strange twist of fate that had caught her up in its knot, caught up everyone she knew and loved. She had put all kinds of families back together, every day for over forty years, ever since Lester had started his nonstop cheating and her picture puzzle addiction had begun, out of sheer loneliness. She had put castles together. She had built massive bridges spanning huge, dangerous caverns. She had created flocks of birds, herds of wild horses, litters of kittens. She had constructed the leathery face of E.T., that ugly little extraterrestrial, as he stared out of a closet full of stuffed animals. And yet she couldn't do a single thing to pick up the Humpty-Dumpty pieces of her son's life and fit them all back together.

She reached a hand into her apron pocket and touched the eyeball piece, still safely tucked into the fold. It gave her a soft kind of comfort, just knowing that it was there. Maybe that's how Sonny felt the day he had hidden that brown piece of Judas's money bag from his sisters. Maybe he just needed to keep it a little while longer before it went off to complete the big picture.

"You need a nap, Mama," Gracie said. She came and knelt before Mattie. Marlene appeared next, then Rita. Marlene reached out a hand and moved some of Mattie's hair away from her face. It was a loving gesture, one that rarely fell between Mattie and her girls. And so, for the first time that she could ever remember, Mattie cried in front of her daughters. Not even Lester's infidelity had prompted her to do such a thing. Instead, she had wept all her tears over Lester in private, thinking that the children needed a safe haven in which to grow up. It stunned the girls, that's what the crying did. They moved like quiet statues, whispering. Gracie hugged her first, and then Marlene came to offer a slack hug. Mannequins hugging. But Rita couldn't bring herself. She patted Mattie's hand, as though it were an interesting thing to find lying there on the table, next to her mother's arm. How had they become such stiff creatures, afraid of touching each other, afraid of unlocking the rusty doors to their feelings? How could mothers and daughters grow up and discover one day that they've nothing left to say to each other, that it's all been said before?

"Come on," said Gracie, gently pulling Mattie up. Marlene found Mattie's favorite sweater and flung it about her shoulders. A sweater in the afternoon warmth! They led her down the tiny hallway of Lester's little blueprint of a house.

"I'll bring you some warm milk," said Gracie. Warm milk in the heat of summer! But Mattie said nothing. Let them nurse her. Maybe it would do them good in some small way.

"Henry wants you to know that he's looking into the arrangements," Rita whispered. "He says to tell you not to worry. He'll see to everything." Mattie nodded. Dear Henry. A quick flash of relief settled upon her. Henry would handle the funeral. Sonny's send-off would be in good hands.

At the door to the bedroom, Mattie turned, looked at the three faces of her children, faces that had already begun to collect their own share of wrinkles, those little nicks of time, those little dents of life. And there was Rita's hair, turning gray, almost as gray as Mattie's.

"How old are you now?" Mattie asked her oldest child. Rita seemed surprised.

"Me, Mama?" she said. "I'm forty-five."

"Forty-five," said Mattie. She reached up and touched Rita's hair, put her fingers on the gray.

"Life ain't perfect," Mattie said softly. The girls waited, respectfully. Now Mattie reached out and touched Marlene's face, touched the little mark beneath her eye where Sonny had hit her with a stick. A scar that needed three stitches. He was seven years old at the time, and it had been an accident. But Marlene never forgave her brother for it, Mattie knew. She had almost protected the scar, kept it as sure proof of how awful Sonny was. They had *all* collected scars, hadn't they? She, the girls, Sonny. But still, they had had so many years to heal, so many years. Funny, but Lester

Gifford was the only one in the family paid for his scars, with that government check sent monthly to wounded veterans. Lester had been the family businessman, dealing in wounds and injuries. Broken hearts and crippled emotions. My God, but Rita, her firstborn child, was now forty-five years old. What had they done with time? How had they squandered it so?

"Mama, are you okay?" Gracie asked. She found Mattie's wrist and checked there for a pulse. This must be something else that they'd taught her in women's studies, how to find the pulse on a woman who's just lost a child to death. Well, good for Gracie. Good for whatever she might learn that could help her out in the world.

"Life's not perfect," Mattie said now. "It's got cracks in it. And some folks, good people like Sonny, they fall into them cracks and they never seem to crawl out. And then one day someone comes along and fills up the cracks and them good souls are lost forever. I don't ask you to love him, but I do ask you to forgive him. For whatever you imagine he's done."

"Try to sleep for a couple hours," Rita said.

"We're taking the phone off the hook," said Marlene.

"Do you want some aspirins?" asked Gracie.

For the first time since Monday, when Sonny had taken his hostages, Mattie slept well, slept the long afternoon, slept away the time of day that used to bring her the RH factor blues. Her dreams were good dreams, dreams in which immense gardens boasted row after row of superb vegetables, tall towering cornstalks, beds of shiny cucumbers so green as to appear unreal, long yellow beans hanging like the earrings Mattie had seen Robbie wear. And everything Mattie stooped to pull up was a color to behold: red radishes, orange carrots, yellow-white parsnips. A garden of colors. Like Mattie had always imagined the Garden of Eden to be. And then there was Sonny, leaning on a hoe the way Lester had leaned on it, in a lazy way, as if the hoe was not a tool for working, but invented for a good-looking man to just lean on. "Sonny," Mattie said, and reached out a hand. It would be so good to touch him. It had been six months since she felt his arms around her at the kitchen stove, while she cooked him a boiled New England dinner, his favorite, and made him biscuits. Would any man ever again put his arms around her, now that Sonny was gone? "Sonny?" Mattie tried again, her tongue finally working in her mouth, her eyes straining hard. Sonny leaning on a garden hoe. What next? Now her dream feet were finally working, her dream feet were taking her places. She would get close to Sonny. She would tell him the best news of all. "I've got my teeth soaking, son," that's what she'd say. But when her dream feet finally took her where she wanted to go, over all those rows of dazzling vegetables, she didn't like what she found when she got there. It wasn't Sonny Gifford leaning on a hoe after all. It was his father, Lester, looking every inch like his son. It was Lester Gifford, looking like a million bucks in his fresh army uniform, asking Mattie out for the very first time. "Run!" Mattie told her dream feet. "Tell him no!" she told her dream tongue. But her feet just kept on walking, and out of her mouth came the very first words she had ever said to Lester Gifford. "Ain't you got nothing better to do than lean on a hoe?" That's what she had said to him, on an August day in 1944, a year before she would marry him. And she had said those words simply because she didn't know, at that point in her trusting life, that Lester Gifford really *didn't* have anything better to do than lean on a hoe.

16

When Mattie finally rose from her bed, leaving Lester behind, hoeing in the Garden of Eden, it was nearly dark outside. She could see stars peppering the northeast sky beyond her window. Voices ran amok in the rest of the house, voices in the kitchen, voices in the living room, the sound of flushing in the bathroom. And voices from the blasted television, one of the family now.

"Our Heavenly Father," Mattie said, her eyes on the black river beyond the row of wild rosebushes, which were now dark creeping shapes, crawling up the riverbank. Would He listen to her if she rang Him up? Or would He be engaged in one of those conference calls with Rita and Rachel Ann? "Dear Heavenly Father, please keep that boy safe in Your bosom. Forgive him for the mess he went and got himself into. Look into his heart, Lord, like me and so many other folks have done. Welcome him into Your arms. If nothing else, he'll bring a little gusto to paradise." She moved away from the window then, moved slowly in the darkness toward the crack of light beneath her bedroom door. *Go toward the light.* The truth was that her heart wasn't in the prayer she had just given. Her heart was lagging way behind. What Mattie really wanted to say was "Beam him up, Scotty. *Please*, beam him up."

In the living room, she met with Gracie first.

"Look who's awake, everybody!" Gracie announced. Mattie blinked at the faces before her, her eyes adjusting to the light, her ears accepting the noise.

"Did you have a nice nap?" Rita asked. "You want something to eat?" Mattie shook her head.

"Where's Henry?"

"He just left," said Rita. "He'll be back soon. They're bringing Sonny home tomorrow. There had to be what's called an *inquest* first. Henry's been on the phone all afternoon."

Mattie sat on the sofa in the living room and stared at the screen of the television. There were new faces now, all discussing Sonny. The words came at her and then flew past, her ears too full to accept any more *developments*, too uninterested now that Sonny was beyond earthly help.

"Uncle Sonny's famous," Josh said to Mattie. He had been asleep when the shooting occurred but now he was animated, caught up in the exciting world of adults and their antics.

"Uncle Sonny never even had a gun," said Lyle. "But they went ahead and shot him anyway. The policeman who done it said he was aiming at the dog." He pointed his finger at Josh's head and fired it. Point-blank.

"Granny, do you think the town will put up a sign or something one day?" Steven asked. "You know, something like 'Mattagash, Maine, Population 410, Home of Sonny Gifford'?" Laughter rocked the room, Mattie's girls finding this notion very amusing. Mattie didn't laugh, however. With Sonny looming so big on television for the past three days, Sonny with his unbalanced grin and his Great Americans list, an underachiever whom the whole country had fallen in love with, considering all that, it seemed like a small thing if the town was to put up a sign.

"I, for one, think he deserves a sign," said Robbie. She was sitting in the recliner, her legs swept up under her. Her little porcelain face was whiter than ever. Of course. Robbie loved her uncle Sonny with all her heart. Mattie had forgotten all about her, so caught up had she been with her own grief.

"Oh, Robbie, listen at you," said Rita. "Sonny's still the apple of your eye, ain't he? I don't want to speak ill of the dead or anything, but Sonny took hostages. Yet people like you see that apple while some of us see the worm."

"That's because people like me know how to look for the good," said Robbie, defiant, her eyes teary. "People *like you* are too busy speaking to God." Rita gasped.

"Roberta, that'll be enough!" Gracie shouted from the kitchen. *Thank you, Robbie.* Mattie realized that she was still tired. Had it been only three days before that life was going on as usual, that Sonny was off somewhere in the world, marrying a woman he barely knew and being generally kind to spiders and old people? Was it just yesterday, for crying out loud, that most of the United States of America didn't know that she, Mattie Gifford, was alive on the planet, that she'd borne a nine-pound, seven-ounce baby boy who would grow up to die on television?

"The whole country is saying good things about him," Robbie added angrily, but Rita had gone back to the kitchen. Robbie got up and stomped into the bathroom, slammed the door. Mattie noticed some dead leaves on her geranium, sere, ugly things. But she couldn't find the strength to reach out and pick them off. They would fall on their own soon, would churn themselves into fertilizer. She tried not to think of Sonny's cold body lying in some morgue in Bangor, waiting to enrich the earth back in Mattagash, Maine. Mattie had already decided to give Sonny her own plot in the Mattagash Catholic graveyard, the one next to Lester. It didn't matter that Sonny wasn't a Catholic. Neither was Mattie. Lester was the only one in the family who was supposed to be Catholic, even though a minister had married him and Mattie. She would give the boy *her* plot. It would be the first time that Sonny and his father ever got together without shouting at each other. She would give Sonny her piece of the American pie. But she wouldn't tell the girls just yet. They'd be all up in the air, saying she was still favoring Sonny, giving *him* her plot instead of one of them. But how could Mattie tell them the things that she'd never forget? Things about Sonny Gifford that only a mother could know? How could she say to them,

His hands were always like ice, even in the heat of summer, and he had a cowlick with a mind of its own. And sometimes, in the dark of night, when no one could hear him but me, he'd cry out, like he was fighting some silent war in his head. And when I'd come into his bedroom, he'd reach out and grab me like I was a piece of driftwood and he was a drowning boy. He done this the last time I saw him, girls. He done this as a grown man, reaching out for his mama, crying like some little baby. He brought me blue flag irises, many times, from the back swamp, and they stunk to the high heavens. But they were so pretty to look at that I kept them in a milk bottle up on the kitchen window, where the sun could hit them and make them blue as velvet, so pretty that the smell didn't matter.

Mattie put the cup of coffee Rita had given her down on the end table by the sofa. It was suddenly too heavy to hold, just like her motherly heart was too heavy. Just like Sonny's terror, whatever it was, was too heavy. She remembered again how limp his child-body felt, limp as a rag, all those nights he'd clung to her in terror. She had let him breast-feed until he was three years old, let him breast-feed while the girls were at school and wouldn't see. What would they say about *that?* She had given him five dollars once, when it was all she had in her pocketbook. So help her God, she'd given it to him so he could buy his own picture puzzle, a moonlighty scene with water fountains full of lilies, and pretty weeping willows hanging all over the place, and a whole parcel of rich folks walking around the lawn, the women wearing ghostly blue-white dresses, the men all smoking cigars. Mattie even remembered the name of it—*An Evening on the Plantation*—she remembered it, and she had given Sonny the money to buy it because it looked like a life he might have wished to live, if he hadn't been born to her, to Lester Gifford, if he hadn't been born in Mattagash, Maine. She had given him the money in hopes that he would cry out a little less in the dark of night. But now she knew she'd been wrong. This was what she would never tell her daughters. She was wrong. She had spoiled him too much. She should maybe have taken a stick now and then and beat him into the reality of what his life was, so that he could settle down to it, bruised maybe, like his sisters were, but at least *able to live*. She would never tell her daughters this, would never give them the pleasure. It would be her last legacy to Sonny, just like that five dollars had been a legacy.

And now, sitting on the sofa, her mind swirling with these thoughts, Mattie realized what her grandsons Steven and Josh had been so interested in, perched in front of the TV as they were. They were replaying the VHS tape of Sonny being shot in a spray of blood and bone, Sonny going down on both knees, his arms rising up in genuine surprise. Humphrey, the dog, arriving at his master's side, licking at the blood spilling out of Sonny's wound. The women hostages being pulled away. Sonny being carried to the ambulance on a stretcher, one arm dangling lifeless from beneath a white sheet. Mattie sat frozen, unable to turn her head away, and watched the replay of Sonny's last stand:

Sonny being carried over and over again, his arm going back up inside the sheet each time Steven rewound the tape, with men taking him *off* the stretcher, Sonny getting up from his knees, the blood going back into his head, all the splatters disappearing back into the future, to the point where Mattie thought it might be a mistake, that Sonny's death could be undone, *rewound*. But then Steven would run the tape forward again, toward its future, and there would be Sonny fulfilling his death, Sonny being carried on a stretcher down from the trailer's front porch by men who were kinder to him than his own sisters, men who saw the good that Mattie and Robbie saw. And Mattie knew then, sitting before the VHS tape of Sonny's Hollywood debut, that for all the rest of her life, she would never listen to anyone say a crippling word about her crippled son. She would never admit to her girls, those big hateful girls, what she knew to be the truth. She would never say, *Listen, you bitches, maybe your brother wasn't a go-getter. But I know this much. Sonny Gifford was like them blue irises that grow down in the swamp. Once you learn to forget the shortcomings, you can concentrate instead on what's pretty.* She would never say this to her daughters.

Mattie turned her head away from the flickering images on the screen. Rita and Marlene and Gracie were now filing into the living room, carrying plates of food.

"Oh, Jesus!" Marlene shouted. "Look what them kids are playing!" She grabbed Steven by the neck.

"Turn that off right now!" Gracie ordered.

"Leave him alone," Mattie said. "He didn't mean nothing by it." Gracie should know that kids these days can't tell the real thing from television. They should be teaching things like that in women's studies courses. But Gracie and Rita had already forgotten about the little mishap, for they were passing out sandwiches. The phone rang. Both Rita and Marlene rushed to answer it.

Mattie stood, her legs wavy beneath her. She stepped over Josh and then Steven. At the sofa she knelt down and patted a hand about on the floor until she touched the sheet of cardboard that held *Easter Rising*. She slid it out from its hiding place and looked down at Jesus with his one pitiful eye.

"Oh, honey," Mattie whispered. "Oh, sweetie." She placed one finger into the gaping hole and then rubbed as gently as she could, caressing the empty socket, the way she wished she could place her fingers into the bullet hole in Sonny's head, could stop that awful gush of bright red blood. She thought of Irwin Fennelson's missing eye, the one he left in Vietnam in 1969, and she knew that God had had a hand in that, too. God even had something to do with the tree branch that had sprung up in front of that old Watertown man's eyeball, all those years ago. "I guess it was God's will," Mattie remembered Martha Monihan saying when they had met the old man on the street one day. It wasn't that Mattie didn't believe in God. She did, she most surely did. She just didn't like some of the things He did, is all.

"Oh, you poor lost boy," Mattie said to Jesus, "with no father there in your life to hold you." She was whispering, afraid Rita would hear her and bring out that blasted Bible again. But it was true. It was what Jesus and Sonny had in common: While their mothers were standing in the background, wringing their hands and crying over milk that was bound to spill, where, pray tell, were the fathers, earthly *and* heavenly? Where were those deadbeat dads? And she would ask Rita this, if she must. But in the meantime, she had to take her share of the blame. She had to admit that maybe it would have been better to reach out and catch that glass of milk *before* it spilled. What good had it done Sonny that she had always been there, like a good motherly soul, like a good *woman*, to mop up the mess? What good had it done for Jesus to see Mary weeping and wailing in the distance, turning up at the Crucifixion while they gave him vinegar on that pitiful sponge at the end of a reed? There had been too many long reeds in the lives of some children, too many ten-foot poles between them and their parents. Yet little Bill Clinton had never even met his father. He had grown up with an abusive man, and yet he had become president of the most powerful country in the world. No, Mattie had to take her share of the blame, there was no doubt about it. Just as Mary needed to take her own blessed share.

She didn't have to worry about Rita giving lectures of a religious nature, however.

"Listen up! Listen up, everybody!" Rita was now bellowing. She had hung up the phone, her face flushed with excitement. "That was a producer from that TV show *Hard Copy*, and he wants to talk to us. I told you all hell would break loose when someone found out Sonny has a family!"

"I can't go on TV looking like *this*," Gracie said. "He ain't coming *tonight*, is he?"

"Do you suppose I should tell him about Sonny's Le Mans Birth Method?" Rita now wondered. "It *was* pretty funny when you think of it. There I was, in the middle of labor pains and no one to drive me to the hospital but Sonny. Then he gets that Pontiac Le Mans of his going so fast I'm afraid I'm gonna have a heart attack instead of a baby. We fly up to the emergency door of the hospital at about eighty miles an hour and Sonny stomps on the brake. My water breaks and water is running down my legs."

"Oh, be quiet, Rita," said Marlene. "You never thought the Le Mans Birth Method was funny until that producer called."

Mattie carefully lifted the cardboard with *Easter Rising* on it and carried it out to the kitchen table. The girls would be busy now, too busy to care about picture puzzles. She reached into her apron pocket and found the eyeball piece. She leaned down to the sad face in the picture, the hair touching the shoulders, like Sonny's own hair—what Rita called hippie hair—and she eased the blue piece of eye gently into the glaring socket. It fit perfectly. Now Jesus looked up at her with two full, serene eyes. There was a great kindness in them, Mattie noticed, now that they were complete. A kindness mixed with that rain cloud of suffering. But everyone who knows life knows that rain cloud. It hangs over all heads.

"There, precious," Mattie said to the calm face on the cardboard before her. "Now you can see what kind of mess you left us in."

She found her homemade sweater hanging on her bedroom doorknob where Gracie had left it earlier. And Lester's suitcase, still sitting like a patient dog in the bedroom closet. She carried the suitcase quietly, back down the narrow hallway of Lester's little Spruce Goose, and out into the kitchen, past her pots and pans hanging from their hooks behind her good old stove with the old-fashioned burners. The girls had now gathered like grackles in front of the television set, waiting for even more follow-up announcements and dispatches and bulletins and reports. Waiting for more calls from producers. Mattie could see Roberta, back in the big black recliner, her face pale with emotion. She had loved her uncle Sonny. Once, he had driven Robbie and her girlfriends all the way to the Fort Fairfield County Fair, when no one else would, and he had paid for them all to ride the big Ferris wheel, until they were reeling with the dizziness and happiness of life. Now Roberta's dizziness was caused by another of life's elements, a baby, a child, another soul to join the planet, to get counted in the census books of Mattagash, Maine. That was all the more reason that Sonny's kindness would become a warm blanket to her, down through the years of Roberta's life, a sweet memory. Looking now at her granddaughter, at the small oval face, Mattie could almost envision Robbie as an old woman, an old woman leaning on a rake and overseeing her yearly garden. "That was my uncle Sonny I'm talking about," she could hear the aged Roberta saying to some child, her own grandchild, maybe. "He was always bringing us kids candy, and surprises, and taking us for rides in his convertible. One year, he even took us all the way down to the Fort Fairfield County Fair, when no one else would, and we rode that big Ferris wheel until we were dizzy with life." Mattie saw this picture movie before her face, watched it unreel as surely as if it had just taken place. She had looked ahead to Roberta's future, with some kind of twenty-twenty vision that sometimes comes on the heels of tragedy. Sonny would live on, kind of the way a yearly garden lives on. There was still hope, Mattie could tell, still a reason for human beings to push forward. Peter Laforest would make Roberta a good husband. He'd never be president of the Watertown Savings and Loan, much less the president of the United States. He'd never own a department store, or a yacht, or one of those little airplanes sportsmen flew into Maine's lakes with pontoons for feet. He'd never fly to Paris on that fast-flying jet, the Concorde. He'd never play golf with bankers, smoke rich cigars from Cuba, go to some island for a winter tan. But he would get a steady paycheck each week, and he would hand that steady paycheck over to his wife, Roberta, so that there would be food and clothing and warmth for his family. And, in the night, he would rise, mumbling and tired from a hard day's work, he would rise to comfort one of his children who had cried out in the darkness, in the terror of a dream. He would wipe a thousand snotty noses, mop up a million tears in his career as someone's father. And every now and then, catching the softness of his wife's face as she sat on the sofa and watched television, he would bring her a cup of tea for no reason at all, other than that he felt a *need* to do so, the push of love. And when the time came for Peter Laforest to take his place in some graveyard, maybe the Mattagash Catholic graveyard, down by that clutch of pine trees that lines the old meadow, *Sonny's* graveyard, there would be no mistresses in the crowd wearing black and weeping. There would be just his family and friends, and they would cry over the loss of him, because in losing Peter Laforest, his family would lose a great earthly treasure. Mattie saw all this, and then the movie of Roberta's life faded away.

"Robbie?" Mattie said quietly to her granddaughter, who looked up, surprised to hear her name in the midst of such commotion. "Come here." Robbie rose from the chair. She stepped over Gracie's Nikes and leggings and Rita's big purse. In the kitchen, Mattie pulled her granddaughter aside, away from the door to the living room. *The living room.* What a place to watch Sonny die.

"What are you doing with Grandpa's old suitcase?" Robbie asked.

"Listen, sweetie," Mattie whispered. "I'm getting away from them Pac Monsters in there. So I gotta say this fast.

You tell Peter Laforest not to worry about saving up that money for a down payment on a house trailer."

"But, Granny," Roberta said, trying to question this. Mattie stopped her by giving her a quick little shake that rattled her long earrings. Roberta fell silent again, her eyes full of deep concern, her face still tear-streaked.

"Just let me say this fast," Mattie continued. "I'm giving you and Peter an early wedding present. I'm gonna get Elmer Fennelson to drive me to Watertown, maybe next week, and I'm gonna have that lawyer, that Mr. Ornstein, make it all up legal."

"A wedding present?" Roberta asked. "Gran, you don't have to do that."

"I know what I have to do and what I don't have to," Mattie said. "Now listen. I'm giving you and Peter this house. It ain't a mansion, but it's a nice, comfortable little home. All Peter needs to do is fix a few shingles on the roof and them rickety back steps. And you could use a new water heater. I've been tempting fate each year by keeping the old one, but don't you two do that. Spend some of that down payment money you saved for fixing everything up perfect as you can. You got something alive inside you to worry about now. You got a baby to think about. Life is as good as you make it, Robbie. So take off them blinders that most folks wear and go at it headfirst." Roberta seemed ready to cry again, but Mattie had no time for any such sentiment.

"Gracie's gonna be mad," said Roberta. "You know she

and Aunt Rita and Aunt Marlene all want to inherit the house. All three of them's gonna hit the roof."

Mattie nodded. "I know," she said. "That's why Peter needs to fix the shingles up there, so the roof will be good and sturdy when they hit it. And that's why I need to see a lawyer first thing next week." She gave Roberta a big hug, and her granddaughter's small body curled into her own, thin and innocent and not really ready for babies and a husband and the rigors of Mattagash winters. Not ready for gossips whose tongues were already warped with whispery news of an early wedding, of a swelling stomach. Not ready for all those years to melt away, as they had for Mattie and Martha Monihan and poor dead Lester Gifford and Eliza Fennelson, just more years of the same, years of softball tournaments in which Peter and Roberta would stand back on the sidelines and watch Mattie's great-grandchildren play ball, years of school lunches, and beds being made up, and clothes being handed down, years of fireflies eating up those same summer nights, thousands of Christmas cards being sent out, millions and millions of snowflakes falling out of those same dark skies, billions of words of gossip flying about like locusts, zillions of gallons of water flowing past in that same old Mattagash River. *This* is what Mattie felt when she hugged her grandchild's little body. This is what she *knew*.

"Gran," said Robbie.

"Listen to me, child," Mattie whispered. "You go on ahead and marry your best friend. And then you two fill up this little house with children and laughter and love, 'cause in its day, there ain't been a lot of the last two things. Now, let this be the best piece of advice anyone ever gave you. Don't let your Mattagash neighbors ruin your life with gossip. Don't you let them fine Christian souls, the ones who talk to God daily, destroy your happiness or your self-respect. And believe me when I tell you that they'll try to do it." Mattie heard Roberta begin to cry, who knows why, over Sonny, over her grandmother giving her the house, over a shiver, maybe, a hint of all those years just lying ahead for no other reason than to be used up and thrown away. Mattie released Robbie from the hug and pushed her back at arm's length so that she could see into her eyes.

"Now go on back to the living room," Mattie said, "and pretend you don't know where I am if someone asks."

"Where you going?" Roberta wanted to know. She wiped her eyes and Mattie saw thin, stringy beads of mascara running beneath each lid. She remembered Sheila Bumphrey Gifford, the daughter-in-law she had never met. She hoped someone kind was with Sheila at that moment. She had seen this woman's face in the crowd. This wasn't Sonny's enemy. This was a woman who had loved him once, maybe still loved him. How could she *not* love him? He had never raised a hand to anyone in his life, male or female. "I'm not a fighter," Sonny liked to say. "I'm a lover." Granted, you could grow tired of Sonny Gifford, Mattie supposed, if you were a woman with children, a woman with a future plan. You could move on from him, even move away from him.

But you couldn't hate him. Only his sisters seemed capable of that.

"I'm going to find my best friend," Mattie answered. "I'm camping out for a spell. I'll be back when the smoke clears."

"But what about Uncle Sonny?" Roberta wanted to know. Mattie stopped her questions. *What about the funeral? How can you not be there? You're his mother.*

"Henry Plunkett has got everything under control," Mattie answered. "I couldn't leave my son's funeral in better hands. Now, as for showing up at the grave, even your uncle Sonny would skip that scene if he could. You can represent me. Kind of like them tag team wrestlers your uncle Sonny loved to watch. You tell him I said good-bye."

Mattie went out the back door and let it close softly. On her front lawn she paused to give her best regards to St. Francis. She had thought to grab her little flashlight from off the counter and now she took it out of her sweater pocket and turned it on. St. Francis glared at her with blank, empty eyes indented in cement.

"Don't take any wooden nickels," Mattie told him. She threw the beam of light before her, then followed it carefully. No need to fall into the ditch that stretched in front of her house, maybe break an ankle. Once on the road, she flicked the light off. Dark was coming on steadily and overhead the stars were glittering and bright. Gracie had told her once that Greek shepherds used to believe that the stars were little lamps. And some folks even thought they were shiny nails holding up the sky. And Gracie said that natives down in Central America believed that their heroes were up in heaven smoking cigars, and that the stars were the glowing tips. Like Henry Plunkett's earthly cigarettes. Mattie liked that story. She looked up at the sparkles hanging in the sky above her and wondered if Lester Gifford was smoking one of his favorite cigars. Maybe he was lighting up a second one and passing it to his boy, Sonny. Maybe the two of them could have that father-son talk they never found the time to have on earth. Maybe now there could be some peace between them.

Since Elmer's house lay west of hers, Mattie felt as if she were following Venus to get to him, the way those wise men followed their radiant star. She could hear the summer peepers creating a ruckus in the swamp, down in that marshy place where Sonny used to pick his irises. Jupiter rose above her left shoulder as she walked—dear Henry and his special knowledge of things—and somewhere up there, not too far away, the nighthawks were circling. Mattie could hear their soft, excited buzz. Just ahead, she saw Lola Monihan's house rise up out of the night like a mighty spaceship. The *Enterprise*, maybe. All the lights were blazing. Lola was most likely at the helm of her ship, answering the phone, sifting through the latest news about Sonny, keeping a sure eye on the television set. Mattie wondered what her own girls were doing just then and if they had discovered her gone. She smiled at the notion. "Don't you let them Pac Monster sisters of mine come down on you like cops on a doughnut, Mama," Sonny had said. Well, she wouldn't. Sonny would be proud.

She clutched the suitcase close to her side as she reached Elmer's mailbox. In the early starlight, she could see that the box was open. She closed the creaking door and heard Skunk bark a response from inside the house. Elmer's kitchen light was on, a soft yellow square of warmth, like a patch of homemade quilt. Yellow instead of lavender. Mattie could see him there, at the kitchen table, his reading glasses perched on his nose. She would tell him quickly: *Pack your things for a week. Pack Skunk some dog food. We'll take the honeymoon first and worry about the wedding later. I'm gonna teach you some stuff Henry taught me. I'm gonna point to the brightest star you ever laid your eyes on and say, "No, that's Jupiter, Elmer. And that there's Venus. They're planets, but ain't they pretty as any star you ever saw?"*

The walk across Elmer Fennelson's lawn was as long as any walk Mattie ever took, even that walk down the aisle with Lester Gifford at her side, in those shoes that hurt her so much, carrying that heart inside her chest that would hurt, too, on all those lonesome nights, back in those days when she was young and crazy and stupid enough to think that planets were stars. But this time Mattie was walking in her old sneakers, the ones she liked to wear when she worked in her garden. *We're gonna live in your house, Elmer, and let my granddaughter have mine. You're gonna teach this old dog the new trick of driving a car. And when the time comes for one of us to die, then the other one will be standing by. Right up until we leave this world, Elmer, we'll always know where the other one is. That's important to some folks, that tiny bit of knowledge. I know it, and you know it. So let's do this crazy thing.*

Mattie climbed up onto Elmer's front porch and heard Skunk go wild inside. It would be a matter of seconds now before Elmer laid his reading glasses aside and came to see what was wrong. He was always coming to see what was wrong where Mattie was concerned. What was it she had promised herself, that first time she stood before the altar and agreed to marry someone?

"I *will* be happy," Mattie said. "I *will* be happy." Then Elmer was opening his front door, the warm yellow of his kitchen rising up like sunlight behind him.

ABOUT THE AUTHOR

Author photo by Doug Burns

Cathie Pelletier was born and raised on the banks of the St. John River, at the end of the road in northern Maine. She is the author of eleven other novels, including *The One-Way Bridge*, *The Funeral Makers*, and *Running the Bulls* (winner of the Paterson Prize for Fiction). As K. C. McKinnon, she has written two novels, both of which became television films. After years of living in Nashville, Tennessee; Toronto, Canada; and Eastman, Quebec, she has returned to Allagash, Maine, and the family homestead where she was born.

A Year After Henry

Available August 2014 from Sourcebooks Landmark

An exquisite new novel from acclaimed author Cathie Pelletier.

Bixley, Maine. One year after Henry Munroe's fatal heart attack at age forty-one, his doting parents, prudish wife, rebellious son, and wayward brother are still reeling. So is Evie Cooper, a bartender, self-proclaimed "spiritual portraitist," and Henry's former mistress. While his widow Jeanie struggles with the betrayal, Henry's overbearing mother is making plans to hold a memorial service. As the date of the tribute draws closer and these worlds threaten to collide, the Munroes grapple with the frailty of their own lives and the knowledge that love is all that matters.

With her trademark wry wit and wisdom, Cathie Pelletier has crafted an elegant and surprisingly uplifting portrait of the many strange and inspiring forms that grief can take in the journey to overcoming loss.

Praise for Cathie Pelletier

"That master juggler of literary tears and laughter is at it again." —Wally Lamb, author of *She's Come Undone*

"Nobody walks the knife-edge of hilarity and heartbreak more confidently than Pelletier." —Richard Russo, author of *Empire Falls*